T0031990

NOTHING IN TRUTH CAN HARM US

A NOVEL

nothing
in
truth
can
harm
us

COLLEEN RENÉ

TIDEWATER
PRESS

Copyright © 2023 Colleen René

All rights reserved. No part of this publication may be reproduced, stored in a retrieval system or transmitted in any form or by any means—electronic, mechanical, audio recording, or otherwise—without the written permission of the publisher.

Published by Tidewater Press
New Westminster, BC, Canada
tidewaterpress.ca

978-1-990160-22-6 (print)
978-1-990160-23-3 (e-book)

LIBRARY AND ARCHIVES CANADA CATALOGUING IN PUBLICATION
Title: Nothing in truth can harm us : a novel / Colleen René.
Names: René, Colleen, author.
Identifiers: Canadiana (print) 20230487386 | Canadiana (ebook) 20230487394 | ISBN 9781990160226 (softcover) | ISBN 9781990160233 (EPUB)

Classification: LCC PS8635.E5395 N68 2023 | DDC C813/.6—dc23

Tidewater Press gratefully acknowledges the support of Canada Council for the Arts

Canada Council   Conseil des arts
for the Arts   du Canada

Printed in Canada

For Emma

. . . it was judged a necessary and the only practicable
measure to divide them among the colonies . . . and as
they cannot easily collect themselves together again, it
will be out of their power to do any mischief . . . I now
send and dispose of them in such a manner as may
best answer our design in preventing their reunion.

GOVERNOR CHARLES LAWRENCE IN A LETTER TO
WILLIAM H. LYTTELTON, AUGUST 11, 1755

. . . be of good cheer! for if we love one another,
Nothing, in truth, can harm us. Whatever mischances
    may happen!

EVANGELINE, HENRY WADSWORTH LONGFELLOW

I
Mathilde

The phone rang in the black night, ripping Mathilde out of her frosted quiet thoughts. She let the ring fill the trailer and build pressure into the walls. A shot of cool pierced through her sternum, expanding underneath the skin of her belly. Dread. The icy floor stung her toes, and she wrapped a flannel robe around her body, seeking out the boiling tone in the kitchen. She gripped the receiver to her ear and heard a bloodless voice.

"*Al allait mourrir. Al allait mourrir.*"

"Who?"

"I'm sorry." Her sister wept.

The car ride to Halifax from Clare took three hours. She drove down the highway, blackened except for the moon hanging like a rib above the evergreens. Snow drifted across the road, fuzzy light sand dancing in her headlights. She didn't flip on the radio. The hum of the wind pushing back against the car asked her if she truly wanted to know. It asked her if she'd rather be sleeping.

The house was unlit. She didn't bother to close the car door. She shut off the engine and bolted. Cold shot up her arm as she banged her fist on the wood. When there was no answer, she found the hideaway key tucked in one of the potted plants. The lock clicked and the door swung into quiet darkness. How cold. How dead. Her boots echoed on the hardwood, and as soon as she entered, she saw a shadow run up the wall behind her and suspend in the corner. It was already a haunted house. She tasted the roof of her sticky dry mouth when she flicked on the light switch. Blood. Not a pool or a drop. Streaks. They curved on the floor. Around from the kitchen and to the top of the basement steps where they descended into darkness. But Maddie followed the blood up, not down.

In movies, dead people's eyes close immediately or remain open, focused and rigid. These eyes were half-opened in a timestamp of death. The pupils had shrunk to pin tips. The whites were crimson. Fear ripped her out of the basement, stumbling up the steps and into the calm street lined by golden lamp light, her throat filled with sick. She stumbled, possessed, until she made it down the hill to the Macdonald Bridge where she stood until the sun rose, shimmering on the horizon. She contemplated what it would be like to breathe salty water into her lungs.

"Are you okay?" A voice hovered over her shoulder.

Mathilde turned and saw a woman standing in a thick winter coat, her cheeks bright red and soft. Mathilde nodded and ungripped her hands from the railing. She looked away from the cold, salty harbour below.

Mathilde sat on a bench in Parade Square and lit a new cigarette with a dying one. Despite the morning sun, flags on the building hung limp while white snowflakes fell silent and full. The trees were skeletons raising their arms up in crooked surrender. She counted the cars. If five drove by, she'd go to the police. If none went by, she wouldn't. She counted the people. If two walked by with red coats, it was only a nightmare. Black, it wasn't. She looked at her watch. If she stopped crying in twenty minutes, she'd walk to the liquor store. If she didn't, she'd walk back to the bridge.

II
Eva

Eva wanted to learn the way the other teenagers did, and so, when she was fourteen, she convinced her aunt Mathilde to stop homeschooling her and put her back in public school. But during her first week of classes, her eyes grew foggy. Instead of looking at the complicated textbooks, she would stare out the window. The teacher's voice sounded like a broken radio and so she would place one earbud in her ear, hiding the cord underneath her long brown hair. She'd press play on the yellow Walkman and listen to Donna Summer's bright, passionate voice.

"Eva," she heard Ms Kaiser shout. Eva looked up and saw the whole classroom staring at her, their judgmental eyes drilling into her skull. Ms Kaiser motioned for her to take out her earbuds. "Not in my classroom."

At lunch, a girl with blond flat-ironed hair shoved Eva against a locker. The metal crunched under the force of Eva's shoulder, and she felt a bruising pain in her arm.

"I bet she doesn't even know how to read," the girl said to her group of friends as they walked away in a cloud of synthetic vanilla perfume. She could hear them laughing. But what was worse, the kids around her avoided making eye contact and strode by. Eva walked to the girls' bathroom, locked herself into a stall and, when she knew she was alone, she cried. She stuffed toilet paper into her mouth to keep her sobs muffled. When the bell rang, she heard kids in the hall scream and laugh, their sneakers squeaking on the speckled tile. As the noise filtered out, Eva pushed herself off the toilet seat and forced her legs to walk into the hall. It felt as if someone had taken a stitch ripper and torn her apart at the seams, filling her body with concrete. Every arm raise, every step, every head turn, was exhausting.

The library was her favourite of all the rooms in the school. It was quiet and small and had a soft, blue couch next to the window. The walls were lined with books and the books were filled with information about anything you could ever imagine. At her fingertips, Eva had the world. Her favourites were the encyclopedias that had pictures in them because she could match the scientific names she didn't know to the images. During lunch, she would sit at one of the tables in the library and flip each glossy page until she made it to the end. She did not want to start with Volume A—too conventional. So she began with the letter K.

Kelp is large brown algea or saeweed that maek up laminariales. There are about thtiry difefrent gnerea.

A kaleidoscope is an otpical itnsurmet with two or more relfceting surafces tidtel to each other at an angel, so that one or moer ojbetcs on one end of these miorrs are shonw as a relguar smymertical partten when vidwed from the other end.

She understood these words in her own way, and even though they would change looks, the meaning never swayed. Eva loved books. But she did not like being tested on books because her teachers always wanted her to write out the words in a way that did not make sense. When she saw the letter D marked in bright red at the top of her first book report, she felt her stomach fill with lightning. But that was not the worst part of school. Math was the worst part of school. Her skin itched when she saw the numbers on the page

4

mixed with letters and her mind got all swirly. Staring at a math equation was like breathing in vinegar. One time, they had a surprise test. All the kids finished early, and she was the only one left in a classroom that smelled of whiteboard marker and Clorox. The teacher tapped her fingers on her desk and stared at Eva, who felt her face balloon with red, hot pressure. Eva didn't know what to do, so she filled in random answers.

Mrs. Graham accepted her paper with a tight smile, looked at her watch, grabbed her shoulder bag and walked out of the classroom. Eva trailed behind the teacher through the empty hallway and veered when she saw that her locker door was open. The lock was missing. She pushed the metal door away and saw that, except for a few loose pieces of paper, her locker was empty. The scarf her aunt bought her for Christmas one year. The extra pair of shoes she kept for gym class. Her jacket. Her hat. Everything. Gone. When she closed the door, she heard giggling from around the corner. But when she went to see if anyone was there, to see if anyone could tell her what had happened, the hallway was empty.

Two painful grades later, Eva saw Leanne, the girl who had pushed her on her first day at school and been her torturer ever since, sitting outside on the school steps. She sat with her legs together, her long flat hair thick over her puffy jacket, surrounded by her clique.

"Why'd you always carry that thing around?" She pointed to the mustard yellow Walkman clipped to Eva's jeans. Eva pretended that she did not hear her and turned Donna Summer up in her earphones. She walked to the back of the school where she liked to wait for the bell to ring. She felt a smack on the back of her head and turned to see Leanne smirking at her. Her friends laughed, their sharp teeth glaring in the sun.

"He hee he hee."

They were pretty girls. Girls with long hair and nice skin. Girls with low-cut jeans and frilly tops. Girls that smelled like vanilla and sugary berries. In another life, Eva imagined that she would be friends with these girls. Leanne shoved Eva and a girl named Molly ripped the Walkman off her body. She felt a fist crunch her right shoulder blade. The eyes of the girls twinkled as they moved in tighter.

"He hee heeee he."

"Leave me alone," Eva said.

It only made them laugh harder. *"Leave me alone!"* They mocked.

Molly opened up the Walkman and took out the tape. "Should I smash it?" She waved it around. Amanda grabbed it and held it up in the air. She dangled it over Eva's head.

"Sing us a song!"

"Smash it!"

"Can you even read?"

"I think she might cry."

"You gonna cry?"

"Look, read this. Dah. Nah. Sum. Er. How lame."

Eva lunged and pushed Amanda to the ground. She felt her knees skinning along the pavement, but there was no pain. She was numb. Her fist collided with the girl's temple, then her jaw and then her nose. Thick smacks and cartilage breaking. She stood up and kicked at Amanda's head, then stomped on her back when she rolled over. Blood on the concrete. Thick, syrupy blood. Eva felt the space around her grow until someone grabbed her under the arms and carried her away while she kicked in the air and felt a low growl leave her chest.

Aunt Mathilde picked her up from school. Eva sat in the passenger seat and watched as the houses drifted by.

"You're the one who didn't want to be homeschooled. You're the one who wanted to be a regular teenager. I can't believe you did such a stupid, stupid thing. Really, Eva, you need to show some self-control."

Eva said nothing.

"She lost a tooth! That's not you, Eva. That's not you."

Eva leaned her head against the cool passenger's side window and smiled to herself, the Walkman and Donna Summer safe in her lap.

That summer, Mathilde sent Eva to live with her uncle Marc in Clare. On the French Shore, the air was thick with salt. It felt as though it blew right through her and knew her insides. The dry, tall sea grass was sharp and when she ran her hands through it, it threatened to slice between her fingers and cut the webbing. She remembered the feeling. She'd been here before. Here, she had to be careful. The French Shore was her mom's territory and she haunted everything.

She'd never met her uncle before. Whenever she'd visited as a child—there were only two times she remembered—he was always away, working in Alberta. He was a man who stood stout and not much taller than Eva. He had white, milky eyes, and when Eva first looked at him, she felt as though she were looking at a demon. He seemed to gaze right through her, and she couldn't tell if his face was kind or malicious. His nose hooked down and his eyes narrowed to a slit when he smiled. It made Eva's skin crawl when her uncle smiled.

Every wave that crashed called to Eva; the dunes on the perimeter with their tall sea grass tails taunted her. The Shore was sandy and grey. The sky was stone and the ocean was stone and the air was salt stone, as if a thunderstorm could erupt at any minute. Eva knew it was fitting for her mother to come from such a lonely place.

At first, Eva would break away from her uncle's home that sat on top of a hill looking out at the ocean. She would run through the beach rose and the primrose, finding herself on the high sandy dunes that looked out at Mavillette Beach. It made her remember the good. Her mother holding her on that same beach, cold velvet sand gushing between her toes. Her mother would wrap her in a rough towel and ruffle her hair until it no longer dripped. Her legs would lift and float up in the air as her mother picked her up and ran, flying her sideways on the shore and making the sounds of a car motor. And then they would lie down on a cool picnic blanket that her mother had made and stretch in the hot sun. Eva would rub her face with the leftover ocean and love the grit it left on her. She refused to wash her hair for days after her mother said that the salt water made her hair so beautiful, buoyant and waved. The good memories of her mother made her hate herself.

Eva woke up in the spare room in her uncle's house and sat in bed until she heard his truck start and roll away down the gravel driveway. She often thought about staying in bed all day just so she would not have to speak with him. She tried to calculate how long she could last in the room without having to eat or drink water, but the more she thought about it, the more she had to pee. The room was painted a sterile white, and the bed's springy mattress squeaked as she pushed herself off it. She listened, making sure nobody else was in the house. But as she opened the door, the smell of caramel wafted up to her nose. On the floor by her toes sat a lonesome cup of black coffee. A peace offering.

Her uncle could speak English, but he refused to. Eva didn't know French. She especially didn't know how to speak Clare French. Was it *quoi* or *tcheu*? Was it *qui* or *tchi*? *Je* or *ej*? With Uncle Marc, she didn't try to speak French or even much English. A part of her didn't want to be misinterpreted.

There would be nothing but the sound of air moving through the sea grass while the two of them mimed. They would communicate by pointing and gesturing, nodding and shaking their heads. Their visual conversations were restricted to the necessities: sleep, food and trips to the ocean or the woods. Her uncle would tap her on the shoulder and point to his truck. They would drive to a stony enclave to forage for periwinkles—little sea snails that stick to the sides of rocks. They would jump from wet boulder to wet boulder until they were near the water's edge. The tide would try to jump into her boots there, where the boulders turned to rocks and the rocks turned to shale that sounded like crunching glass underneath her feet. The blue-grey shells were smaller than a truffle in a Pot of Gold chocolate box.

Eva kept her eyes and ears open to the crash of the waves. She remembered being told about staying off the black rocks, but this was different. This wasn't child's play. This was a transaction. Eva felt commercial in her rubber boots against the waves. She knew when to clutch onto a dry edge. She knew when to look at her uncle to see if he flinched—then she would really know if she were in trouble. But her uncle would always stand on the shore, smiling, a hooded figure alone in front of kelp-covered rocks, his blue-white milky eyes staring off into the distance. He looked like death waiting. When Eva arrived back on shore, he'd put the harvest of periwinkles into the hood of the sweater she wore. At first, a joke. Then, an easy solution to forgotten buckets.

Before they ate their harvest, she watched her uncle bring a pot of water on the stove to a boil. Then, he poured in the snails. He took another, smaller pot and tipped in a generous pat of butter, melting it so the smell drifted in the night air. Eva sat at the table in the kitchen and picked at the skin around her fingernails as she watched him, in his red plaid shirt, dark blue jeans and a ripped green baseball cap, stirring the snails in the water. When they were done, he strained them and dropped them into a yellow Pyrex bowl and placed them on the table along with a small dish of the melted butter.

Marc tipped a blanket of toothpicks out onto the table and sat down across from her. His smile was no longer anything but love. Picking up a snail, he held the toothpick with his other fingers and picked away the small piece of shell that protected the meat. He stuck the toothpick into the shell, pierced the meat, and pulled out the slug in one long strand so that the muscle jiggled. The end tip sprang like a pig's tail. Marc held the slug lollipop in front of Eva's face and then pointed to the melted butter. Eva took the toothpick and then dipped the meat into the butter, coating it in a golden gloss. The taste of salty fat was followed by a nutty, almost smoky flavour of the chewy escargot.

Uncle Marc took apart boat engines and cars to see if he knew how to fix them. He usually did. The house was filled with pieces of engines and old washing machines and the innards of boats. Marc's hands were big and calloused, his wrists ringed with welts that came from the mitts he wore while on the boat. The mitts shrank in salt water and tightened around his hands as he pulled up the icy traps or dug around in the slosh pile. He showed her the copper bracelets he wore to prevent them, then threw them on the worktable and shook his head.

Eva tried to learn French on the Shore. She listened to her uncle shoot words back and forth with neighbours while they drank iced tea. Eva would sit on the front porch in her bare feet while the marsh grass lulled in the lazy salt breeze and listen to the words that she understood in her own way. Even though the sounds would change, the meaning did not.

He never mentioned her mother. One time, she heard her mother's name spoken into a sentence by a neighbour, and Eva's eyes locked onto her uncle's face. But he only shook his head. The neighbour's words hung like a noose between them.

Gabrielle.

Her skin tanned that summer and she felt older.

"You have his number," Aunt Mathilde said during the car ride back at the beginning of September. "You can always call."

But Eva knew it wouldn't be the same. She watched the ocean and the beach grass and the sand and the rocks slip away as she and her aunt drove back to the city. Memories of her mother fell away from her mind along with Clare.

She did not go back to school that September. Instead, she found a job in the dish pit of The Crown in downtown Halifax, a restaurant that hired kids with no experience.

"If that's what you want," Mathilde said before taking a sip of her red wine. Her eyes had grown darker since Eva had gotten back from Uncle Marc's place, and her voice seemed deeper and defeated. She stared at a blank canvas that stood on her easel in the living room, hand on her hip underneath her billowing linen shirt. "Save your money. Don't be stupid."

Eva kept her head down. Her boss, a lumbering man with big eyes and tiny teeth did not mind that she was young and did not question why she wasn't in school. He let her clock in, work, and clock out. The dish pit was a deep stainless-steel trough and had an elephant trunk hose dangling from the wall above it. She would pinch the nozzle on the hose and pressure-wash red sauce, Caesar salad dressing and ketchup from the plates before loading them into a steam-filled sanitizer that was so tiny she had to keep it running throughout her shift. Her hands were decorated with pink knicks from loose knives and red burns from boiling water. She wrapped them in bandages and salves after her shift and would sit on the edge of the tub to soak her aching feet in warm water while mint tea bags floated by like tiny boats. The mint was a trick Mathilde taught her. "It helps relax the muscles."

On her free days, Eva went to the library. The walls wrapped around her like a hug. She sat in felted chairs in silence and hid her face with pages of words that had shifting letters she could eventually decipher if she tried hard enough. Sometimes the library would host guest lecturers, professors from Dalhousie or Mount Saint Vincent, and Eva would sit in the far back of the auditorium and listen to the sounds coming out of the speaker's mouth. There was something so safe about listening to a person talk about things they knew so much about. It was like being guided by a strong hand down a treacherous path with no hope of light. In those lectures, Eva felt wrapped up tight in a warm blanket. She learned about extinct plants and animals. She learned about some poet named Rumi and how tectonic plates shift. And the words and the sounds of the words finally made sense.

III
Gaby

"When I get out, we're going to have a party," Gaby said. "I'm going to throw a big party and she'll be there."

Outside in the prison yard, Gaby sat on a bench and leaned back with her arms folded across her chest, smiling. Lisa paced in front of her, shaking her head. Lisa was a little bit older than her, thin with short blond hair. She liked to wave her hands around when she talked, which Gaby found irritating. The air was getting colder, and the grass was changing into a dull yellow. In the distance, she could see a large dark storm cloud growing bulky and rolling in.

"When was the last time you saw her?" Lisa asked.

"Twelve years ago. But I've sent letters and things."

"Has she answered them?"

"I know she reads them. It's probably hard for her, you know?"

Lisa kept pacing, turning her head every now and then to look back at the group of women smoking in the designated area off to the side of one of the buildings.

"How long has it been for you?" Gaby asked.

"Two months."

"Not bad."

"She hasn't answered your letters but you think she'll want to see you?" Lisa pointed her finger at Gaby, who tried to ignore it.

"I'm sure it will take some time for her, but she'll come around."

"I dunno, Gaby. When I got out the first time, my daughter couldn't even look at me."

"That's too bad for you," Gaby said.

Lisa looked back at the smokers and wrapped her arms around her body. She kicked at the dirt.

"Are you on a patch or anything?"

"Cold turkey."

"That's rough."

"Look, all I'm saying is that you gotta be realistic."

"Why do you care?"

"Because you're thinking crazy."

"You don't think she'll want to see her mother?"

"I think you need to understand—"

"I think you need to shut your mouth."

"You haven't seen her in over a decade."

"Are you serious?"

"Do you have a brain?"

Gaby lunged at Lisa, feeling the anger boil in her belly. She felt the thud as the body hit the dirt and she felt bones underneath her thighs as she sat on top, crushing the throat with her hands. It felt like squeezing raw chicken thighs tight, the muscle thick and the skin bunching up. Lisa's face grew red, and then purple as she squirmed beneath Gaby, who couldn't hear the shouting or the guards running. She didn't fully understand what she was doing until she felt someone grab at the back of her head and pull. The clawed fist in her hair. The tight, strong fingers. When she looked up, a guard stood over her with an angry face shouting an order she didn't know how to obey. She only felt the memory of the hand on the back of her head, tugging at her hair.

The segregation doors were gigantic slabs of metal. There was a slot the size of a sandwich stuck in the middle with a flap over it. The three windows in the room were as big as beer cans, all lined up in a row. In segregation, they talk to you through the slot. In segregation, they push food through the slot. In segregation, you don't ask the guards if you can leave. In segregation you pace back and forth and back and forth. Gaby woke up to blood pooling under her back. She saw it on her hands and screamed. She rocked herself back and forth and back and forth. She heard someone shout for her to shut up, but Gaby wasn't there. Gaby wasn't anywhere. Gaby was trapped in a dream world where dead Adam was smiling, eyes open, under her bed, waiting.

Menstrual pads were dropped through the slot later, but Gaby had already bled through her clothes, the blood coagulating in her underwear, dripping down the front of her pants. She felt like a child who'd pissed themselves, made to sit in their own urine as punishment, a hot pool turning cold. The entire day was blank, except for the one hour she was handcuffed, wrists behind her back, and taken to an open space, not quite outside, not quite inside. She sat on a bench, looked down and saw the burgundy-red butterfly pattern between her legs. She didn't even notice the sun shining on the back of her neck like a soothing hand. An hour passes slowly when you're forced to be out in it. They didn't give her anything, just some more time to think. She could hear them laughing. She could hear them talking. Gaby was taken back to her cell, her hour of freedom was over. After three attempts at falling asleep and waking up and falling asleep and waking up, a new pair of pants was thrown into her cell.

IV
Eva

On the eve of her eighteenth birthday, Mathilde informed Eva that they would be moving to Montreal in a month because "that is where artists are appreciated."

Mathilde rinsed her paint-covered hands in the kitchen sink, crimson and lemon melting together under the hot stream and wilting away down the drain. She wiped her hands on her shirt, pulled her thick curly hair up into a bun and rubbed her eyes hard. "Maybe you can finally learn French."

Eva tried not to care about leaving. She thought about all the things she hated about Halifax. The ninety-degree hills. The cold wind that blew sideways. The fear that no matter what bus she got on, the route would change, and she'd end up far away from where she intended to go. The dark streets she'd walk down at night, crickets and heat bugs filling the silence around her. Each house dimly lit with sunken driveways, figures looming in pockets of gloom.

Halifax was a city, but it never lost its forest feel. At least not at night. Not with those old trees. Not with the overgrown shrubs covering abandoned houses and the heritage houses and the garden sheds with the swaying weeds in front that hosted shadows that looked like memories of murder. Halifax was a ghost town after midnight, haunted by groups of unsexed men leaving sports bars and drunkenly shouting, decked in their boat shoes and blue denim bootcuts, plaid shirts, greased hair flipped in front of their foreheads, sweating out the beer they had inhaled and deserved because their girlfriends or wives had nagged them too long about something or other earlier. They reminded Eva every time she walked home that the city was not hers and never would be.

In July, when it would have been her prom, Eva finished her last shift at the restaurant. She saw all the kids from her grade in the Public Gardens, wearing long dresses and suits, big smiles plastered across their faces. Their parents held cameras and helped readjust ties and straps. One girl wore a beautiful emerald gown that showed off her shoulders and long, pale neck. Eva stared at her from across the street while she waited for the bus.

The morning they left, Halifax was foggy; the damp air seeped into Eva's bones and made her stomach feel sick. It was the aftermath of a storm, the water taking its revenge on the air with a thick blanket of grey. She took all her belongings out of her aunt's apartment on Creighton Street in the North End and set them on the curb before hauling them into the car. She hoped nobody would see the teddy bear's foot sticking out from one of the boxes covered with a homemade quilt that was ripping at the seams. She hid the Donna Summer cassette in her backpack so Mathilde wouldn't see it. Eva didn't like her stuff out on the street as she loaded the car. It made her feel dirty. She tried to move faster.

"Don't slam the damn thing," Mathilde shouted as Eva closed the trunk. "Five hours each until we get there. How's that?"

"Fine," Eva said, sliding into the passenger's seat and pulling the hood of her sweater over her head. She had forgotten to pack tissues for her nose that always dripped in damp weather, but she knew her aunt was eager to leave, so she used the sleeve of her T-shirt instead. Mathilde angled into the driver's seat and slammed the door. The engine revved and rattled Eva's skull.

"Hey," Mathilde said, touching Eva's chin. "It'll be good for both of us."

Eva remembered when her aunt saved her. After her mother left.

Eva was six when she woke up in her home for the last time, the snow outside blanketing the ground forcing a damp silence. She heard someone move in the hall beyond her bedroom door. Then a man stood tall in the doorway. He had a vest over his torso, puffing him up like some kind of bird. He still had his boots on, which Eva did not like. He spoke to someone out of view in a hushed tone. When he stomped into her bedroom, she saw his badge and then his gun.

"Where did Mom go?"

"She'll be away for a while."

"Can I see her?"

"No."

She didn't understand why, from then on, people spoke her mother's name as if they were eating sour candy. Downstairs, there were more grownups and Aunt Mathilde was there. Her eyes were puffy and red and her mouth downturned. It looked as if she were wearing a mask of her own face and it gave Eva a panicked feeling in her stomach. A woman in a maroon-coloured blazer told her she needed to get dressed and helped Eva pack her backpack with jeans and tops and underwear. When the woman was busy talking to one of the policemen, Eva went into her parent's bedroom, took the Donna Summer cassette tape off the dresser, and shoved it into her bag.

She was told that she would have to live with another family for a while. The man was a doctor and the woman was a minister. Mr. and Mrs. Abbott. Their church had a stage and a drop screen where they projected slideshows of pretty flowers and song lyrics. People played guitar and sang joyfully, swaying back and forth with smiles on their faces. Kids were invited to come up and sing along with the music, shaking jars of beans and tambourines, praising Jesus. It made Eva squirm in her seat to see people so comfortable. There was no burning frankincense. No Jesus dying on the cross. The priest didn't even wear robes. When one of the kids held out their hands, beckoning Eva to join them on stage, she almost let out a hiss.

Months went by—Eva didn't know how many. It was before her birthday when Mathilde appeared at the Abbotts' house. Mrs. Abbott had packed Eva's things into a Barbie suitcase that was standing by the door. Aunt Mathilde's curly hair was pulled up into a bun at the back of her head. Her linen pants swayed as she told Eva to get in the car. As they drove away from the strange family, Mathilde shook her head.

"Pick-and-mix Christians," she muttered.

"Are we going to Clare?" Eva asked.

"No, *chère*. I have an apartment in Halifax now. We're staying here."

"Is Mom in Clare?"

"No, *chère*."

"Where's Dad?"

Mathilde's mouth opened and her tongue flicked back and forth over her teeth. Her neck grew thick, and Eva saw redness come back to her eyes. Eva did not know what this meant, but in the absence of words, she felt as though she too should not speak.

The new apartment looked anything but new. The front door opened into the kitchen, but if Eva tried to open it too far, it would smash into the stove. The floorboards creaked and slanted; when Eva once dropped a ball, she saw it roll all the way to the small living room. Before Eva could sleep in her room, Mathilde had to clean out mould that was growing in the far corner. She attacked it with bleach and rags, wearing a mask over her mouth and clear plastic goggles over her eyes.

"Keep your things off the floor," Mathilde said. The moisture from the harbour city would eat through anything worth keeping if it were not kept elevated.

The apartment was much smaller than Eva's house and always smelled like vinegar. For the first few nights, she slept under a quilt on the couch. Once her room was set up with a new bed, Eva refused to leave it. Her skin stuck to the sheets, her body sunk into quicksand. The pain came as quickly as an inhale but as unexpectedly as a hiccup. She'd feel her stomach flutter and her throat tighten. Anything would set her off. A song. A smell. The smell of lilac drifting through the air into her open window. Mathilde would have to drag her out of bed.

When a woman at the grocery store shot her the same look her mother used to give her, Eva convulsed with sobs all the way home, blinded by salty tears. Mathilde let Eva watch whatever she wanted on the three channels she had to offer. They cried together. Her aunt clutched her body close to Eva's in those moments, wrapping her arms around Eva tightly as their vocal cords rusted from grief, wishing in their own way that the loved ones in their lives hadn't been stolen. But then, in the morning, it was as if nothing had happened.

"You have to go to school, Eva."

But Eva would not move. She would curl up under the covers in her bed and stick to the sheets like a wart. She would force herself to sleep because, in her dreams, she was still in her home and her mother and father were there.

"Eva! Get up!"

But she would not get up. She would only cover her ears and close her eyes tight.

So Aunt Mathilde let her stay in the apartment, and Eva didn't go to school.

As Eva grew, the name Gabrielle was erased from all parts of her life until her mother turned to vapour. Her father, however, was brought up constantly. Mathilde mixed blues and reds and yellows and whites together on her palette as she sat in front of a gold-painted canvas. Her aunt's hair was wavy and longer now than it had been when they first moved in. She'd gotten rounder, though she hid her body with flowing pilled cardigans and wide-legged trousers.

"Your dad was so special," she said. The paint transformed into the colour of pale skin as she loaded her brush and smoothed it over the gold into an oval. She turned to Eva and smiled. Her eyes had grown darker and hollow.

"Do you remember his curly hair?" She dipped her brush into a walnut-brown dollop and swerved the bristles around before dabbing them onto the canvas. "And his beard?"

"I remember."

"And his eyes," Mathilde said. "He had kind eyes."

She swapped brushes, leaning forward to grab a small one with a fine, pointed tip. She dipped it into wheat, and then a glossy espresso. She lingered on the orbs, swirling them around and around with her brush, hypnotized. "Kind eyes."

"Mom had nice eyes too."

Mathilde froze. Then, she cleared her throat and kept painting. "Your mother," she said, "did not have kind eyes."

"I think they both did."

Mathilde turned. Her eyebrows knitted together, her face wrinkled and harsh. The look shot fear down into Eva's stomach.

"Your mother," she said, "was a poison." Her voice scratched rough as she spoke low and slow.

Eva watched her aunt turn back to the painting and methodically dip her brush into a container of water, flicking it around so that the excess paint circled hazy and floated on top.

"*T'es okay, chère*. Your mother is in a better place."

V
Mathilde

Mathilde couldn't stand the sight of cigarettes littering the sidewalk and trashed coffee cups falling out of public garbage cans. She did not like the style of French that came lilting out of people's mouths. She did not like the women who walked fast out of the metro with their leather bags slung over their shoulders and heads held high. She did not like the confrontational sexuality that dripped out of storefronts and clubs downtown from young people with tight clothes and exposed skin. The smell of foreign food did not tantalize her and she did not get a rush of pleasure window-shopping or passing overflowing boulangeries along Saint-Denis. She could only feel her hands shaking and her heart beating fast as the cars sped by honking loudly.

One afternoon, while walking home from the art supply store on Sainte-Catherine, a woman called to her from a doorway. She was seated cross-legged, and her hair was cut short, pieces of it sticking out the way a child's does when they cut it themselves. Her big, dark, brown eyes stared up at Mathilde like a sad puppy's as she held out her palm. With her other hand, she pulled the neck of her shirt down to expose her left breast. It made Mathilde's stomach churn. But, as much as she did not like the city, it was better than staying in Halifax and risking Gabrielle forcing her way back into their lives.

The new apartment sat on the corner of Rachel and Drolet. The neighbourhood, much to Mathilde's liking, was at least somewhat quiet and allowed her to paint uninterrupted throughout the day whenever she wasn't working as an instructor at the local community centre. The kitchen and living room were one large space with two windows opening up to a massive stone church that sat on the opposite side of the street. Mathilde would sit at the window in the morning with her easel and canvas, small tubes of oil paint lined in a brilliant row at her side, waiting to be picked up. Some were squeezed more than others, but Mathilde had a rule that if she purchased a set of paints, she must use all of them at least once or else it was money wasted. Prussian blue was her favourite, and when she squeezed it onto the palette, it made a squishing and bubbling sound. Typically, she painted rolling green pastures and large blue waves, golden hues of hay cascading down hills into small villages dappled in bright reds and yellows and purples. She loved painting the sky in its light blue and white. Her ability to blend colours into realistic shadows and make light appear out of nowhere was a gift and what she was known for by the small collection of admirers who bought her paintings or commissioned pieces. But in the past few years, she'd been dreaming of a face. The face that appeared behind her eyelids. At first, a soft outline, and then, illuminated features that transfixed her and wrapped her in so much warmth that she despised waking up in the morning.

Mathilde picked up her paintbrush and swirled it into a glob of pale yellow, slowly folding in crimson red. She wanted to recreate his face from memory first, and then find the picture of him in her closet. She wanted to prove to herself that her memory of him was real and that she could capture him better than any photograph.

The summer of 1989, Mathilde was twenty-one and renting a small apartment in Digby, an hour's drive from where she grew up in Mavillette. She helped teach art to kindergarten students during the school year, and in the summer worked at the community centre, showing kids how to dip old newspaper into a concoction of flour and water to make papier-mâché. Mathilde hated how the dried bits of flour would stick to the webbing of her fingers. To her, the mess was not worth the fun that the children apparently had.

She was running her hands under steaming hot water, scrubbing them with soap to remove the bits of paint and paste stuck underneath her fingernails when the phone rang. Her mother's voice was impatient and annoyed. "*Ta soeur m'a callé auhordi,*" she said. "She doesn't sound good."

"I'm busy."

"*Oh, arrête avec c'te sacrée marde là.* She can be yer problem too ya know. Get down here."

Her mother lived in the same trailer Mathilde had grown up in. It was larger than most mobile homes but, with two siblings, it had never been large enough. Ever since Mathilde moved out to be on her own and her brother Marc moved to Alberta for work, concern for her sister had consumed all the air in the trailer.

The mid-August heat stuck to Mathilde's skin and everything felt like a hazy dream. The trailer, fire-engine red, sat on a plot of fried, dry grass near Mavillette Beach. The air was so thick with salt water coming off the ocean, her skin had crusted, leaving granules that she would rub and pick. Down the slope and over the road, the ocean beat against the sand hugged by bright green bushes and tall grass.

When Mathilde pulled in, the weeds scraped the side of the car like boney skeleton hands gripping at the paint, trying to drag it into the ground of the property. The gravel crunched under her tires. The chicken coop to the side of the property had been vacant for years but the barn to the right bloomed with rusted farm equipment, art supplies, old car parts and shotguns. The guns that sat on the outside of the property were always loaded, and the ones that sat on the inside of the barn had bullets that were not far away.

Two ATVs, one for her mother and the other a spare, sat parked on the side. They used to ride them everywhere around Clare: to the dollar store, the Frenchy's, Comeau's Farm Market. One time, a pack of them rode along the old train track all the way to Digby to pick up what they had heard was the best fried chicken. When they parked their ATVs in the lot and walked into the restaurant, covered in dust and clicking off their helmets, the waitress commented on their tenacity. "*C'est point trop pire*," her mother always shrugged while retelling the story. "We really wanted chicken."

Inside the trailer, Mathilde's mother and three friends sat around the kitchen table, all wearing big round glasses and perms and blue eyeshadow. They perched on either side of a large blue and red quilt that sat flat in the middle, working meticulously by threading needles and pinching the side of the soft fabric. A dark pot of tea sat steeping on the counter. Mathilde hugged the other women before hugging her mother, using only one arm and wrapping it around her neck. Her mother did not stand. Mathilde sat down on the orange velvet bench opposite them and listened as the women gossiped about their sons and daughters and that boy up the road who wasn't right in the head. *And did you hear about Joey going up to Calgary? Lost another one.*

Mathilde looked out the window. There were barely any trees in the small community, and the other houses were in clear view. At one house, up the hill, cars pulled in one by one and people gathered on the front lawn, plumes of smoke rising in the air. A fire pit glowed orange.

"I think she's there," her mother spoke into the quilt, then squinted up at Mathilde. "Have you been talking to her?"

"No."

Her mother set down her section of the quilt. Mathilde stared through the screen door of the trailer. The sun was sinking low in the sky and shadows from the houses stretched up long on the overgrown grass. Heat bugs rattled in her ear. The wet salt that dried on her face made her feel as though she had a second skin to shed. "Find her." Her mother returned to the quilt, picking at it with her needle.

"*Ej va. Ej va.*" Mathilde turned and rolled her eyes when her mother couldn't see. The screen door slammed as she walked along a back deck surrounded by driftwood handrails. The grass hadn't been mowed and the driveway was indistinguishable from the rest of the property. She stood with her hand on her hip desperate for a cigarette, knowing her mother hid a pack underneath the deck, but she could feel eyes peering out at her from the trailer window.

Mathilde's car was a used Chevy hatchback. When it rained, the radio stopped working and she had to keep cloths in the back seat to wipe down the fog that accumulated inside. She drove the short distance up the hill to Philip and Manon's old house and parked next to the other cars that saturated the lawn. The house was big and should have been vacant, seeing how it had no running water, no bathroom inside, and walls that apparently were still coated in lead paint. But she could hear live music.

A couple sat on the patio drinking beers and smacking their knees as they leaned over, laughing at some joke. The tall grass tickled her ankles as she walked around the back of the bright blue house, paint peeling off the side and weeds growing high. That's where she found Gabrielle starfished on the grass underneath a clothesline, staring up as the fresh linen swayed in the hot breeze, closing her eyes when it whooshed over her nose. Her stomach was strong and thin; her arms, exposed by an orange crocheted halter top, gangly and tanned. Mathilde hovered over her sister, and when Gabrielle noticed something had eclipsed the sun, she opened her eyes and smiled.

"You came." Her voice was sing-song, like a child's.

Mathilde crossed her arms. "Mom told me to."

"Do you want a drink?" Gabrielle sat up and clutched her

denim-clad knees, inviting Mathilde to sit. Her sister handed her a sweating amber bottle that Mathilde popped open with her car keys. She took a short swig.

"What are you doing?" Whooping laughter shot from the house. The sound of a glass bottle falling to the floor and shattering shot into Mathilde's ears.

Gabrielle shrugged. *"N'y avait trop de racket là d'dans."* She motioned to the house. "I think I took too much."

"Too much what?"

"Shais poinne. Tcheudzonne avait tcheukaffarre pis j'croyais que ça f'ra un beau jeu." She cradled her chin with her hand and a lazy smile spread across her face, eyes half-closed. "I thought it'd be fun."

Mathilde eyed Gabrielle and took another drink. *"Es-tu alright* though?"

"Yeah."

Mathilde stood up and walked toward the house.

"Where are you going?"

"Getting you water."

Inside, the walls looked exactly like the outside, paint chipped and raw. People shouted over fiddle music and the smell of mildew filled her nose. A woman sat at the kitchen table peeling a potato, the hem of her dress pulled up over her thighs. Her knobbly knees were wide, her toes spread out on the worn wooden floors, her heels up like a country ballerina. On the table, one sweet chocolate square on a ceramic plate had been cut into halves, then quarters, then eighths, then sixteenths until there was only a sliver left so nobody could feel guilty about taking too much. Mathilde squeezed her way through the crowd and grabbed an empty glass. She turned on the tap, forgetting that the water would not run.

"What are you doing?"

She heard an English voice and felt a hand on her shoulder. When she turned around, a man with an unkempt beard met her eyes. He was wearing a red plaid shirt with the buttons undone, exposing coarse, brown hair.

"Trying to get water," she said.

"Here," he reached into the fridge and pulled out a jug, placing it on the counter. He had large hands.

Mathilde thanked him. She twisted the top off and poured the cool water until the glass turned frosty.

"Not going to drink it?"

"It's not for me."

"No?"

"My sister."

"Who's your sister?"

She looked out the back window and pointed. Gabrielle was stretched out on the grass, laughing to herself. The man nodded.

"She looks like she needs it."

Mathilde excused herself, but as she walked out of the kitchen, the man trailed behind her. She turned.

"Do I have a shadow now?"

"Do you want one?"

The screen door rattled in time with their feet stamping the wooden steps. Mathilde heard a cricket somewhere in the grass, turned around to see the man's face, and saw that he had bright apple cheeks that stuck out from his beard when he smiled. The grass made soft swishing sounds, holding the cool glass up to her chest she could feel herself blushing. She wanted to know what his fingers felt like on the nape of her bare neck. She handed her sister the glass of water, and Gabrielle reached up with two hands like a child. The man sat down in the grass next to Gabrielle, legs stretched out long, shoulders broad. Mathilde saw the way he was looking at her and knew immediately. A glance down at her chest.

"Do you know each other?" Mathilde asked.

The man shook his head. "Adam." He held out his hand to

Gabrielle. When her sister was done drinking her water, she fell back on her elbows and closed her eyes, letting the last bit of sun in the sky fall on her chest, leaning her head back so far her neck arched. Mathilde became too aware of the matronly dress she was wearing: square neckline and tough cotton. It felt like burlap. She gripped fistfuls of grass between her fingers and ripped them out of the ground.

"I haven't seen you before," Mathilde said, breaking the silence partially filled by a distant heat bug warning of a sweaty night.

"I'm visiting," Adam said. "Came down to see André."

"You're military?"

Adam nodded.

"You're not from here," Gabrielle spoke up into the sky and cackled.

Adam smiled. "I'm not from here." His face was shaped like a diamond, skin tanned and hair thick. His ears stuck out. Almost too much, she thought at first, but it disarmed him and made him seem vulnerable.

"That explains it." Mathilde wanted to know how his skin felt. She wanted to know what his face looked like in the morning. She wanted to know what he did by himself, when he was all alone and thought nobody was watching.

"I was always told to watch out for sailors on leave," Mathilde said.

"We're not all the same," Adam said. Gabrielle scoffed, falling to her side. She propped her head up with her hand, breasts cupping under her halter, revealing the freckles on her chest that she'd earned.

"That's too bad," Gabrielle said.

A fast banjo and a sporadic drumbeat from a makeshift snare filtered out from the open door and pulled Mathilde and the other two inside. She had to hold out her hand for her sister to grab.

"Don't fall, Gabrielle."

Full guitar strings held the rhythm and the entire room together. Without it, everyone would have flown out the windows. Short clips of the strings got Adam's foot stomping and a fiddle bow sawed the air, forcing Mathilde to start clapping. Laughing big and sitting on his lap, her chandelier earrings swayed in time, face pink with staccato tones, breath short from the quick doubling of notes. With the break into a bridge, she came crashing down on Adam's thighs, face hot, teeth protruding from her lips, hips swollen between his big hands as they swayed to a key change.

O'toi ti monde, moi j'connais hier au soir, tout partout y'où
moi j'étais, pour te 'joindre ma jolie cœur,

And everybody sang.

Hé-y-yaille, la promesse tu m'avais fait, elle a mieux aimé
m'tourner l'dos, s'en aller en rejoindre un autre.

With the song at an end, Adam's eyes grew hazy, and Mathilde saw that the neckline of her dress had dipped too low for her liking. She shot up and pushed through a sea of shoulders to find fresh air. She sat on the rough wooden stairs that led down to the grass and let the air and the vast black expanse of the country muffle the voices inside. She heard the music pick up again with the creak of a rusty hinge as Adam took the spot beside her and lit a cigarette. He smelled like campfire and ginger.

"How long are you here?" Mathilde asked.

"Two weeks."

"Are you coming back?"

He took a drag with half-moon eyes. "I'll be gone a few months."

Then, his bristle-pad beard tickled her chin and his hands gripped her tight. She broke away, down to the grass, and waited for him to follow. She held out her hand just as her sister called from the window.

"Mathilde!" Gabrielle leaned out, her torso suspended in the air while her arms waved up high. "Come back!"

Mathilde tried to hide, but it was too late. She'd been spotted.

"I'm tired," she shouted back.

"But it's just starting."

"I'm tired, Gabrielle."

"Don't be like this."

"Like what?"

"Boring! Mathilde, come on. *T'es si tant platte.* Come have fun with me!"

"I'm . . ." Mathilde glanced back at Adam who was leaning up against her car, half hidden in the shadows. "I have to work in the morning."

"Oh, come on," Gabrielle said. Mathilde could tell her sister was in the clouds. "Come on. I want you to stay. *H'ai besoin de toi.*"

"*Tu va être okay,*" Mathilde said.

She heard Adam chuckling, his hands up over his mouth. "What are you guys saying?"

Gabrielle's shoulders slumped and she folded her arms. She made a face Mathilde was all too familiar with—an angled lip pout and a cocked brow. Unimpressed. She wouldn't back down.

"Gabrielle, *va rinque back en d'dans.* Go back inside and find some guy."

"What?"

"Bye, Gabrielle."

"At least I know how."

"What's that supposed to mean?"

"You're the one who's never had one." Gabrielle leaned out the window. "You wouldn't even know what to do with it."

Mathilde prayed Adam didn't hear, but there was no way he didn't. She tried to breathe through the rage of always having to be the mature sister. "I need to work tomorrow," she said calmly. "I know you don't know what that means."

"Bullshit," Gabrielle snapped. "You think you're a saint because

31

you work? Nobody works harder than you, right? Martyr Mathilde. *La Sainte Vierge*. Don't wait too long—you'll be all dried up down there." Gabrielle hiccup-laughed so hard she almost fell over.

Mathilde felt rage boil up inside of her like waves crashing up over a levee during a storm. She couldn't stop it. "You're going to die on some dirt road with *ton corps rempli d'pills*, and I'm not going to feel sorry for you one bit. *Point du tout*. Because that's all you're good for. That's all you've ever been good for."

Gabrielle stared at her, mouth open like a dead cod. She pulled herself back in through the window and slammed it shut. Mathilde let the gentle sounds of crickets and cars in the distance echo around her body. Lost in the sound of the ocean crashing on the shoreline, she looked over at Adam, but his face had lost its good-time feel. His arms were crossed; he was staring at her fiercely. He saw her for the girl she was. One who, when backed into a corner, would bite.

Forced out of her half-dream by the sound of something hitting the wall in Eva's bedroom, Mathilde rubbed her eyes until she saw hazy stars behind her lids. In the kitchen, she scooped ground coffee from a tin and jumped again when more clatter came from her niece's room. She paused, the coffee scoop in her hand, as Eva slammed open her bedroom door and hauled out a neon green bike with an awful milk crate on the back. She was covered in a slick sweat, her hair frizzy and winding over her face.

"Sorry," she said, out of breath. She leaned the bike against the wall and stepped toward the bathroom but tripped over her feet and smacked her knees on the hardwood. Mathilde heard Eva swear under her breath, letting out a groan before pushing herself to stand, staring at Mathilde with her arms long by her side. "I'm late for work."

Her niece's hair was short and tousled above her shoulders, and she knew that it had not been brushed in a very long time. Mathilde watched Eva struggle to get out the door with her bike, scraping the walls with the handlebars and leaving a long thin black streak on the white paint. Her face remained cold as stone. *Too much like her mother.*

VI
Eva

Champ de Mars was an ageing brick hotel in Montreal's Old Port on a corner next to a busy street known for having bicycles fly down it with no regard for cars or human life. Eva had convinced the owners that she would make a great chambermaid, even though she had no experience, didn't speak French and couldn't lift her own bicycle above her head without straining a muscle in her neck. Maya and Mirac Yildiz were a young couple and had owned the hotel for a little under five years, taking over the business from Mirac's father. Much to Eva's joy, they did not particularly care about having good maids, as long as they did not gripe about the money.

She undressed the beds, cleaned the bathrooms and washed the linen for eight dollars an hour because that's what people made if there was a possibility for tips, even if the tips were a nickel, a bread tag, a shoelace or three loose beers. The job sent Eva's lower back and legs home with a beating, but she didn't mind. She liked being alone and working with her hands. It was a job that let her see results right away. She measured her success in cleaned-away used tissues and sparkling porcelain tiles. On her hands and knees, she scrubbed the bathroom floors with bleach and watched as she erased grime one tile at a time. She loved the smell of bleach. She loved scrubbing a toothbrush in the grout lines and watching as blue and grey scum lifted and melted away. The bathtubs were covered in stringy, wet clumps of hair she picked up with pieces of toilet paper and flushed down the toilet, wiping everything down with Clorox. Then she moved on to the bedroom. All the blankets, sheets and liners were stripped off the mattress and thrown into the hallway. The mattresses were lifted to check for drugs, sex toys or condoms. Once cleared, Eva tucked in the fitted sheet and the top sheet, threw the duvet over along with the pillowcases, and then added a staple of all hotel stays, a velvet beige throw neatly folded at the foot of the bed. The rooms smelled like a mix of synthetic wild berry mist and the memory of cigarettes.

She felt the sweat drip under her armpits and saw the dry skin on her hands crack as she checked all the drawers and then the mini-fridge. Sometimes people would leave boxes of cookies or packaged cakes, either because they forgot, or the treats were a regrettable impulse buy. Eva always took them, no matter how plastic they tasted. In other rooms, she found cold beer. She loved finding cold beer.

She vacuumed her way out into the hallway. Hidden among the fibres of the carpet, Eva always found crumbs and bits of gravel no matter how long she vacuumed. Some things refused to budge. She threw all the dirty towels and linens into black garbage bags and dragged them along the floor to the maid's staircase and heaved them forward, watching them tumble down the steps to the laundry room below, which was really an unfinished basement with one dinky washing machine and a dryer. She sat underneath the only window on the carpeted landing and cracked one of the beers, feeling the muscles in her back spasm. The carpet was grey and scratchy, but bright and warm from the sun. The beer tasted like tinny water, and it was cold and quenched a deep, aching thirst.

When all the garbage bags filled with soiled linen and dirty towels were thrown to the bottom of the stairs, Eva made her way down to the empty restaurant.on the ground level of the hotel and casually walked behind the bar to rummage through the breakfast leftovers in the fridge. Mirac hurried into the empty restaurant with two phones in his hand and waved to get Eva's attention.

"Can you add kitchen towels to your laundry?" he asked.

"Sure."

Mirac disappeared into a back room behind the bar and came out with a large black garbage bag filled with what Eva assumed were grease-stained kitchen towels and rags.

"Sorry," Mirac said. "Don't stay past five. I can pick up from there."

Biking home down a side street that evening, Eva got lost. It was early September, and the heat was still oppressive and the air smelled like gasoline and Portuguese chicken, but the lush green trees offered her relief from the heat as she wiped away the sweat that had collected on the back of her neck. When she made it up the hill and into the Plateau, low buildings and cobblestoned streets made her feel as if she were living in a village—each alley she biked down was like a new world, lonely and expansive, a portal where voices called to her through adjacent walls.

Music played from open windows, and she could smell evening coffee and ginger root. Rows of wrought iron spiral staircases were packed with people perched like cats, smoking and sitting close together. She followed the smell of tobacco and slowed to the sound of laughter and bright music. A group of kids about her age, crowded the back lot of some apartment, drinking beer and smoking. They were dressed like people Eva had seen in the American Apparel signs that hung outside the store on Spring Garden Road in Halifax: leather jackets, sheer leopard print blouses and velvet bodysuits tucked into high-waisted black jeans. They looked as if they'd just walked out of a 1960s album cover and had something to prove. A boy glanced over and stared at Eva, then he grabbed a beer from a cooler.

"Hi," he said.

"Hey." She liked his hair, which was brown and curly.

"You okay?" He twisted the cap off the beer and handed the bottle to her. "Come on—we don't bite." And he gestured with his own beer for Eva to follow.

She leaned her bike against the fence and stepped into the lot. She took a sip of the bitter ale. Between the building and a fence, a girl crouched, her bright cellphone screen so close to her face it made her skin appear yellow. She had a mane of mousy hair that thinned at the tips, and she was lipreading a message off her phone. The boy who'd given Eva the beer said something she didn't register and he slipped out of her vision. The girl on the ground looked up at Eva and raised her open hand as if to say hello. Eva levitated forward until she was hovering over her.

"I'm dead," the girl groaned. She smacked her palm against her forehead, knocking her head on the back of the fence. "He hates me."

"Who hates you?"

In the light of the cellphone, Eva could see that her whole face was covered in freckles. She wasn't wearing makeup, or at least it didn't look like it, except for sticky red lipstick. Her fingernails were chipped with dark blue nail polish, and she was wearing jean shorts and ripped tights. Her jacket was dark camo green and long, covering her body.

"My boyfriend. We had a fight. Do you have a smoke?"

Eva looked over at the guy who had handed her a beer. "I can get us some."

She went back over to the boy and smiled.

"Do you think I could have one?"

He winked and pulled out his pack.

"What's your name?"

"Eva."

"Oh, yeah?" He held out a smoke. "Hi, Eva."

"What's your name?"

"Thanks, Matthew!" The girl appeared at her side and snatched the cigarette out of his hand before Eva could grab it. Then she took Eva's arm and pulled her into the dark corner of the alley.

"That guy's a creep, don't talk to him," she said. She lit the cigarette and took a long drag before handing it over.

"I'm Alma," she said. "Do you drink a lot?"

"Not really."

"Hmm."

"Why?"

"My boyfriend Dexter says I drink too much. We had a big fight last night."

Eva didn't know how to respond, so she didn't. She took a drag and sat down next to Alma on the cool pavement, gliding her sensitive palms along the coarse ground, back and forth.

"He's, like, my soulmate though. I love him so much. We just moved in together." She eyed Eva. "How old are you?"

"Eighteen."

"A baby."

Eva would have despised this response from anybody else, but when it came out of this strange girl, she felt nothing but joy. She pictured the inside of her chest glowing bright orange.

"First year? Concordia or McGill?" Alma asked.

"Concordia," she lied.

"Me too," Alma said. "Third year. English."

Eva rubbed awkwardly at her neck. After Alma was done with her beer, she pulled an amber bottle out of her jacket pocket. It looked like cough syrup.

"Don't worry," Alma said. "It's gin."

Eva felt pulled into this new girl's skin, as if she held all the secrets to the world. She watched as Alma picked herself off the ground and offered Eva a sip from the repurposed bottle. It burned her throat.

"What classes are you taking?" Alma asked as she tossed the dying cigarette to the ground and stomped it out with the toe of her black boot.

Eva stalled. "The basics."

"The requirements in first year are all boring. Just stuff we learned in high school. Are you in Shakespeare? We could go to class together. I put it off for so long and now I have to,—"

"Yes!" Eva startled herself with her sudden interjection, but Alma seemed unfazed. She took another sip of gin and then offered some to Eva.

Her aunt was taking a nap on the couch when Eva arrived back at the apartment. She dug through her backpack and found the parmesan she'd taken from the hotel kitchen and clumsily grated it on a cutting board, her eyes struggling to focus. She put a pot of water on the stove and, when it was boiling, added dried fusilli.

Swaying in front of the frying pan, she added pink cubed bacon to the sizzling oil, smelling the maple smoke. Mathilde coughed herself awake, eyes squeezed tight, lips snarled. She pushed herself up off the couch and reached for the glass of water that Eva had placed on the coffee table. Eva scooped the noodles out of the water and tossed them in the frying pan with the bacon and grated cheese before plating the pasta and placing it on the coffee table in front of her aunt.

"Where were you?" Mathilde sat up.

"The other girl was sick," Eva lied. "I had to stay longer."

She sat cross-legged at the coffee table and faced her aunt. She stuck her fork in the pasta, stabbing the little screws. A peppercorn crunched between her teeth and melted into the salty, creamy cheese. Mathilde stood up from the couch and grabbed two glasses and a bottle of wine from the fridge. She brought the cold white back to the table and poured. It was later than usual for the two of them to be eating, and the apartment was dark and glowing gold from the floor lamp.

When Eva and Mathilde first arrived, there had been a strong cat smell explained by trays of cat litter in the cupboard under the sink and the bathroom had been covered in a strange purple grime they still couldn't get out of the grout. Garbage bags had lined the floor around the windows and random pieces of furniture—an armoire, three bookcases, two coffee tables with knife marks etched into them, and a desk missing a leg—had cluttered the living room. They saved what they could repurpose and everything else went out onto the street for others to find.

She watched Mathilde swirl her fork through the pasta. Since moving to Montreal, Eva had noticed that her aunt seemed to have lost interest in food. That evening the fridge held only a few bottles of wine, a chunk of cheese that sprouted fuzzy green mould and a limp batch of parsley. In the past month, inspired by hunger and Mirac's instructions, Eva had taken over responsibility for the evening meals. Fruits and vegetables had been sorely missing from her aunt's diet, so Eva tried to incorporate them into her cooking, although she always fell back on the basic ingredients of any traditional French dish: carbs and fat.

Mathilde's favourite dish was coq au vin, so Eva experimented by making it with white wine, adding small potatoes and carrots. Another of Mathilde's favourites was rappie pie: grated and squished potatoes, stock and shredded chicken. Eva used the leftover potato shreds and stock for fricot. In the hot Montreal summer, both dishes made their faces swell from the salt and heat, rouging their cheeks and leaving them sweating and wondering why they didn't choose to make something more refreshing. Mathilde had joked that Eva should make *fromage à la tête de cochon.*

"When I was growing up, the farmers used to slaughter their pigs in November. I don't remember why." Mathilde pulled out a book from her bedroom closet and flipped through it. "They would salt all the meat and the tendons so it would last through the winter."

"Including the head?"

"Of course."

Eva took the book from Mathilde. It had hand-written recipes scrawled on its pages, in French. Her aunt took it back and translated: pig's head, onions, carrots, peppercorns, salted spring onions. Boil the head in a pot with everything and skim.

"The snout will poke up at you," Mathilde said with a glint in her eye. "Just ignore it."

After two hours, strain and remove all the meat from the skull. Don't forget to remove the thin, gelatin membrane off the tongue.

"Reduce the broth left in the pot and pour over the meat that's now shredded and lined in a baking dish. Leave to gel." Mathilde translated. "Serve cold spread over toast."

It wouldn't be the hardest thing for Eva to do. Travelling with a pig's head on her bike would be the most difficult part of the process.

After finishing their pasta, Eva stood up and went to the kitchen to wash the dishes, chewing on stringy bits of bacon fat she'd saved from the frying pan. Since she was little, Eva loved chewing on the leftover fat of whatever meat they were eating. She wiped down the counter with a rag while Mathilde sat on the couch and looked up at the ceiling, her empty wine glass in her hand.

"Are you going to study your French tonight?"

Eva said what she always said, "It doesn't stick. You know that." The wine buzz filled her head.

"You know whose fault that is."

"I know."

"It's in you. You'll get it one day."

"I know."

"We should make lobster one night."

"Why? It's so messy."

Mathilde chuckled and shook her head.

"What?"

"My mother was so stubborn," she said. "Whenever anybody asked for butter for their lobster, she'd wag her finger." Mathilde pointed her finger and put her hand on her hip, squawking, "*Respecte le goût.*"

"Sea bugs really need that much respect?"

Eva poured her aunt another glass of wine.

"What else would she do?" Eva asked.

Her aunt looked up at the ceiling. "Oh *chère.* I couldn't touch her tea bags. She wouldn't let me throw the used ones out. She'd let them sit in cold water until they bled."

"Did she only speak French?" Eva asked, leaning on the counter.

"No, she knew both." Mathilde trailed off, staring at the place where the floor met the wall. "Papa didn't speak English though."

"What was he like?"

Mathilde looked at Eva with an impish smile. "Oh, he was bad. He was a character, that one." Her aunt steadied her hands on the coffee table and shook her head, laughing at an inside joke. "Always causing trouble." It looked like she was gearing up to tell a doozy of a story, but deflated instead. She looked at the top of the table, then at her unpainted fingernails. She took a long drink. Eva's mouth felt dry, so she poured herself another one too, picking up the cleaning spray and wiping down the counter again.

"You know," Mathilde said. "You should learn how to make jambalaya."

"Jambalaya?"

"We had cousins visit from Louisiana one time and they shared a recipe." Mathilde was smiling with her eyes closed, clutching the glass of wine to her chest. "I remember it being so spicy. Like nothing I'd ever had before."

"Jambalaya. Like the song."

Mathilde's eyes lit up. "Like the song! You know the song?" She beamed. Eva loved seeing her aunt's face bright like that. Warm. It was rare to see her genuinely happy.

"*Jambalaya, crawfish pie and a filé gumbo,*" Eva sang. "*'cause tonight I'm gonna see my share of meatloaf.*"

Mathilde looked up, confused. "Eh?"

Eva put down the rag. "What?"

"Sing it again?"

"Why?"

"Tell me what you just said right there."

"*Jambalaya, crawfish pie and a filé gumbo,*" she sang.

"And the next part?"

"Why?"

"I need to hear what you said."

"*'cause tonight I'm gonna see my share of meatloaf.*"

"*Amio?*"

"Meatloaf."

Mathilde's head swung back and she cackled. "*Chère. Ma chère amio.*"

"It's not meatloaf?"

Mathilde couldn't stop laughing, rocking back and forth, eyes closed and slapping her thigh. "*O, ma chère. Tu me fais pitier.*"

"I don't get it."

Mathilde calmed herself and wiped away the tears that had collected under her eyes. "*Ma chère amio,*" Mathilde said. "It's *ma chère amio.* You didn't get that? I call you *chère* all the time."

Eva's smile dipped. "Oh, yeah. I get it now. I get it."

"I needed that," Mathilde sighed, pushing her brittle hair away from her face, collecting the last bit of happy tears with her fingertips. "That was good. You know, your mom almost named you Yvonne, after that song."

Eva looked up. She didn't say anything. She didn't want to spook her aunt while she was talking about her mother. Mathilde was still smiling, like a child remembering a day at the carnival, while she looked down at her feet. "She wanted to call you Yvonne."

Eva put down her wine glass and folded her arms across her chest. She leaned up against the counter, making a conscious effort not to look at her aunt. She felt her mother in the room peering over her shoulder. Silk soft skin. Baby powder. Jelly soaps and candy.

"Why did she choose Eva? Evangeline?"

But Mathilde was lost in thought. Unblinking, staring at her toes and breathing slow. "I don't remember." She rubbed her thighs.

"Oh."

"I think your dad chose your name, actually."

"Oh."

"It makes me happy that she's no longer in our lives. It's a good thing, eh?"

Eva remained silent but nodded her head.

"Well," Mathilde said through a yawn. "*Shu fatiqué*."

She struggled up to stand, made sure her glass was full of wine and headed to her bedroom. As the door opened, Eva caught a glimpse of the bed, which was covered in unfolded clothes. The floor was a sea of still unpacked boxes. The room looked like a dimly lit cave, and Mathilde smiled gently as she closed the door behind her.

Eva's eyes hung heavy and felt full of sand, and she decided that what she needed was to take a bath. The muscles in her legs and shoulders tenderized and she sank deeper into the water. She hugged herself, feeling like a belly-up turtle, trying to breathe in the steam. When she was a kid, her mom would run baths for her. She remembered always hearing the kettle on the stove scream whenever she was in the bath. In the lukewarm water, Eva sat with her Barbies and her facecloth, jelly soaps and her mom's pumice stone. Her mom would come into the washroom and hot water would plume around Eva's legs as the kettle tipped into the bathtub.

"Habit," her mother would say when Eva asked why she boiled water for her bath. "We didn't always have hot water."

She remembered being on her back in the water, her mom swishing her small body up and down along the bottom of the tub rinsing her hair and singing. The warm water caressed her head, and she remembered the feeling of the water sloshing up onto her forehead, but never getting into her eyes. Her mother cupped water into her hair, rinsing out the shampoo that tingled her scalp. She could close her eyes and trust she'd never have to open them again if she didn't want to.

Dors, dors, p'tit bébé
C'est le beau p'tit bébé à maman

But sometimes, her mother's hand would slip on the wet porcelain and dunk into the tub, splashing water everywhere. And sometimes, her speech would slur. And sometimes, Eva would smell a sour, fermented stench float off her breath. It scared her, and she would ask if she could leave the tub. Her mother would smile softly and open up a large, fluffy towel and envelop her in her arms and shake her until Eva forced a laugh. And then, her father would be there, outside the door, and he would tell Eva to wait in the hallway with her hair soaking wet and dripping down her back with her once warm body now growing cold. Her knees would shake while she watched her father open up the cupboard in the bathroom and take out an orange pill bottle. He would tell her mother to hold out her palm and he would shake the small white pills into her hand and pour her a glass of water and watch her swallow them.

One time, she saw her mother slap her father in the kitchen. Her father looked right into Eva's eyes and clenched his jaw and told her

45

that everything would be okay. Her mother was having a bad day, he said.

The next morning, her father sat with her on the living room floor. He cut a long strip of blue construction paper and taped it together creating a loop. He placed it on his head and made a silly face, pouting his lips and speaking in a British accent.

"I'm the Queen of England!"

Eva giggled so hard her stomach muscles cramped.

"Want some juice?" He asked, pushing himself to standing. Eva watched as her father went to the kitchen and poured three bright orange drinks. He pulled open one of the drawers and Eva saw him take a pill and crush it before spilling the powder into one of the glasses.

"Shhh." He put his finger to his lips, then waggled it at her. "It's okay. Your mom has trouble remembering sometimes, and we have to help her take her medication."

Eva got out of the tub, pushed a glob of toothpaste on the end of her toothbrush and stuck it in her mouth. She wiped away the steam from the mirror, her skin slick and faintly grey. Her short brown hair fell just above her shoulders and curled from the steam. Her face was round and full. Too full, she thought. She disliked how the dark brown colour of her eyes almost completely camouflaged her pupils. When she opened up the towel to look at her naked body, she was disappointed to see that her legs were still muscular and that her hips were still nonexistent. Her skeletal upper body made her look as though she had a bobblehead, and she resented the fact that her fat never sat in the correct places. She thought about all the times she went to bed hungry as a kid, although she didn't remember why. She remembered their nice, big house, that her bedroom was pink and that her dad went to work every day. Each Friday, he'd bring home a new toy that they would play with together on the weekends. She remembered asking her dad for a Mermaid Barbie, specifically Midge, with her bright turquoise bedazzled fish tail and long auburn locks. Her dad pranced around the kitchen in his thick leather jacket, getting her to chase him as she ached for the packaging held above his head. She remembered loving him the moment he handed her the shining box, Midge's bright eyes staring blankly up at her with her golden crown. But Eva still remembered the gnawing feeling of hunger at night and didn't know why. When she was told to stay in her room and not come out.

Eva wrapped herself back up in her towel, spat in the sink and rinsed her toothbrush. In her bedroom, she pulled a clean oversized shirt over her head and climbed under the covers. She rolled over, reached down underneath her bed and pulled out a wooden box. She put it on her lap and opened it, revealing tiny individually wrapped chocolates, a clementine and a small pepperoni stick. She could smell the phantom fragrance of jasmine in the room. It smelled like her mother.

VII
Mathilde

Exposed brick met the palm of Mathilde's hand as she leaned up against the south wall of her room, a thin line of sweat dripping down to the small of her back.

Her room was in complete disarray with clean clothes mixed with the dirty ones thrown about all over her floor. It had begun with a gentle unpacking of her belongings. While Eva had unpacked within days of arriving in Montreal, Mathilde was less keen. She'd left her suitcases open on the floor and picked out pieces as needed. Boxes of books and knick-knacks remained sealed and hidden in her closet. The only items that were removed with care were her paints, brushes and canvas. The rest were ignored and left to be dealt with later.

The one box that Mathilde had been wanting to unpack, waiting for the right moment, was the one that sat in the back of her closet, covered by a purple silk scarf. It was a small box, no more than six inches by six inches, smooth caramel-coloured cardboard taped perfectly. Mathilde waited, listening to her own heart beating and the sound of her short, shallow breaths, before reaching into the closet and removing the box. With a sharp paring knife, she slit the tape in one clean line on all four sides, pulling the cardboard flaps open. Inside sat a photograph of Adam as a young man, a porcelain cross and a small heart-shaped rock. What made Mathilde's heart skip a beat was not the contents of the box, but what was missing. The envelope. She could have sworn she'd packed it.

What if?

After exhausting her search through overflowing suitcases, hastily folded bed sheets and kitchen supplies, Mathilde wrapped her shaking hand around the handle to Eva's room and creaked open the door. Eva was still in the bathtub, and Mathilde paused—listening for the sound of water sloshing and a plug being pulled. Eva's room was like ice. A perfectly smoothed sheet covering her twin bed. Clean walls. Mathilde knew it was wrong, but she couldn't stop herself. Pushing away the bubbling feeling in her belly, she felt like a child again, snooping through her mother's room for lipstick and blush, applying the makeup in the mirror to feel what it felt like to be beautiful. She pulled open the top drawer, revealing Eva's underwear and socks. White cotton socks were rolled neatly together and placed in bundles on one side and pretty lace underwear—blue, pink, purple, and black—cuddled on the other. Mathilde almost forgot why she was there in the first place; the underwear stared up at her and told her something about her niece that Mathilde had not thought about before. It startled her, leaving her arms numb. She pushed the soft lace underwear aside to look underneath, seeing nothing but the bottom of the drawer. She gently closed it and opened the next one. Shirts and sweaters neatly folded with nothing underneath. The other drawers contained nothing but jeans and leggings, which soothed her nerves. The lack of anything gave Mathilde a calm feeling until she remembered that the envelope was still missing and could be anywhere for Eva to find.

She looked at the perfectly made bed, its crisp cotton sheets spread tight. Mathilde felt along the bedding and then reached beneath the cool, soft pillow. Her fingertips touched the sharp edge of something, and she pulled out a glossy photograph of a young Gabrielle, smiling, her eyes squinting into the sun and her hair flowing down along her shoulders. The picture was a voice, talking as if cotton was stuffed into its mouth, a low hum and a cadence of warning. It spoke to her of the evenings when Eva took too long to get back from the hotel. It spoke to her of strange noises in the night. It spoke to her of Eva, sharpening a knife before hacking into a whole, raw chicken.

She's still Gabrielle's daughter.

Mathilde remembered the small drops of blood.

She was visiting her sister at the large house in Halifax. Eva couldn't have been more than four and Gabrielle had gone off her medication. She'd pushed Adam out of the house. He tripped and fell down their back patio steps, smacking his face on the stone. Gabrielle had accused him of cheating.

Adam went to Mathilde after Gabrielle had gone to bed early. He had tears in his eyes. "Her moods," he said, his black eye fresh on his face and tender to the touch. "I can't keep up with them."

Gabrielle complained the medication made her drowsy and scrambled her memory. To Mathilde, this was a small price to pay for a happy husband. Mathilde placed her hand on his. It was warm and calloused. He was so strong.

"I can't control her," he said.

"You don't have to. She should be taking care of you. And Eva."

"She won't take her medication."

"Maybe it would be better if . . ." Mathilde said. But she couldn't bring herself to finish the sentence or the thought. "Make an appointment for her tomorrow. We will try together."

They ended up packing her into the car under the pretense of going to see a movie. Mathilde sat in the front seat while Gabrielle sat in the back with Eva. Once Gabrielle had figured out that they were actually going to the doctor's office, she started to scream, reaching for the seatbelt and trying to unbuckle the clasp. Mathilde reached back and tried to grab hold of her sister's arms to hold them down, struggling with the bounce back of muscle and the knowledge that this is what her sister had become. Eva sat in her car seat, big doe eyes and chubby cheeks staring as her mother writhed.

"You can't make me take them!" She shouted. "You can't make me!"

Adam angled the car into the curb and shut the engine off. He unclipped his seatbelt. As he walked around to her side of the car, Gabrielle went quiet, tears still falling down her cheeks. Her eyes were red. Adam opened her door and knelt down while cars drove by, oblivious. His shoulders rounded and he looked up at Gabrielle. His hands clasped together over her thighs like a prayer. "I need you to do what I tell you." His voice was calm and focused. "You have to."

Mathilde loosened her grip and pulled away while Gabrielle's neck slackened, and her head tilted back onto the headrest. She closed her eyes and said nothing, no longer fighting. Adam and Mathilde looked at each other and nodded in agreement; this was Gabrielle's way of acquiescing.

They made it to the doctor and Gabrielle went in with Adam. Mathilde sat in the waiting room with Eva who picked up a magazine from the coffee table and roughly turned the pages, ripping at them with her chubby, strong hands. The pages were filled with pictures of women posing in luxurious clothing on a beach and in a farmhouse and next to a large perfume bottle and by a pool. Mathilde gently pulled the magazine out of her niece's hands and traded it for a colouring book, setting a box of crayons on the empty seat next to her.

Back at the house, Gabrielle boiled potatoes while fat raindrops smacked against the windows. Mathilde watched as each slimy peeled potato slipped out of her sister's hand and dropped into the water. She made monotonous movements as if possessed. Eva sat small at the table, her baby belly jutting out from underneath her top while she held a bright orange carrot in one hand and a vegetable peeler in the other. The entire house filled with steam, a balloon that could burst at any moment. The sound of rain echoed inside the sterile kitchen, painted cream white and devoid of character, tile bleached white as if nobody had ever used it before, but for some reason cleaned daily.

"*Patate*," Mathilde said to her niece. "*Patate*." She held up a potato and waved it. "*Dis-la. Prononce-la.*" But Eva stared blankly, dark circles under her wide eyes and her little pink lips pushed into a pout. Much to Mathilde's disappointment, her niece was not learning French. She noticed a food stain on the toddler's T-shirt.

"*As-tu besoin de d'l'aïde,*" Mathilde turned to her sister.

But Gabrielle didn't turn around. Her back was stiff. "I don't need any help." She spoke to the pot.

Eva's tiny hands worked over the orange flesh of the carrot, juice staining her fingernails. The handle of the peeler slipped through her fingers, and she caught it by the blade.

"There better be carrot left," Gabrielle said over her shoulder. "Only peel the skin."

The upstairs radio flicked on, and the wooden spoon fell from Gabrielle's hand and clattered on the stovetop. She froze, ears perked. Listening. She still had not taken her medication. Mathilde could see it. She could see the childishness in her sister as she tensed her back and jumped at every sudden sound. Eva sat silent with her heels propped up under her bottom, so her belly button squished into the side of the table. She looked at her mom and then at Mathilde as if trying to discern the mood.

"Are you going to school next year?" Mathilde leaned across the table and put her face directly in front of the child's. "*Tcheu grade t'es dedans?*"

Eva didn't say anything. Her face was deep olive and round and she had small puffs under her eyes as if she hadn't been sleeping. The dark hair on top of her head, soft wisps.

"She's going into kindergarten," Gabrielle said, still looking at the pot.

Mathilde made a warm, surprised face. "Kindergarten! *Ça c'est un vraiment bon grade.* Look at you."

Eva looked like she wanted to smile back, but instead, her tongue flicked out of her mouth, reaching toward the bottom of her chin as if trying to lick a speck of forgotten chocolate. She looked at her mother's back seemingly waiting to be fed a line. The handle of the carrot peeler looked like it was digging deeper into her belly as she slid the blade down the length of the root.

"Gabrielle." Adam's voice shouted from the bedroom upstairs.

"What's your favourite colour?" Mathilde leaned in closer to Eva and pulled a pack of crayons from her purse. "What would you like me to draw?"

"Gabrielle." Adam's voice grew louder.

"*Comment c'que tes tchums s'appellont?*" Mathilde asked. But Eva continued to stare at her mother.

"Gabrielle!"

Eva flinched at her father's angry shout. The peeler slipped through her fingers and clattered to the table, then to the floor, skidding across the tile to Gabrielle's toes. Gabrielle whipped around from the stove. She grabbed Eva's shoulders and squished them so tightly the child was hoisted off the chair. Mathilde saw the veins in Gabrielle's thin arms pulse and her lips curl, revealing sharp teeth.

"What did I say?" She growled low as Eva's eyes grew big. She dropped Eva back on the chair and grabbed her cheeks between her thumb and finger, squeezing them like a vice. Then she smacked her upside the head before returning to the stove.

Mathilde let out the breath she'd been holding when Gabrielle removed a colander from the cupboard and drained the boiled potatoes into the sink, steam rising into the air filling the already heavy room. Eva looked at Mathilde, mouth open in a grimace the way children look when they're not sure if they're allowed to cry, baby teeth set in her gums like Chiclets, face red. Her hair was bunched in the spot where her mother had smacked her.

"Don't start." Gabrielle glared at Mathilde as she strode out of the kitchen toward the stairs. Mathilde bent down and picked up the peeler. Blood bubbled on Eva's tiny finger. She took Eva's little hand and helped her off the chair. Inside the small bathroom, Mathilde locked the door. She ran a wad of toilet paper under the faucet and gently dabbed it on Eva's finger. Some of the blood had dripped onto the white tile. Her nails were barely the size of an eraser on the top of a yellow pencil, and Mathilde admired them while dabbing away the blood.

"*T'as des beaux ongles,*" she said. "I wish I had nails like yours."

Tears bubbled up in Eva's eyes.

"You're okay," was the only thing Mathilde could think to say. "You're okay. Don't cry. Oh, *chère*, don't cry. Let me see that smile. Yeah, there it is. You don't have to cry, okay? *C'est point* that bad. *T'as point besoin de brailler.* Maybe you can come stay with me, eh? It's okay. It's okay. Oh, sweetheart, it will be okay."

Remembering Eva's tiny face scrunched up in fear made Mathilde's hands tremble. She rushed back to her bedroom and waited, listening as the water from Eva's bath drained. She held her breath as it quivered at the top of her chest, silently waiting for its release. When her niece finished in the bathroom, Mathilde snuck in and tugged on the roll of toilet paper, ripping off a few squares and squishing them into her eyes. She refused to buy tissues and allowed the toilet paper to dissolve in her hands as more tears fell. She ripped up the photograph of Gabrielle and threw the scraps into the garbage can. She paced back and forth through the kitchen, accidentally kicking the full blue recycling bag. The cans and bottles inside made a sharp clinking noise against her toe. Eva was supposed to have taken them out. Mathilde heaved up the bag and staggered outside, where the air smelled of smoke. The curb was lined with blue and black bags and when she dropped hers down, there was the sound of breaking glass. A woman walked by and smiled; Mathilde imagined her face distorting, lips falling off and black eyes rotting in her head.

In the kitchen, the calendar that hung on the wall above the stove reminded Mathilde of why they'd moved. It was coming soon. With every new sunset, a growing shadow loomed over her and Eva. She grabbed a pen and sat at the kitchen table, pulling out a sheet of paper from her stack of art supplies by the window.

I never knew my sister. Not in the way other sisters do. We were not connected by some spiritual tether, and if we ever were, it was cut early and quick, so early and quick that we never knew it existed in the first place. Gabrielle was the youngest, after our brother and me. She was a spark. Full of life. I knew she was one of those people who believed that the world was created for them. I must admit at one point I was jealous. But after what happened, after what I learned, I was forced to reconcile with the truth. I saw all the things she kept hidden from us. The abuse, the deception, the manipulation. It completely broke me. I didn't truly know my sister. I only knew an idea of her. I take responsibility for not recognizing her danger. What I once believed was zest for life was a complete disregard for safety. What I once believed was charm was calculation. What I once believed was confidence was selfishness. Gabrielle was destined to travel down this path because she was born without a conscience. She is unfit to be released. I believe that if she's let out of prison, she will make the same choices again. We need to be protected from her.

VIII
Gaby

Days are meaningless in segregation. Time served is meaningless.
It doesn't mean a goddamn thing. Gaby lay on the blue mattress
on the bolted-down bed and pretended to sleep, knowing a demon
slept underneath. She wouldn't touch her toes to the ground without jumping a few feet first. And when she sat on the toilet, she'd see
his face under the bed, looking over at her, grinning a toothy grin.
His eyes hollow and grey. They never shut off the light. She could
always see him. He never blinked.

Once again, they brought her out to the yard. Gaby sat, once
again, handcuffed and head down. She was so tired that being tired
was pointless. Her eyes closed unintentionally, but she never slept.
Her head just lolled to one side, and then the other, threatening to
snap her neck like a wafer. But at least outside the air felt different.
Cool. Fresher than the cell.

She remembered when she was sixteen. It had been the eighth
anniversary of their father's death. Maddie was there, baby-faced
and stubborn as always. Gaby and Maddie curled up in bed and
listened to an Edith Piaf record that their father had found at a yard
sale. They were both quiet, looking up at the ceiling until Maddie
spoke.

"I think we're cursed," she squeaked. The corners of her mouth
turned down.

Gaby scoffed. "God doesn't care enough about us to curse us."

"How could you say that?"

It had stuck with her, the way Maddie always fixated on the darkness. She was terrified of God. She was so caught up in feeling guilty about doing wrong, she could never focus on what she could do right. Gaby had seen her sister scrub her hands raw after watching a movie with a sex scene or one that had too many curse words. Perfect. Saintly. Those were Maddie's aspirations. For a while, she painted nothing but scenes from the Bible. The birth of Jesus, with light shining out of the cradle and Mary looking down at him with love. The Sermon on the Mount, Jesus holding up his right hand on a cliff surrounded by a large crowd of listeners.

Gaby remembered leaning against the wall while Maddie painted, dipping her brush into pots of thick paint, some of which were so old they had dried, and Maddie had to add drops of warm water to the pots to loosen up the pigment. She sat at her desk, smoothing the paint onto the board.

"*Ça icette c'est assez plate*," Gaby said.

"It's not boring."

"Come on, let's go to the beach."

"I'm busy."

"I can steal some of Mom's beer."

"Go with Marc."

"He's not here."

"Go by yourself."

"You never want to do anything fun."

"Oh, Gabrielle, you're such a leech."

"I am not!"

"I want to be alone."

"Maddie, come on."

"*J'veux être tout seule astheure!*"

The rejection hit Gaby like a weight to the gut. She could feel her face getting hot. She eyed the unfinished painting on Maddie's desk. It looked like it was going to depict the Cleansing of the Temple, as she'd sketched out a raised fist clutching rope. Before Maddie could react, Gaby snatched the painting off the desk and bolted. She could hear her sister's footsteps barreling behind her down the wooden steps of the porch and out onto the gravel driveway. She hopped across the grass, almost tripping over her bare feet, leaping over rocks and sharp weeds and poison ivy. Sinewy legs and arms splaying up into the air. She cackled like a witch as she ran. Maddie shouted at her to stop, running behind her all burly, her arms puffing at her side. Gaby kept going, clutching the painting in her hands, twisting at her thin waist to look back at her sister struggling.

"Catch me!" The wind felt free on her face and adrenaline pumped through her veins better than any drug. They ran through their neighbour Joe's backyard and landed on the hot tan beach, running as if in a dream. Gaby's feet sank deep in the wet, low-tide sand but she kept moving until the icy waves splashed up on her legs, soaking her jeans and dragging her heavily into the brine. With one swing of her arm, the painting flew up into the air and landed face-down in the water.

Her sister screamed and dove after it. Gaby stood waist-deep in the water, waves crashing up against her as she watched her sister bobbing up and down in the ocean, reaching for the now soaking canvas. Giddy, she jumped into an oncoming wave and tumbled around under the water before coming up for a breath. She floated on her back, face up to the bright sun, and breathed in the salt air. She felt like a mermaid. That's when the sun disappeared and she felt hands grip around her neck.

Maddie was overhead, blocking out the sun with her body and choking her. Gaby thrashed in the waves, trying to find her footing, digging her toes into the sand and trying to stand. The waves continued to flow, uncaring, threatening to drown them both until

Gaby felt support underneath her back. They'd made it to shore, but Maddie's hands were still wrapped around Gaby's throat. Her sister's face hung over her, dark and round, hair dripping at the ends and splattering salt water. Gaby couldn't breathe. She flopped like a dying fish on the sand, legs whirling in the air, hands clawing at Maddie's arms. Their neighbours, Philip and Manon, along with Sherri and Pam from up the road, stood in the distance, hands over their mouths looking on. Maddie let go just as it felt like Gaby's head was going to pop. She fell back into the wash and inhaled deeply, coughing up salty pools. She felt hands on her arms and shoulders, lifting her up with frantic voices.

"As-tu besoin de d'l'aïde?"

She stood, jeans heavy and thick, threatening to fall down. She felt so small on the expanse of the sandy shoreline. The sun sank low on the horizon and she watched as Maddie grew smaller and smaller, shrinking away.

"Maddie!" Gaby cried after her. "I was only playing!"

But Maddie didn't turn her head. She walked up over the dunes and back along the boardwalk, leaving splotches of wet in the dry sand. Gaby pulled a thin strand of seaweed off her forearm and let the sea grab and pull it away. The neighbours dispersed. Gaby was left to walk back along the shore alone, her jeans and T-shirt heavy from the weight of the sea.

The sound of grating metal preceded a voice.

"Lawrence. Out."

It was time to go back.

IX
Eva

Eva biked up Rue Rachel, passing the small park with the concrete arch where the leaves were changing from bright green to crimson. She dodged orange and white plastic construction cones scattered down the street, her leg muscles sore but strong. Detour signs and fencing that had seemingly been placed at random had been knocked over by the wind or frustrated commuters. In the down-hill bike lane, she switched to autopilot, Walkman clipped to the top of her jean shorts, black cord winding up to small earbuds. The warm afternoon air taking her in its hands and filling her lungs with oxygen. Along Maisonneuve, she rode through the belly of the city. Cars revved, moving and halting without warning while kids on skateboards weaved in and out of traffic, defying stop signs and broken limbs. Eva flew by slower bikers with ease, a yellow traffic light a dare, and when she reached Concordia on Bishop, she slowed.

The university consisted of multiple buildings spanning several downtown blocks, sandwiched between Sainte-Catherine and Maisonneuve. Eva made her way through the doors of the Hall building and into a sea of students, who swarmed up through the tunnels from the metro, packing the escalators and the hallways. Eva felt like she was being swept along by an academic current. Walking up the broken escalators to the fifth floor, she found the lecture hall she wanted. Students waited on their phones for class to begin. Eva sat in the fourth row and attempted to save a seat for Alma, but two people flanked her and locked her in. She took out her notebook and a secondhand copy of *The Norton Shakespeare Tragedies*.

Professor Moore was a frazzled man with waxy skin and tousled short red hair whose round glasses always seemed askew. As he entered the auditorium, he dumped a briefcase, a stack of papers and a sportscoat onto the desk in front of a whiteboard. As he fiddled with the clasp on his briefcase, his elbow accidentally knocked the stack of papers off his desk. Some students laughed and Eva felt embarrassed for the poor man. She was surprised when he laughed too and then made a small kick with his sock-and-Birkenstock-attired left foot, following up with a jerking motion with his hands. Two students in the front row helped gather the papers off the floor.

"Well, thank you, friends," Professor Moore said. "Best men oft are moulded out of faults, eh?"

In the three lectures Eva had attended, they'd covered almost all of *Hamlet*. While she recognized most of the individual words, trying to decipher their meaning made her head hurt. But she enjoyed listening to Professor Moore and what other people thought of the story. Their ideas came from a place Eva couldn't name, and she sank lower in her seat, like a bird settling into its nest.

She'd discovered the Shakespeare class thanks to Alma, who'd texted her the day after they met. *Are you in Moore's class? We can meet up.*

I am. But I forgot my schedule. What's the room number?

Although terrified she'd get caught, Eva told Alma she'd meet her. When she walked into the lecture hall and heard the professor talk about a strange place in Denmark she'd never heard of before, she was mesmerized.

Every day she wasn't working, Eva would go to Concordia and wander the halls, listening to passing clusters of students talk about

Alejandro Jodorowsky and John Milton. She'd meander until she found larger classes where it was easier for her to go unnoticed. She learned about modernity and Buddhism. She learned about the Dead Sea scrolls and Gentileschi's *Judith and Holofernes*, amazed by the painting cast on the lecture hall's huge screen. The golden hue of her skin, the strength of her arms, the blood flowing down the white linen. How many painters had depicted the beheading?

"Did you know there were female painters back then?" she asked her aunt that evening as they ate a steak Eva had found on sale. But Mathilde only narrowed her eyes and stabbed at the overcooked meat.

"And did you know that the earliest known named author was a woman? Enheduanna. She was from Iraq. Or what's now Iraq. She was a priestess."

One time, Eva wandered in on a lecture about female sexual dysfunction and learned about a woman who had an electronic device implanted into her pelvis because she heard it could help her achieve orgasms, but it ended up making her leg spasm at random. Eva felt as if she had landed on another planet. Like she'd gained access to a secret society. She wanted it all. The plush seating in the lobby. The sparkling chrome on the escalators. The smart blazers the professors wore, the wine and cheese events, the rich-smelling textbooks. Eva wanted to complain about the elevators being broken and have it be the worst part of her day. She loved watching the students with home-bleached hair and matte black platform creepers and oversized graphic tees and 90s polyester shirt dresses banter with professors.

But it was delicate. There was always fear. Fear that her secret would come out and she would be caught and shamed. She became a rat, running from room-to-room evading capture. Because it was more than just witch trials and Charlie Chaplin movies and women painters and the meaning behind forgotten religious iconography. It was something else. It was the feeling of belonging. The feeling of the plastic chairs and the excitement in a professor's voice. It was the tension of sitting next to a boy, handsome with thick blond hair that waved up over his head—did he glance her way? It was the wealth of knowledge that surrounded her. Sitting among so many people who also wanted to learn.

Alma walked down the aisle of the lecture hall just as Professor Moore was talking about Ophelia with the same frantic energy that seemed to electrify the air around him. Alma's thick hair bounced as she took a seat a few rows away and gave Eva a little wave.

"Sit with me," Alma whisper-shouted. She patted the chair beside her.

Eva shook her head, but this only made Alma work harder. "Come on!" she mouthed.

Eva rolled her eyes and stood up, gripping her backpack and books tightly to her chest. She slid between her chair and another student, wobbling her way so as to not smack anyone in the head. She could feel the professor's eyes tracking her, but he continued with the lecture.

Alma wasn't wearing a bra under her white linen blouse. She smiled, and Eva noticed for the first time that her front teeth were crooked, folding over each other like messy stacks of white paper. Eva felt a desire to shrink down until she was tiny enough to hide in Alma's horribly cared-for nailbeds. She wanted to see what Alma ate, what she read, how she applied her makeup. Did she use a brush? Or did she smear foundation on her fingers and mush the product into her skin? How often did she smoke? Did she steal clothes? Alma knew how to speak Portuguese. Alma was smart and a mess. Eva looked down at her own nails, trimmed and clean.

"Are you coming tonight?"

"I might," Eva said.

"It's at a friend's place. I'll send you the address."

"I might."

Alma took out her pen and tapped on Eva's pages. "You have nice writing."

Eva forced a small smile and rubbed the tips of her fingers across her forehead, looking down at her secondhand textbook with someone else's notes in the margins.

The flyers were red and had a drawing of a crumbling building sketched in black Sharpie. Calls to keep education accessible and affordable flanked the image—a threat or a prophecy, Eva couldn't tell. She hung back outside the student café while Alma kept walking. One of the students handed Eva a flyer.

"How much does tuition cost?" she asked, then flushed as she realized her mistake. But the student only gave her a sour look, causing Eva to back away and almost trip.

Outside on Mackay Street, Alma paced back and forth smoking a cigarette.

"Can I have one?"

Alma fished the pack out of her bag. Eva picked one out like a piece of candy, and Alma lit it for her.

"So, you coming to the party? I want you to meet Dex."

Eva let the smoke slowly leave her lips. Her brows furrowed. "I want to do well in school."

"Why?" Alma spread her arms wide. "We live in a city where eighteen-year-olds go to retire." She had the biggest grin on her face. Eva gave a tight smile, flicking the ash. The sidewalk moved in and out of focus as she stared off into the distance, letting the nicotine buzz take her.

"Are you okay?" Alma gave a nudge.

Eva shrugged.

"You go out last night?"

She shook her head. "No, I stayed in."

"You seem off."

"I'm not. I'm just . . . I don't really go to parties."

"Just come drink, you'll be fine."

Alma took a long drag and looked down at her toes. She kicked a rock and watched as it skipped down the sidewalk.

"What's Dex like?" Eva asked. Alma's cheeks went pink and she dropped her cigarette, killing it underneath her toe.

"You'll love him."

"What should I wear?"

"That's a yes!" Alma did a small jump and gave Eva a punch on the arm. "See you tonight!"

Eva watched as her friend strode away with her nose high in the sky, tiny leather backpack swinging from her shoulders.

When she walked into the party, Eva was confronted with a narrow hallway plastered with paintings and charcoal drawings of emaciated bodies and rough sketches of hands and faces. Mud caked the uneven hardwood floors. Eva watched a thin boy in black jeans with no shirt lick a small tab of paper off his middle finger. He locked eyes with her, his face and chest covered in glitter. She smelled burning hair. In another room, a girl wearing a crop top over a viscose mini dress poked someone's bare leg with an inky sewing needle. People passed around manifestos and artwork while kids discussed the ramifications of gentrification and railed lines of coke off small mirrors. Two girls walked around handcuffed together to "bring awareness about a new wave of digital feminism." Eva listened to the conversations ringing around the room.

"What's the increase?"

"Ten percent I heard."

"The French schools will fight it."

"It's nothing."

"It might not be."

"They can all go to hell."

"Who?"

"The ministers. Fucking trash."

"My friend said he heard people already have a campaign organized."

"A campaign? To do what?"

"Eva!" Alma called over from the middle of the stairs, moving her arm in a way that told Eva to come quick. Alma grabbed her hand and pulled her up the steps and down a hall into a small bathroom. She locked the door. Eva leaned up against a towel rack, feeling the metal dig into her back and smelling freshly sprayed lavender Febreze. Alma strained to look over her shoulder at her back in the mirror.

"Am I bleeding?"

"What?"

"Can you see blood?"

"I can't see anything."

"Thank God. I felt warm. I thought my tampon leaked."

"There's nothing there."

Alma turned and faced the mirror, fluffing up her hair and then tilting her head into a goofy smile, teeth sticking out underneath her forced thin lips. She locked eyes with Eva, who erupted into laughter at her new friend's silly face.

"You're so pretty," Alma said. It caught Eva off guard. Alma's eyelids were thick and heavy, parted lips smiling.

"You think?" She pulled her eyes away from Alma and stared at herself. She was wearing light blue jeans and an oversized T-shirt. Next to Alma, who looked effortlessly cool in all black, she felt bland.

"Very," she said. And then she left, so casually, opening the door and disappearing into the hall, leaving Eva to stand alone in front of her own reflection. As if people said those things without expecting anything in return. As if she had ever been made to feel beautiful.

She opened all the drawers, unsure of what she was looking for. She pocketed some tampons because she knew she was starting soon. In one drawer, she found a dark purple shade of lipstick. She rubbed the top layer onto a piece of toilet paper before smearing the clean pigment onto her lips. A brown purse next to the sink was unzipped and open, displaying a fat wallet. Eva picked it up and flipped through: a student ID for someone named Abi and a grocery store gift card. Eva took both.

In the hallway, she heard what sounded like someone crying behind an almost closed door. It was dark inside and Eva listened to see if she could hear the voice again, but all she heard was breathing, hard breathing, and something knocking back and forth. When she peered in, she saw a man on the floor in a pushup position with his shoulder muscles round through his shirt. Eva thought she saw a wig on the floor, but realized it was a girl, head to one side and hair splayed out long. He had blond hair, and his head was facing the wall, but his eyes were closed and the muscles on his face were twisted. The girl moaned again. Or was it a cry? Eva didn't move. She saw him lift one hand off the floor and grip the girl's skull, grabbing a clump of hair. Eva felt herself breathe in sharply and then backed away from the door, unsure of why there was a horrible sinking feeling in her stomach, as she saw his head turn toward her.

She found Alma downstairs in the living room talking to a boy with short red hair and thick, dark glasses. Everyone was shoulder to shoulder, hollering over a booming sound system. They were talking about Mac Demarco's tooth gap and whether Naked & Famous jeans were worth it. She touched Alma's shoulder and she turned, lips stained purple and pulled into a big grin. That's when Eva felt something hard touch her wrist and heard a clicking sound. She looked down and saw a handcuff dangling. She looked up and saw the two feminists smiling. Alma laughed and held out her arm.

"Me too!"

The girls clicked the other cuff around Alma's wrist. Alma let out another manic laugh, tilting the bottle of wine into her mouth.

"Let's go scare Dex." Alma pushed people aside, pulling Eva along, the metal handcuff digging into her wrist. Eva had only seen handcuffs once in real life, and they'd been wrapped around her mother's wrists. She looked down at the bright metal that twinkled in the low light. Alma held up her hand once they had maneuvered their way to the kitchen.

There he was, the same blond hair. But his eyes were open now. His neck was slick with sweat, and he was out of breath when he bent down to kiss Alma on the lips.

"Looks like you'll have to take us both home," Alma joked, holding up her handcuffed wrist. Eva stiffened. Dex appeared unamused, the muscles in his jaw clenching. His eyes flicked to Eva and then back to Alma.

"Why would you say that?"

"It was a joke."

"It's not funny."

"Oh, whatever. Eva, want a beer? Dex, get her a beer."

Dex opened the fridge and pulled out a beer, handing the cold, sweaty bottle to Eva. He took one for himself, twisted it open and tilted the bottle into his mouth for a short sip.

Eva felt like the handcuff was getting tighter on her wrist, and she looked around the party to see if she could spot the feminists and convince them to unlock her.

"Hey," Dex said. He tipped his bottle toward Eva's and clinked the neck of his beer to hers. He gave her a wink. "Cheers."

He took a long swig. Alma turned and touched someone's shoulder, leaning away even though her hand was still chained to Eva's. Dex was tall and soft blond chest hairs peeked out from the top of his shirt, along with the flash of a thin gold chain. She noticed he had dark moles on his neck that trailed down into his collar like constellations.

"Oh, woah," Dex said. "Do you want another?"

She was confused by the question until she looked down at her empty beer. Strums from a guitar erupted from the next room and she saw two people picking up electric guitars and throwing the straps over their thin bodies. They both had thick, black hair and wore bulky leather jackets and bobbed around while they waited for their drummer to take a seat. The drummer smashed his sticks on a cymbal and moved back and forth on the stool like an excited kid. Eva heard a screeching noise blast out of the amp and a horrible, out-of-tune note ring. She turned to Alma, who rolled her eyes.

"I think I need to go," Eva said, but Alma couldn't hear her.

"I need to leave!" she said louder. She felt the handcuff tug at her wrist.

Alma gave her a pleading look and shouted at Dex to get Eva another beer.

Dex had not taken his eyes off Eva and only stared at her, blinking once. He looked at her as if he were trying to place her, decoding her eyes and excavating her face shape. She'd seen the same expression on other people's faces. Eva saw the familiar click in Dex's eyes when he connected the dots. Although this felt different. Dex wasn't recognizing her as her mother's daughter. He wasn't recognizing her from some news story. He was placing where he first saw her—half an hour ago, upstairs in the hallway.

"Alma, I'm gonna go home."

"No stay! Stay, come on. The band gets better. Sometimes."

Eva tried to pull the handcuff over her wrist, but it was too tight. She felt caged, panicked and annoyed, willing to rip their skin apart to be free. Alma's eyes were stormy and strange, about to burst with rain. She could feel Dex's eyes boring into the back of her head and her heart was in her throat. She stepped away, but Alma yanked at the handcuffs. Eva tugged back. They tugged and tugged until Eva couldn't bear it anymore and pushed the sharp metal over her skin, thrashing back and forth, digging the cuff into flesh until her bones stung and her hand was raw and bleeding. When she was free, she ran out the kitchen door and found herself in an alley. She bent over, hands on her knees, gulping air to stop the black tunnel forming in her vision. Then she walked to the street, empty except for the echo of voices from other buildings. Music and voices blended like a howl. The language she didn't understand. She could feel her shadow stretching up the street but knew she wasn't alone. Eva turned and caught sight of the illuminated cross at the top of Mount Royal. It taunted her.

X
Mathilde

The crows that October were relentless and called to each other in clusters on the small strip of concrete outside the community centre, waiting for the children to drop bits of crackers out of their mouths or for the return of the old man who carried around pieces of bread in an old Bon Matin bag. Mathilde hated the crows and would kick at them when she walked by. Her foot would never make contact with their oil-slicked black feathers, but she would get close enough so that they would spread their wings wide and hop away, clearing a path to the front door.

The community centre smelled like crayons and digestive cookies, and the room that she worked out of lacked natural light, which made directing the children to choose the right colours for their paintings difficult. They would mix horrendous shades of coral with mint green, or daffodil yellow with cool lilac. When one child told Mathilde that she wanted to paint a dog running through a park and she wanted to paint the dog pink, Mathilde corrected her. "Dogs," she said, "are not pink."

"But I want this one to be pink."

"Then it will be a silly painting. Do you want to be a silly painter, or do you want to be a real painter?"

It had made the child scrunch up her little mouth and look back down at the box of paints that sat at her feet next to her hot pink glitter-covered sneakers. The rest of the children in the classroom did not look up from their own paintings and diligently worked in silence, the way Mathilde liked it to be when she herself was painting. And when the class was over, she praised the children for working very well and hard and in silence. But that evening, she received a phone call from Brenda, the woman who ran the arts program at the centre. The child with the glitter sneakers had gone home in tears, crying to her mother that the mean old art teacher wouldn't let her paint her dog pink.

"They're children," Brenda said.

"I'm teaching them."

"We need to cultivate their creativity."

"They need to know the difference between the right way and the wrong way."

"Oh, Mathilde, if a seven-year-old wants to make a dog pink what's the harm?"

"I'm teaching a craft," Mathilde said. "When they learn the craft, then they can break the rules."

But Brenda would not bend, and she let Mathilde off with a warning that if she continued to stifle students' creativity and make them feel bad, she would have to find somewhere else to teach. "Make them feel bad," she muttered to herself while pouring a glass of wine. Now teaching children one of the oldest and most respected art forms was considered harmful to their delicate emotions.

When Mathilde was a child, her mother would beat her with a wooden spoon whenever she cried. After her father drowned while out on a lobster boat, her mother stopped eating and Mathilde had to learn how to pull food together for her sister. Gabrielle was eight years old and thin as a rail, and her knees and feet were always covered in dirt. Marc was no help. He disappeared inside himself and would leave for weeks at a time. Mathilde didn't know where he went. She picked berries and plants in the woods across the highway, learning which ones to steer clear of and which ones were safe to eat. She scrubbed the floors, tended to the chickens, did laundry and dishes, darned socks and mended clothing.

The following year, when she turned twelve, she learned how to make a simple, filling soup by boiling potatoes and adding salt and chunks of beef into the water. She'd salt and dry the fish bought fresh from the men who parked their trucks at the head of the road, and they would give her a deal because they knew that her father Jean-Marc LeBlanc had been a good man. On canning days, she'd boil jars and lids and stuff them with jams and vegetables and meats so the family would have enough food to last the winter. In the fall, Mathilde caught rabbits in makeshift snares and hunted gophers with her brother's gun.

When Gabrielle had a toothache one evening, Mathilde put cloves in her sister's mouth to numb her gums. She'd rub menthol cream on her back and chest when she had coughing fits in bed all night. She boiled the kettle and gently poured the steaming water into Gabrielle's bath while she bathed to keep the temperature up when they ran out of hot water. She taught her sister how to file her fingernails into an oval to avoid hangnails and to keep them clean even after she'd been rummaging around in the dirt. She told Gabrielle how important it was to apply lotion right out of the shower and how to pat, never rub, her skin dry. "If you rub," she said. "You'll get wrinkles."

Their mother continued to sink into bottles of beer, her mood shifting from jubilance one moment to complete chaos the next. Whenever Mathilde tried to get her to eat, she'd curse at her, and greasy strands of hair would sway in front of her face. Her mother haunted the trailer like a ghost, roaming back and forth and muttering and singing and shouting that she was going to burn the place to the ground. Their father's body was never found, but his friends held a funeral, burying an empty casket on church grounds.

They etched his name into a large plaque that sat atop a rocky cliff that looked out onto the thundering waves. Mathilde saw it there, among the others. She thought it looked like a grocery list, the names of items you'd pick out from the aisles. The dates of death, their price.

She'd found painting by accident. Her mother told her to go into the barn and find her father's old work shirt because she wanted to smell him again. Mathilde rummaged through boxes that were so dusty they made her throat itch and her nose fill with thick mucus. There were more boxes up high on one of the shelves, so she grabbed a ladder and propped it up against the wall. At the top of the ladder, Mathilde reached for her father's old shirt, which was stuck underneath an old dusty crate. She gripped the fabric and pulled, releasing a cloud of dust into the air. She sneezed, and her right foot slipped off the rung. Mathilde tried to grab hold of a piece of wood that was sticking out of the wall, but she wasn't fast enough and she tipped backward and fell on her backside, raising more dust. But down there on the floor, Mathilde saw a box filled with small cylindrical bottles of paints. She picked up a moss green colour and held it up in the dust-filled light that streamed in from the one window in the barn. She smelled the sawdust and the chicken feed and realized she could breathe again.

In Clare, she became known as *le p'tit peinturier*. Wherever Mathilde went, she carried her box of paints and a few brushes she found at a yard sale, trading a jar of homemade blueberry jam for them. She couldn't afford canvas, so she dragged home old pieces of wood or scrap metal at the junkyard down the road, or she would find white fabric and nail it to boards and pretend it was real canvas. She would hide in the room she shared with Gabrielle and revel in the comfort of glossy blues and earthy greens. And the jewel tones. The jewel tones made her think about kings and queens with their purple garments that flowed down from their shoulders. In her paintings, Mathilde recreated stories from history and the Bible, borrowing art books from the library and copying scenes on her pieces of found canvas. *Girl with a Pearl Earring* was painted on a piece of an old door. She painted *Madonna and Child* on the back of an Acadian flag, using tinfoil covered in yellow to mimic gold leaf. *The Last Supper* was recreated on a table that had been ripped from an old, decaying boat. Of course, the early renditions were hokey and blotchy. Mother Mary was merely a blob of pale blue in her early works. But as she grew and studied the masters on her own, her lines sharpened and her attention to detail heightened, enough so that she could move on to original works of landscapes or portraits of people in her town. The man with the sad eyes. The woman with wrinkles above her lips from smoking too many cigarettes. The hands of the men on the docks. She created her own world—no longer did she have to sit and ache for a different Mathilde, a new Mathilde, a stronger Mathilde.

Those children in her art class got upset if she made the smallest criticism of their efforts. They went crying to their mothers, saying that Mathilde had told them the worst thing she could tell them when, in fact, she'd held back.

Mathilde still couldn't find the envelope that she'd misplaced and began to worry that Eva had found it and kept it hidden. Surely she wouldn't read something that wasn't hers to read. But if she had read it? If she saw what her father had written, would Eva ever look at her the same way again? She took the small box off the shelf in her closet once more to make sure her mind hadn't played a trick on her and that the envelope was in fact missing. She always made sure to stop and listen for footsteps. A lock clicking. A sheet rustling. A sign of her niece hovering in the doorway, speculating. Blood rushed as she opened the box and breathed in the past. The smell of his old cologne still lingered, and it smelled of cinnamon. Mathilde sat in the middle of her closet with the flickering light above igniting her memory of *almosts* and *if onlys* and *maybe somedays*. But the letter still wasn't there.

Deep down, Mathilde knew that this would eventually happen. Her memory would slip or things would begin to go missing. It wasn't intentional, it was how life moved away from dead things. People are forgotten bit by bit and their possessions that are inherited are misplaced, not by reckless hands, but by hands that need to keep moving in order to survive. She tried to recite the letter to herself from memory, pulling her sketchbook and a graphite pencil out from her bedside table. She sketched the waves in his hair.

I'll leave her one day. Soon, my love.

And his sharp chin. A thin line from the bottom of his ear lobes that shot at an angle to the tip. When he was thinking, the muscles in his jaw would round and pulsate.

It could have been something. I didn't know my mistake would cause so much damage.

She'd only ever seen his eyes in the morning one time, and she hoped that if she ever lost her memory, the image of his eyes in the morning would be the last thing to go.

Don't give up on me. I need you. You know me.

She wished she could capture the sound of his laugh on paper. The way he would throw back his head and let the full force of his pleasure erupt from his body. His neck thick and strong and filled with a deep voice that commanded Mathilde.

You know me.

You know me.

You know me.

In the back of her closet, Mathilde pulled out another box, this one dark blue. Inside, forgotten lines written in desire and never sent. She breathed in. The rose perfume she'd sprayed on them still lingered, though faint. The smell settled into her skin, and in that moment, hidden away in a quiet corner of memory, nothing could harm her except the thought of Eva discovering the letter.

What if?

Mathilde sat at the kitchen table and fiddled with an empty glass under the dim light of the overhead lamp until Eva stumbled in, glassy-eyed, almost tumbling to the floor before ripping off her jean jacket and letting it slump to her feet. Eva tilted back and forth as if a boat on the bay; Mathilde could smell the alcohol from where her niece stood. It was almost two in the morning. Eva never stayed out until two in the morning.

This would have to stop. Eva smiled foolishly as Mathilde poured a glass of whisky. "Drink," she said, pushing the glass toward her niece.

Eva lumbered over, collapsed into the chair, and held the glass of amber up to the light. Mathilde gave a tight smile and watched Eva open up her throat and accept the liquid. She filled her glass again. "Fun night?"

"Just a few drinks."

"Where were you?"

"Out."

"And?"

"I don't feel good."

Eva took the newly filled glass and held it out as if sighting a bullseye before firing a dart. She downed the shot and set the glass on the table.

"What happened to your wrist?"

"I fell."

"Eva."

"It's nothing. Don't worry about it."

Mathilde held out the bottle of whisky again, but Eva held out her hand in protest.

"Come on," Mathilde teased. "Big city girl."

Eva pressed her lips together and closed her eyes, her shoulders swaying to inaudible music. Mathilde poured more whisky.

"New friends?"

When Eva looked up, her eyes were unfocused. Heavy hollow sockets. She had puffy red cheeks, and when she yawned, her mouth grew so wide it forced her to bend her neck down to the table. She took another sip of whisky before slamming the glass down and hunching forward. The chair squeaked, Eva shot up and ran to the bathroom.

She listened in satisfaction as her niece emptied her stomach into the toilet, liquid dumping into liquid. She came out of the bathroom wiping her face. "I feel better."

Mathilde tilted her own glass of whisky into her mouth and let the smoky liquid sit on her tongue. Her cheeks tightened as if sucking on a lemon. "Get some rest," she said.

She watched her niece, legs like a newborn deer, stumble to the kitchen sink. She flipped on the faucet and stuck her head underneath the heavy stream, opening her mouth like a baby bird and sucking back the water. Mathilde placed her hand on her niece's back and shut off the tap.

"I'll get you water, *chère*. Go to bed."

Eva turned and wrapped her arms around Mathilde's neck. She felt cold, wet lips on her neck, heard a sucking smack and smelled cigarettes in her niece's hair. Mathilde patted Eva's back, watched her stumble-walk to her bed and collapse. She grabbed the trashcan from the bathroom and placed it on the floor next to the bed, then took Eva's feet, one at a time, in her lap and untied her shoelaces before pulling them off and placing them neatly by her closet. In the bathroom, she ran a washcloth under cold water, rung it out and folded it into a long strip.

Eva was lying on her back when Mathilde walked back into the room. She tapped her on the shoulder. When that didn't wake her up, she slapped the side table. Eva's eyes shot open. "You have to sleep on your side, *chère*."

Eva rolled. Mathilde wiped at the marks on her niece's wrist. They were only surface wounds. She placed the cold facecloth on the back of Eva's neck. She pulled the covers up to her shoulders and left the door open a crack. Returning to the kitchen for a glass of water, Mathilde paused. She looked over at the bottle of whisky that sat on the kitchen table, and then at her own glass, half empty. She held the glass up in front of her, transfixed by the glittering amber. She downed the rest, poured more liquor, swaying her hips and drinking it back.

What if? The voice hushed to a whisper in the unsteady dim light. She gripped the window latch and pulled, thrusting it open. The sound of Montreal filled the air around her. Dipping her head back, the voice spoke so softly.

What if? What if? What if?

She tried to drown it with the drink. She tried to bury it in the sound of the city. She hummed to herself, sitting down in her chair with her feet up on the table, rocking back and forth until the voice grew, shouting in her ear. She threw her hands up, cupping the sides of her head, bending over and whispering softly to herself.

H'ai t-y un ombrage astheure? Mon amour mon amour mon amour mon amour.

Show your face.

Show me your face.

XI
Eva

When she woke up, she was on her back and sweating. Moisture pooled in her navel and underneath her breasts. She wiped it away with her hand, feeling her skin hot and slick. She'd had a nightmare. Alma was her roommate and Eva walked in on her cutting off a man's head in the kitchen. She watched as nightmare Alma folded the man's body into a black garbage bag and heaved the sack into a bin. She stared in horror as Alma grinned, her hair greasy and stringy and wilting on her face. Alma had cut the man's face clean off his head and packaged it on a Styrofoam plate, wrapped in plastic like a fillet of salmon.

"You want it," she said. "Eat it."

Alma stored the packaged face in the fridge and Eva had to stare at it whenever she reached in to grab a carton of milk or some eggs. She picked up the packaged face and held it upside-down, feeling the pressure of wet skin and flesh under plastic sink into her fingertips. She could smell something rotting. She held the face and saw a row of flat, white teeth before jolting awake.

The veins in her head all seemed to be filled with molasses. They throbbed and forced her to move slowly, the cold floor sending shivers up her legs as her toes touched down. The smell of coffee wafted under her nose and beckoned her into the kitchen where she saw her aunt sitting at the table, writing. Eva could only muster a grimace when Mathilde asked her how she was feeling. Her stomach made the sound of a marble rolling around in a large wooden bowl and she felt her arm sting. The red track marks on her wrist and hand made her remember. *The handcuffs. Dexter's eyes. The girl moaning.*

"Here." Mathilde stood up and opened the fridge. She took out a glass of something pale yellow. "Might do you good." Eva took a sip. Flat ginger ale. She watched as Mathilde leafed through loose papers, picking up a pen and clicking it incessantly.

"What are you writing?"

"Oh, nothing." Mathilde flipped the page. "So," she said, "last night?"

"I was out with friends."

Eva felt as if she had clamped her teeth down on a metal fork. Her bones vibrated with pain. Mathilde gave her the look she always used when she suspected Eva of lying.

"Are they friends?"

"I think so."

"Mmmhmm."

Eva took another sip of ginger ale. "I'm gonna shower."

"Are you even looking at your French books?"

"Yeah," she said. "Every now and then."

"You know, you can find free classes. It's really not that hard."

"I know," she said. "I know it should come easy."

"Can you help me clean up the apartment today?"

Eva looked at the kitchen counter and then at the living room. She'd done a deep clean the day before and the place was spotless.

"I have some things I need to sort for Goodwill," Mathilde explained.

"Sure." She turned, but then her aunt's voice stopped her again.

"And, um, did any of my boxes end up in your room?"

81

"I don't think so."

"Okay, well, if you see anything that . . . if you see something, let me know."

"Are you missing something?"

"No, no. I mean, well, yes. I misplaced some papers. Paperwork."

"I'll let you know."

"Okay," Mathilde smiled. "And why don't you stay in with me tonight? We can watch a movie."

"I think I might meet a friend."

"You think or you know? Come on, I've barely seen you. And you must feel horrible after all that." She waved her hand in the air.

A thick bead of sweat dripped down the small of Eva's back. Thick goo bubbled up her throat. She ran to the bathroom and dry-heaved, watching as the room began to tilt sideways and spin. She heard the floor creak behind her, so she turned on her knees and fell back on the floor, leaning up against the tub.

Her aunt stood in the doorway, light shining behind her like an angel.

Eva wiped the sticky residue from her mouth, swallowing down the pinching feeling and the sour taste that dripped from the back of her nose. The way that Dex looked at her last night had released a dormant feeling from her core. An ancient, sleeping feeling that had been stirred and, when it woke, extended its roots down inside Eva's gut and reminded her that she was not safe. When she thought about telling Alma what she'd seen, she felt a shiver crawl up the nape of her neck and a sudden feeling that she was being watched. No, not watched. Hunted.

Eva took a shower to wipe away the dried sweat and the stench that floated up from her armpits. When she stepped out of the steam, she saw that her face was puffy, and her eyes were bloodshot.

Mathilde was in the kitchen humming to herself while the coffee machine bubbled out brew into the carafe. Eva patted herself dry with her towel and pulled on a pair of shorts and a white shirt. When she went into the kitchen, she saw stars appear before her and grew light-headed. She had to sit at the kitchen table and wait for the stars to disappear. She took in a deep breath and let the air out between pursed lips, squishing her eyes with her knuckles. She took another breath and played with the papers on the table where slices from an old, lightly browned apple sat on a plate. The flesh was grainy on her tongue and very sweet. While she let the juices fall over her tongue, she flipped over the pages on the table, casually glancing at the words until she saw *Gabrielle*. Like a whisper from another room. Like seeing a wolf while walking through the woods. As if the name would leap off the page.

Gabrielle
    sink its fangs into a vein
I saw the truth. The way she treated him
    how evil she is
complete disregard for safety
    blood in her ears
        without a conscience
            murder.

"Eva?"

She shot up and heard the shatter. Broken ceramic on the tile and a puddle of coffee sliding in between the grout lines.

"Sorry. I'll clean it up."

"No! Don't move!" The panic in Mathilde's voice vibrated her skull. She watched as her aunt pulled on shoes and grabbed a broom. "It's okay, *chère*. Don't move." She swung over to the table, eyes wide and frantic. The back of Mathilde's head swayed as she leaned over and swept the pieces into a dustpan. She swept the floor until every bit of glass was in the bin, and again, even when nothing could have been left.

"I think you got it—"

"Stop it!" Mathilde looked up with a fierceness usually saved for others.

Words caught in Eva's throat, and she wilted, trapped between sharp objects.

XII
Gaby

Gaby remembered when her mother first showed her love. She'd given Gaby a bottle of beer and they were sitting outside in the summer night, soft and dark with nobody else around. She could hear the sound of the ocean waves crashing on the sand and cars driving slowly by. The grass was tall and slick wet from the rain that had stopped earlier that evening and Gaby could smell the fresh wet mud and leaves from the weeds. She had just graduated from sixth grade. She was proud to sit with her mother on the back porch while Maddie and Marc were away with friends. She had her mother all to herself.

"Hand me that," her mother said in her low voice, pointing to a lighter. Gaby grabbed it and handed it to her mother who lit the end of a cigarette and breathed in deep.

"Your sister wouldn't like this," she said, leaning in with a wink and a smile. "You know how she is."

Gaby nodded, knowing exactly how her sister was. Maddie disliked touching her own dirty socks.

"This will be our secret."

Gaby held the amber bottle up to her lips and took a small swig. It tasted like metal and thin molasses, and she let the liquid sit on her tongue before swallowing.

Her mother let the cigarette smoke lazily flow out between her lips. She held out the neck of her bottle. "Cheers, *chère.*"

Gaby knocked her bottle against her mother's and heard the glass clink.

Almost every evening for the rest of the summer, they would drink and smoke together. When her brother and sister were out with friends or sleeping, her mother would stumble in and whisper with a wink. "Ready?" And Gaby would grin.

One time, Maddie almost caught them when she stumbled out of the trailer in her pajamas, rubbing her eyes. "*Cache-toi! Vite!*" Her mother whispered to Gaby, who ran through the wet grass in her bare feet to hide behind the trailer. She heard her mother whisper to Maddie to go back to bed. After that night, they both decided that it would be better for them to have their little parties in the old barn.

Gaby saw her mother in her true light. A funny woman. A strong woman. A woman who loved to sing. Almost every night, after her fifth bottle, her mother would break out into song, standing barefoot in the small barn that was filled with her father's old lobster traps, shotguns, and half-filled cans of things that Gaby did not recognize. With her feet wide apart and a bottle in hand, she would sway and sing her favourite Jacques Brel song. *Ne Me Quitte Pas.* Gaby would applaud and crack open a fresh beer for her mother, who drank the entire thing back in one long pull. Gaby knew that when she grew up, she wanted to be exactly like her mother. Fun. Devoted to a man even after his death. Drinking beer in secret late at night while her siblings slept, Gabrielle knew she was loved.

It had been weeks since she'd been let out of segregation. The light from the yard outside shone through Gaby's bar-covered window. She lay on her bed, her forearm shielding her eyes from the fluorescent light overhead, so she could focus on the window. Her window was beautiful, and she never wanted to cover it, even at night, so she left the shade up. Even though the unnatural shimmer from the floodlights kept her awake, even though it was barred, even though it was too small, she loved her window.

She had pulled a muscle in her lower back that morning and rolled from side to side and stomach to back on the thin mattress trying to find a position that didn't leave her in pain. Standing in the kitchen, peeling potatoes for hours on a hard floor with awful shoes had done her in. When she reached down to pick up another sack, her lower back had crunched and another woman had to come over to hold her up.

The guards couldn't give her anything for the pain. They told her to not go looking for anything either. So, Gaby shut up about it. It wasn't that bad. She could manage. For the next month, she had to be a ghost. She didn't want her parole hearing pushed. Gaby had to be a whisper of a prisoner, and when her release date came, she wanted everyone to be surprised she was even still around. She had to learn to blend into her surroundings so nobody could mess with her. That had always been her issue. She was always too noticeable, always too available, always too alive.

The Nova Institution for Women had a playground outside for kids when they visited. It had walkways so inmates could stroll the grounds with other inmates during their hour of free time. It had a semi-flourishing garden with red geraniums in the summer, and in the winter, hardy green shrubs. Cells weren't really cells, they were bungalows or large apartment-like buildings with bedrooms, a shared common space, and shared bathrooms. The prison had a kitchen where inmates could cook for themselves or one another. There was a laundry room and a TV room and a place where you could sit and read. The inmates were paid a wage so they could purchase groceries from the prison store. Gaby had plants in her room that she cared for, and she worked in the kitchen where the knives were tethered to the wall and went for daily walks even when it was raining. She'd been moved there from a maximum-security unit a few years ago, and compared to the other prison, it was a dream.

The mixed prison out of province was a factory-like building. When she'd arrived with a cohort of other confused and tired women, she heard the men shouting, whooping for them to strip as they tracked through the concrete block. Their maximum-security quarters were the old psychiatric unit refurbished to hold women, a corner block curtained off with five cells, each with a single bed, a toilet and a sink. They had painted the walls pink.

The cells led out to a common area with tables and a stationary bike, but the women mostly sat at the tables and rolled cigarettes. Gaby decorated the cell wall by her bed with pictures of Eva. Mostly, she played cards to kill time. Mental health and addiction programming was available, but it was in the men's unit, and she didn't like walking by them every time. She felt like a butchered cow dangling from a meat hook, being pushed down the line of a slaughterhouse. So instead, she walked in a circle in the grime-covered common area while the other women smoked or sat in their cells with blankets or sheets draped over the open iron bars. One afternoon, she heard shots outside her window and thought someone may have tried to escape. But the outside courtyard was lined with targets, colourful bullseyes painted on the middle of cut-outs of torsos. The guards were practising.

As the years went on, Gaby realized the women mostly hurt themselves. She saw women cut down from tangled bedsheets. One woman stabbed herself in the gut. Gaby watched in horror as a homemade knife, a melted and sharpened plastic brush, dug into the flesh and twisted; an unsettling whine ached from the woman's mouth. She folded over and blood dripped down her pant leg. After the woman was carried away, the only sounds left were creaking pipes, withdrawal moans and the echo of steel.

When Gaby was transferred to the medium-security facility in Nova Scotia, she brought all the memories with her. She applied for a job in maintenance where she cleaned corridors and offices and the newly vacant rooms to prepare them for new inmates. She liked cleaning the rooms the best, not to welcome new women but to remove traces of the old ones. But Gaby hated cleaning underneath the beds. Underneath the beds, blood soaked the floor. Underneath the beds, her husband's corpse lived in the dark, head turned to its side with a grin.

In the new facility, some women were allowed to leave on day passes to see their families. One woman, while on her day pass, was taken back into custody out of the blue. She was accused of stealing, though they wouldn't explain what she was trying to steal or from whom. She was sent to solitary for four days. She'd been up for parole, but because of the theft charge her hearing was cancelled. Gaby heard her crying at night—low, long wails. Because even with a garden and bungalows and walkways and playgrounds, the bedroom doors were still locked from the outside and the windows were barred.

Gaby turned onto her side. Her lower back shot pains through to her right leg. As she closed her eyes, she thought about her mother and those nights they would drink and laugh together, and fell asleep.

In the morning, she tried to call Maddie on the communal telephone that hung in the hallway, a tweed-covered chair sitting too low underneath the receiver. Maddie rarely answered—there were a handful of times a few years ago when she'd pick up for bite-sized conversations. Sometimes, she'd hear Eva's voice in the background and Gaby's heart would turn so warm and full she could almost feel it beat out of her chest. Maddie wouldn't let Gaby talk to Eva, but her daughter's voice in the background was enough to make the calls worth it. One time, Gaby heard Eva say the word "butterfly." It was the best word she'd heard all day. She went around saying it under her breath as she walked through the halls of the prison. She searched for butterflies in the courtyard, looking up at the big grey sky and through the bushes that lined the fence. Gaby had made a mental note. *Butterflies. She likes butterflies.*

But this time, all she heard was a mechanical "The number you have dialled is not in service."

She called Marc next.

"*Elle a mové. Montréal,*" he said.

"To Montreal? With Eva? Why? Do you have her new number?"

"*Non.*"

"Lawrence, off the phone. You're meeting with Cheryl."

Gaby turned to see an officer standing in the hallway. One time, the officer said he didn't see prisoners as humans, and Gaby respected him the most because at least he was honest.

Cheryl was her primary worker. She was young and had bright purple hair the texture of straw. She was rail thin, and her nails were long pieces of brittle glass. After her fruitless phone calls, Gaby sat with Cheryl in a windowless white room, stacks of paper at her side—every piece of her past like bullets waiting to be loaded into a gun.

"You'll have rules if your parole goes through. No drugs. No travelling. Get a job and help around the halfway house. You can handle that?"

"What about seeing my daughter?"

"Is she in the province?"

"I'm not sure."

"You don't know where your daughter is?"

"Well. No. I . . . My sister has her."

"If she's an adult she can choose to make contact. If she's not, or if she's out of province . . . You know, I wouldn't worry about that right now. Focus on this." Cheryl tapped the pile of papers in front of her. "You need to show them that you've learned from your mistakes and that you feel sorry for what you did."

"But if she's out of the province and she does want to see me, I could drive to her."

"No, you couldn't."

"Why?"

"Because that's part of this," she tapped the papers again. "Gaby, you need to listen to me. You can't leave Nova Scotia."

When all the prisoners were sent back to their room for count, Gaby paced. Her sister moved. Her sister *moved Eva*. She felt her teeth clench. She stood in front of a picture of her daughter that was taped to her wall. Eva was three and sitting on the floor in grey overalls playing with a doll. Her hair was short and messy and made her head look twice as big as it was. Her cheeks were bright pink, and she was looking over her shoulder, confused. She always made that face when she was distracted from playing.

Gaby knew the night she first met Adam he'd been eyeing Maddie. She could tell by the way he looked at her, his eyes narrowing whenever she shot him a glance, her olive skin reddening and a thin layer of sweat pooling underneath her nose. Gaby thought that, to Maddie, he was like a passage from the Bible, too sacred to speak. It was pathetic. At first, she didn't even see Adam as a person. He was a knot of hair from a shower drain, less than dust. That night at the party, she only wanted her sister's attention. But to get her sister's attention, she had to take something away that she wanted.

You're going to die on some dirt road with your body pumped full of pills and I'm not going to feel sorry for you one bit. Not one bit. Because that's all you're good for.

After Maddie drove away, Adam stayed. He offered Gaby a cigarette and she remembered trying to balance the hazy summer dream world with reality after watching her sister, purple-faced with rage, slide into her car. She heard windchimes singing a lullaby in the blackened night, notes like stars dancing with the crickets in her head. The cigarette smoke filled her brain, and she felt her skull creak and expand. The pills she had taken earlier didn't work. She still felt the sting of Maddie's words and that's when she truly contemplated Adam.

He told her she was the most beautiful thing he'd ever seen, and Gaby's skin bloomed into apple blossoms, pink and white oil dripping from her fingertips. She pinpointed it as the exact moment she fell in love. Falling into Adam's chest was easy. He smelled like cardamom and honey. His smooth skin, his thick muscles filling the gaps in her hands that were desperate to hold onto something real. He made her laugh. Not a fake laugh, but a laugh from her belly that forced her to choke. He took her to movies and fancy restaurants in Halifax and drove her to meet his parents who lived in a new subdivision outside the city where people had four-car garages.

If she had to choose the moment she knew she was going to marry him it would have been the time she realized they were born on the same day. They were drinking wine in a dark café on Barrington Street and the rain splattered outside, soft in the liquid black. It was the most romantic thing she could have ever imagined. She melted at his every word, each syllable water nourishing growing fruit.

Your eyes are so beautiful.
I could marry you right now.
I've never met anyone like you.
We're meant to be together.
Let's get married.

Gaby's wild heart calmed, and she found what she'd always been looking for. Love and attention. She wore a white dress with lace trim and the officiant offered them both cigars on the steps of the courthouse that had moss growing in between the ridges, giving off a faint scent of mould. Gaby had wanted to be married in a church with a priest. She wanted her family to attend. But Adam said he couldn't wait. *All that matters is us.*

His parents gave them a house they owned off Quinpool Road in the South End as a wedding gift, so it made sense for them to live in Halifax, not the French Shore. And besides, what was Adam going to do there? Work at the mink farm? Fish? Cut down trees? In Halifax, Adam kept his job as a lieutenant in the military and Gaby worked at a pub as a waitress. Adam told her she didn't have to work, but at the bar, she delighted in the light of newfound friends, in their cooing over the massive diamond on her finger and admired the stories of their own lives. Jill, one of the bartenders, used to be a longshoreman. She worked on the docks long enough to save up for a home, until she busted her knee. Jill had a laugh and a ruddiness about her that reminded Gaby of her mother.

Brandon was another bartender who had a full beard and would wrap her in a big bear hug whenever they ran into each other outside of work. She built a cohort of people she could lean on, busting their backs together slinging beers and burgers until the late hours. When they closed down the pub, every now and then Adam would show up and join them for a nightcap. For Gaby, this was paradise.

Two years went by and during this time, Adam told Gaby that he no longer wanted to be in the military, disliking the long hours away from her. Eventually, he left his job and decided to open his own business as a mechanic, a trade he'd learned while serving. She beamed with pride when she told her new friends how her husband had opened up his own shop and started making money so quickly. He bought her expensive jewellery and wrapped it so delicately in beautiful gold paper, presenting it to her as she woke from a deep, restful sleep. The first was a necklace with a dangling heart pendant; their initials engraved in the back.

He draped it around her neck and clasped it in the back. "You like it?"

"I love it." Gaby stared at her reflection in the mirror. Gold looked good on her. She would never again have to paint her rings with clear nail polish to prevent her fingers from turning green. She didn't have to worry about cheap earrings scratching her lobes. She would never have to choose the cheapest bracelets at the mall. She had a man who gave her real jewellery. She had a man who made her look expensive.

One time, Adam appeared out of the blue while she was cleaning tables at the pub, holding another small box wrapped in blue paper and a silver ribbon in his hand. Gaby eased into his embrace and lingered on his cologne.

When he pulled back, his hands still holding her arms, he looked down at her chest. "Where's the necklace I got you?"

Gaby felt her bare chest. "I thought it was too nice to wear here. You never know what people might do."

"What do you mean?"

"You know. Steal it. I could lose it or get it dirty. I want to save it and wear it on special occasions." She smiled at him and made a move to turn away, but his hands gripped her arms tighter. His eyes looked odd, as if he were staring through her.

"Are you okay?" She gently touched his hands.

Adam blinked and licked his lips, loosening his grip. "Sorry," he said. "I don't know what happened. Lost in thought." His eyes roamed over her body while he chewed the inside of his lower lip. He parked himself at the bar, ordered a drink, and stayed there until the end of her shift, taking his eyes off her only to order more beer.

The suggestion was as casual as a raindrop.

"What if we had a baby?"

He swept into the kitchen one evening while Gaby was packing her purse getting ready for a shift.

"Wouldn't it be nice to not have to work?"

"I like working." Gaby smiled. She brushed the idea off at first since Adam had told her from the beginning he had no interest in children. But Gaby always wanted to be a mother. And an image of tiny shoes hovered in front of her face like a carrot. The smallest socks. Plump pink lips partially opened while the little potato slept cradled in her arms. The look of pure love. She'd have to quit drinking and late-night "whatever drugs" as she called them. It couldn't be that hard. Not for something that needed her.

Adam moved in close, one hand on the small of her back, the other gripping her thigh as he pushed her up against the kitchen counter. He convinced her to call in sick that evening. He convinced her to call in sick that week. He convinced her to spread her legs and let him drift his smooth lips along her soft neck down to her chest, buckling her knees and letting him move in close so that his hips rubbed up against her inner thighs. The way they had to go about it made sense. Even if they were sore. Even if she were torn. If they were serious about it, she had to stop working too. If she wanted a baby, this is what it took. Chubby little fingers. Fresh baby powder. Sharing secrets with other mothers and angelic baby laughter. Her friends at the bar would be fine without her—it wasn't permanent.

When Gaby finally got pregnant, she felt so lucky. Hearing of women trying for years to no avail, hours spent on treatments and money poured down the drain over medicinal tinctures and hormonal spells. So many stories from her own mother and aunts about miscarriages. Babies dying in the womb. Babies dying once they were born. Babies dying a year after they were born. Gaby took a test alone in the bathroom. When she saw the double lines, she cried. She told herself they were tears of joy. But they were not. They were tears of something she couldn't name.

XIII
Eva

The weather grew colder in Montreal as the leaves changed colour, rusted, and gave way to the ground, covering the sidewalk like the temporary tattoos Eva used as a child, sticking them onto her skin with a damp paper towel and waiting for the image to transfer. But she always misjudged how long she needed to leave the wet paper towel there, or how wet the paper towel should be in the first place, and she would peel back the plastic and see that the ink mixed with the adhesive and had dissolved with the water, and the image supposed to be tattooed onto her skin slipped away.

Eva did not like winter. She hoped that winter in Montreal would be forgiving.

On her way home from work, she walked in the rain from the hotel to the Berri-UQAM metro. The air smelled like cigarettes and wet compost. As she got closer to the station, she heard the clamouring of metal and buzzing, hollow horns. Eva saw red banners spread over the heads of what seemed like thousands of people who came into view as she drew closer. A woman dressed in a jean jacket and black slacks wrapped a red bandana over her mouth and let it hang long. Police in full riot gear flanked the massive crowd. Eva stood on the sidelines and absorbed the enormity of the group that seemed to be growing by the second, with posterboards taped to wooden sticks bobbing up and down like apples in water. Eva didn't understand the French on the placards—she tried to decode the words but only caught a few. She felt her face grow hot at not being able to understand and watched as the throng moved down the street. Someone shouted into the air and the rest of the crowd erupted into a cheer, slamming noisemakers together and blowing into long plastic horns that trumpeted out a vibrating moan. Fat raindrops pelted the top of Eva's head, and she ducked into the metro, hearing in the distance a police siren and a loudspeaker amplifying French music.

The next evening, while reheating leftover chicken casserole she'd cooked the night before, Eva heard on the radio that four people had been arrested. The announcer said it was the largest student protest in the province's history with almost 30,000 people. Student leaders said more than two hundred thousand students had voted in favour of boycotting classes.

"I was practically in the middle of that," she said to her aunt.

"What have I done? Orange doesn't belong in a field of French lavender!" Mathilde put down her paintbrush in annoyance and reached over to the radio, changing the channel to a music station.

"Did you know about this?" Eva turned to Mathilde, who was now pacing around the living room.

"I try doing something different and of course it comes out wrong."

"Did you hear about that protest?"

"What?"

"The protest that happened yesterday. I think universities are going on strike or something."

"So? What's that got to do with you? Look," Mathilde gestured to her painting. "Why do I even try? I've never even been to France."

"Can't you dab it out with water?"

"Water," Mathilde let out a laugh. "I can't use water. The only thing I can do is let it dry and paint over it."

"That doesn't sound bad. At least you can afford the paint."

"But that means there's going to be a noticeable change in texture in that region."

Eva gave up. "Do you want any casserole?"

Mathilde stood with her arms folded over her chest, hand underneath her chin as she stared at the imperfect painting. "I'll have a small bowl."

Eva pulled two bowls out from the cupboard, set them down on the countertop and scooped out the creamy chicken bake. Soft bits of snow began to float outside the window against the blue night and it didn't take long for the ground to be covered in a light dusting.

The next day, there was a desert of snow mixed with bits of gravel outside their apartment. When Eva stepped outside that afternoon, her nose began to bleed from the quick shot of cold, and on her way to the metro, she slipped on a thick patch of ice.

When Eva arrived at the university, she saw students standing outside with picket signs displaying their opposition to rising tuition costs and somebody named Charest. While she pushed her way through the angry sea of red, they shouted at her.

"Who will fight for you?"

"Traitor!"

"Education is key! It should be free!"

"You're spineless! Fuck you!"

"Scab! Scab!"

The words stung. She wanted to shout back that it wasn't true, but Eva knew it wouldn't make any difference.

Alma sat in her usual place in the lecture hall that had become increasingly empty.

"What's happening out there?" Eva sat down next to her and pulled her hair up into a small ponytail.

"I don't know but it's crazy."

"Do you think they'll cancel classes?"

"How can students go on strike? Strike from what? Snorting lines?"

"Do you think they'll start taking attendance or something?"

"Why would they do that? They'll probably just kick everyone off campus."

Eva's breath caught in her throat. She turned to look around at the empty seats and feared that the professor, who must have been running late, wouldn't appear at all.

"They can't cancel class."

"Who would I see every day?" Alma asked, mostly to herself. "What would I do? Sit at home?" She looked down at her phone and cursed under her breath.

"What's wrong?"

"Dexter cancelled on me. He has an essay that's due tomorrow and he hasn't started it."

"He's starting tonight?"

"You've never done that before?"

Eva looked down at her hands. She cracked her knuckles and thought about the way Dexter looked at her the night of the party. She thought about how the girl on the ground looked lifeless, almost like a doll. Maybe it had just been a doll. Some strange prank his friends had forced him to play. She hadn't seen the girl the rest of the night. Or maybe she had and didn't realize; she hadn't gotten a good look at her face. Maybe she left early with some friends or simply blended into the crowd with the other laughing girls. Eva told herself this and knew most of these assumptions were wrong, and the rest were only hopes. She tried to think about how to compose her next sentence to Alma, whether she wanted to begin with an accusation or a question about her relationship. But, as she thought about this, Professor Moore walked in and the class finally began.

After class, Eva waited in the hall for Alma who had ducked into the bathroom. When she came out, she was wielding two empty black garbage bags like prizes from a hunt.

"Hey, you wanna go sledding?"

Eva gave her a puzzled look.

"With what?"

Alma held up the garbage bags higher, her eyes twinkling.

They jumped the turnstiles at the Guy-Concordia metro and ran down the concrete steps, flying through the closing doors, laughing wildly as they tried to catch their breath. When the train stopped at Mont Royal, they shot up the stairs and ran up the avenue toward the mountain, the winter cold stinging their eyes and mixing with their sweat. Light snowflakes melted on Eva's eyelashes, dragging down her eyelids, but her body vibrated with life. She pushed through worn-out thigh muscles, matching Alma's speed along the snowy sidewalk, slipping only once and catching herself by grabbing onto a stop-sign pole. When they arrived at the base of the mountain, Eva held tight to her garbage bag, following Alma as they hiked up the crisp snow in the dark, the tops of her thighs burning as if she were running through sand. When Alma found a satisfactory spot, she dropped the bag, sat directly on top and lifted her knees up to her chin. Eva watched as she slid a few inches, her hair covered in white flakes.

Alma looked over her shoulder. "Give us a push!"

Eva shoved her whole body into Alma's back and watched as she flew down the hill like a shooting star shrinking smaller and smaller, flying. Her scream was muffled by the sound of cars sloshing by on the road below. They were the only two on the mountain.

With the light shining from the streetlamps, goosebumps on her arms and adrenaline pulsing, Eva decided to give it a running start, jumping and landing on her stomach. She shot down the slope and flew into the back of Alma's knees, knocking her over. They both splayed out, laughing the kind of laugh that paralyzes, no breath left to move or even inhale. She thought she was going to pass out as she rolled over.

Alma turned and looked up at the cross on top of the large hill and asked quietly. "Do you believe in God?"

Eva caught her breath. "I think so. My aunt does."

"The whole city is drenched in it."

"Is it?"

"You see that, right?" Alma pointed to the cross.

Eva tried to focus, but she kept hearing Mathilde's voice in her mind. What would she say? *Pick-and-mix Christians. To one without faith, no explanation is possible. While the world changes, the cross stands firm.* "I guess," she said. She didn't want to disagree with Alma and decided it would be easier not to say anything else.

"I'm freezing," Alma said.

They decided to leave the snow and search for food. They found Patati Patata on the corner of Saint Laurent and Rachel, a small restaurant that served hamburgers and fries. The scent of fried bacon and beef and toasted buns hit Eva's nose and her stomach growled. The people behind the counter stared at her and Alma with bored eyes, and she realized how cold she felt, the heaviness of her wet clothes. She caught a glimpse of her reflection in the dripping window and saw that her face was dappled with melted snow and her skin was frosted pink. Eva looked down at her fingernails and saw that dirt had crawled underneath. They sat together on the high stools at the bar, each ordering a burger and Coke, watching the employees dunk baskets of fries in hot oil and slap uncooked patties on the grill.

"You know, they have a cot under the counter." Alma turned to Eva.

"Hmm?"

"They keep a cot under the counter so employees can sleep before and after their shifts."

"Really?"

"My friend told me. Some of them stay for weeks and never go home. They get paid in Patati bucks and can only use the money at the restaurant."

"Oh, yeah. That makes sense."

"Jesus, Eva. You believe me?"

"Oh," she said, then belatedly giggled.

"You're so gullible."

The guy behind the counter placed a basket of hamburgers and fries in front of them and they each dug in, Eva feeling the squishy bun underneath her raw fingertips.

"It wasn't a surprise to me," she said. "People sleeping at work." Part of her still kind of believed it. She imagined a submarine bunk bed compartment underneath the counter right by her feet with two people curled up and snoozing.

They ate their burgers in silence. Eva melted at the sour mayo and pickles, the crisp salt, the taste of processed cheese and chuck. She inhaled fries that tasted like vinegar and allowed the salt crystals to linger on her tongue before washing them down with iced cola.

"Are you going back anytime soon?" Alma asked.

"Where?"

"Nova Scotia."

"No."

"Do you want to?"

"No."

"Why? Aren't you guys always pining over it? The ache for the Atlantic or whatever?"

"I like it here."

From the bar, Eva could see the kitchen workspace. A tall stainless steel soup pot sat on top of the stove with a ladle sticking out of it. She heard something bubbling.

"Are your parents still together?"

Eva shook her head and stared at the backsplash above the cook-top, covered in grease stains. Tinfoil wrapped over the pipes along the deep fryer and sink.

"My mom would kill me if she saw me eating this," Alma said, looking at her half-eaten burger. "What are your parents like?"

Eva took a long swig of Coke and cleared her throat. "My dad was fun," she said. "I remember playing with him a lot. He wore these old motorcycle jackets and fixed dirt bikes."

"Was?"

"He died in a car accident when I was a kid," she lied. "He was kinda tough, you know? Like, not really into girl stuff. But with me, he'd make candy. From scratch. He'd wear the floral apron and everything. He'd boil the sugar and whatever else goes with it. And then when it cooled down, we'd stretch it. That's what you have to do. You have to stretch it by pulling on either end, and I would stand at one end of the kitchen and he would stand at the other end. And I'd put all my weight into it—are you laughing? Picturing me as a little kid? I'd fall over all the time. Ha! I remember pulling really hard on that candy rope with him on the other end. And I remember him straining, like, really really hard, pretending that it was tough for him, you know, trying to build me up. Build my confidence. Make me feel tough or whatever. It made this sticky caramel that he would chop up into little pieces."

Eva looked up at the ceiling and then down at her burger. She felt bloated and sick. "But then, after he died, my mom didn't want me."

She smeared the grease off her lips with the back of her thumb. She thought hard about how to pivot the conversation away from her parents, feeling as though she said too much. But Alma seemed to take her sadness as an open door she should gently push open, and Eva never knew how to stop prying eyes.

"Why wouldn't she want you?"

It was a question from a child used to receiving unconditional love. Eva knew there were many reasons to not want a child. They're expensive. They're loud. They take up all your time. They're annoying. They smell. They grow up to despise you. During the course of Eva's childhood, she made a mental list of all the reasons why nobody would want her, including her mother, to make sense of what had happened.

"Aren't you mad?"

She finally looked up into Alma's face and saw pity. It made her stomach convulse. "I tried to be."

Alma stuffed the rest of her hamburger into her mouth and chewed, her cheeks bulging like a chipmunk's.

Eva could hear her heavy breathing. "What are your parents like?"

"They're fine. My mom's obsessed with exercise because she's scared of getting fat and my dad's addicted to work. They're still in Toronto. I have an older brother and an older sister. They left home pretty early on. I don't see them a lot."

"That's sad."

She saw something real in Alma's face. It came on slowly, an old black-and-white silent movie, Alma the background actress. Her eyelids heavy. Her arm, bent at the elbow on the counter, her wrist limp and dipping under her chin so that her cheek rested on the back of her hand. But it was only for a moment. The tinkling music from an old piano faded. The film blackened and slowed. The lights cut out and it was only the two of them sitting in a nearly empty burger joint with fluorescent overhead lighting.

The snow had let up and it was completely dark outside when they paid their bill and left. Eva had a chill deep in her bones and looked forward to going home, taking a bath and relaxing on the sofa with Mathilde. But as she slowed at her street corner, Alma turned.

"Do you want to come over? We can watch a movie."

Eva knew her aunt would be worried. She should have been home hours ago.

"I have wine. And Dex is away" Alma said with puppy dog eyes. Eva couldn't say no.

The apartment was a loft on the third floor of a large brick building. The front door opened to a living room with a huge L-shaped leather couch and a flat screen hanging on the wall. Behind the couch, three massive square windows stuck out from an exposed brick wall. The air smelled like Pine-Sol and oranges. The kitchen was around a corner, slightly hidden and flanked by a wooden island with a sink in the middle of it. Sandy wooden beams stretched over the ceiling and down the sides of the apartment. Eva couldn't tell if they were necessary or just decorative.

Alma told her that she could leave her shoes on, which made Eva deeply uncomfortable because the floor looked cleaner than any plate she'd washed in the dish pit. Alma disappeared into a dark corner of the loft and flicked on a soft golden light that illuminated a brick wall painted white. Eva watched as her shadow danced up against the wall, arms lifting over her head and peeling off her damp shirt.

"Do you want dry clothes?" Alma shouted.

Eva scrunched the water out of her T-shirt, held it in her hand and wiped it back onto her pant leg. "Sure."

Alma emerged wearing grey sweatpants and a grey sweatshirt; her hair wrapped in a towel. She threw a pair of clean sweats at Eva who caught them and gently fingered the soft, clean fabric.

"The bathroom is there." She pointed.

Eva followed the line of her finger and walked through a slim wooden door that slid to the side. The bathroom was covered from floor to wall to ceiling in small aquamarine tiles. There was a chrome showerhead that hung in the middle of it, which Eva thought was odd, as there was no shower curtain, and the toilet was out in the open. She peeled off her wet clothes and used a soft folded towel on one of the shelves to pat her skin dry. Her legs felt like ice cubes, so cold they were almost numb. After she pulled on the comfy sweats, she wrapped her hair up in a towel and met Alma in the living room where she was sitting with two full glasses of red wine, her legs crossed on the sofa.

"That was fun." Alma beamed.

"You and Dex live here?"

"He had the place before we met. His parents are loaded." Alma took the glass and held it by the base, looking directly down at the wine as if staring at her reflection in a pond. "It's nice, isn't it?"

Eva didn't speak. She nodded her head and looked around some more, trying not to make it obvious that the whole place took her breath away. She thought apartments like this only existed in movies; she didn't realize people actually lived in them, let alone people in their twenties. While the place was filled with stylish furniture and expensive-looking paintings hung on the walls, and there was a warmth from the dim golden lights that made Eva feel hugged, there was an emptiness.

She couldn't put her finger on it until they were halfway through the movie that Alma picked out: the story of a young graphic designer whose dreams overtook his waking life. There was a scene where he and his neighbour decided to create an animated film about a forest that grows inside a boat. They're unsure how they're going to create the sea, until the neighbour turns on the faucet and pale blue cellophane pours out into the sink, the sound of rushing water crinkling with the texture of the plastic. This excites them to no end, and they run to find materials that could act as clouds, throwing around big puffs of cotton that are sustained in the air by slamming down the correct chords on a piano. It wasn't until that scene that Eva knew why the apartment unsettled her. It was devoid of Alma. The Alma that was willing to throw herself down a snowy hill on a garbage bag was not the art on the walls. The Alma that poured gin into empty bottles of cough syrup was not in the immaculate aquamarine bathroom tiles. The apartment was unfinished with Alma's light.

When the movie ended, Eva tried to look for traces of Alma. A book peeked out from underneath the couch, the corner beckoning her to pick it up. She reached down. It had a French title, and the picture on the cover was of a girl sitting with her knees together and her head tilted to the side. Her hands were up underneath her chin, and her little black dress spread out at her sides like wings.

"Oh," she heard Alma say. "That's nothing." She grabbed the book out of Eva's hands and tucked it between her legs. Pink flashed across her cheeks.

"You know French?" Eva asked.

"Of course."

"I don't."

Alma looked down at her legs and let them relax, falling away to let the book slide back out. She opened it and gently flipped through the pages. "She's pretty good," she said. "I like her."

"What's it about?"

"Short stories. Love."

"Can you read some to me?"

Alma eyed her. It was a pointed look. "You don't know French."

"I can't learn," Eva said, taking the book back gently. "I'm too stupid."

"Hey."

"What?"

"Don't say that about yourself."

"Why? It's true."

"Eva, you're not stupid. That breaks my heart."

"I should know it by now."

"You can't say that about yourself."

"There's a lag in my brain." Eva paused. She did not feel like she was going to cry. She felt numb. She looked down at the open pages and then closed the book. "I'm tired anyway."

Alma sighed before grabbing the book out of Eva's hands. She flipped through the pages and landed on a section she seemed content with. She spoke each sentence in French, then translated each sentence into English. The story was about a painter who was newly married to a Spanish woman. He fell in love with her because she resembled a painting by someone named Goya. Because she was Catholic, the light had to be completely out before they made love. But the painter persisted and eventually convinced his wife to pose for him nude.

Eva closed her eyes and listened to the deep hum of Alma's words. She instinctively stretched out her legs so that her toes touched Alma's thighs. She was reminded of when she was a little girl and her mother would read to her in bed and rub her feet, pressing her thumbs gently into the arches. She could feel her eyelids grow heavy; once or twice her head twitched and she realized she'd been dreaming. The warmth in Alma's voice and the weaving of her words made Eva stretch her tense leg muscles. She allowed herself to give in to sleep.

XIV
Gaby

The tape recorder sat nestled in Gaby's pocket. When she first got the idea, her hands wouldn't stop shaking. It was the only way she could be sure.

Maddie didn't make it to Gaby's baby shower, which had consisted of Jill and two other women from the bar who brought her gifts she could only use after the baby was born—a giant bottle of Scotch, a box of cigars and a gift certificate to a sushi restaurant. Gaby thought it was the sweetest thing in the world. But after her friends cleared out of the house on Quinpool, Adam appeared from the basement, a devastated look in his eyes. He held the box of cigars in his hands, looking down as if about to cry or scream.

"You wouldn't," he said.

"It's a joke," Gaby pacified. "You have nothing to worry about."

But his face shifted. The box sailed through the air and crashed into the wall, brown cigars scattering onto the pristine white floor. Gaby felt her heart beating in her ears. Her skin froze but her blood ran on in her veins, tingling her forearms and forcing her hands to clench. He put his face square in hers, his jaw tense, his eyes pools of anger and worry. She thought he might say something when his lips curled at the corners, but he turned instead. With a slam of the front door, he was gone.

It was their first fight of many. After each, Adam told Gaby she was crazy.

Babe, it was an argument.

Babe, we were just talking.

Babe, you really love to make things a problem.

Babe, come here. That was called an adult conversation.

So, Gaby bought a tape recorder. Just in case she wasn't crazy. When Maddie arrived at the house a few weeks later, she played a recording of Adam shouting an accusation that she had been unfaithful.

"Well, did you?"

"Did I what?"

"Cheat."

"I'm pregnant!"

"Don't be sexist. Pregnant women can cheat."

Gaby poured her sister a cup of tea and placed the porcelain pot back down on the counter, nestling it into its cozy.

"He's going through a lot," Maddie said. "It can't be easy losing a wife."

"Losing a wife? I'm not dead."

"You know what I mean. Pregnancy affects them too. I think you're fine. *Toute va alright.*"

"Don't say that," Gaby whispered, listening for the sounds of Adam's footsteps. "He doesn't like it when we speak French."

When she didn't hear anything, she leaned against the counter and chewed at her lips. It had become a habit recently to rip dry flakes from her lips with her teeth and pick at the jelly fat inside her mouth. Her mouth tasted like pennies.

Maddie shrugged and sipped her tea, speaking into her mug. "It is his home."

It was true. Adam gave her spending money. He gave her a home. He was stable. Secure. Adam loved the routine of going to work and coming home to a cooked meal. But her shoulders tensed whenever he walked into the room.

He gave her the child that was now growing inside of her like a little bean sprout. But Gaby's dream of pregnancy had not played out the way she'd hoped. There were no pregnant women sitting cross-legged in a circle in her living room talking about morning sickness and their weird cravings. She didn't go for walks with her friends—they rarely came over to visit. Gaby never saw her mother because her mother couldn't drive to Halifax and Adam always had the car. She asked Adam if he could pay for her to go to a child birthing class or some kind of women's group, but Adam said she didn't need to do any of that. He said her body knew what to do. It was natural.

But it didn't feel natural sitting at home every day by herself listening to her own thoughts, watching the same soap operas over and over and over again. She tried to distract herself with her favourite cassette tapes. Carly Simon. Donna Summer. Prince. Her round baby belly grooving as she jumped and twisted to "Bad Girls" while folding tea towels in mid-afternoon or strutting to "She Works Hard for the Money," scrubbing a cheese-caked casserole dish in the sink with a Brillo pad.

To carve out the true aching boredom of her days, she'd go for walks alone, waddling down the streets of Halifax in early spring, the sun high and bright. She decided to make it her mission to always have a purpose for her walks. Every Friday afternoon she'd pick up milk and orange juice. Every Wednesday afternoon she'd travel to the corner store to purchase cigarettes for Adam, holding her belly and joking with the cashier. *Oh, don't worry! They're not for me!* And every Tuesday morning, Gaby would treat herself at the café on Quinpool where the barista always greeted her with a big smile. He looked not much younger than she was; his face showed memories of acne and rosacea. She always ordered a decaf caffè

mocha and sat by the window, enjoying the warm drink and looking out at the busy street while the chocolatey sweetness embraced
her tongue. After a while, the guy behind the counter started her
order the moment she walked through the door. He always eyed her
stomach with what Gaby could only describe as suspicion, but he
never said anything until one day she decided to put him out of his
misery.

"I really miss caffeine," she said while patting her belly. She felt as
though she were putting on a show for a little kid. "I can't wait for
this little one to crawl out of me so I can poop normally again."

The boy turned beet red and sputtered a laugh. From that point
on, whenever she made her regular stop at the café, he would ask
her one question about the baby.

Do you know if it will be a boy or a girl?

How far along are you?

What happens if the kid doesn't want to come out?

What's the first thing you're going to do when you're not pregnant?

What should I get my girlfriend for her birthday?

Well, most of the time the questions were baby-centric.

When Robby would ask a question about life, Gaby was happy to
answer, although she wondered why he thought she knew anything.
After all, he was the university student—he told her he only worked
part-time, to pay for his courses at Dalhousie.

If it was a slow day, Robby sat with Gaby at her table while she
drank her hot chocolate that was pretending to be coffee.

He'd been with his "long-term girlfriend" for over seven months.
"She's the best," Robby would say. "She's fearless and funny and she's
smart. I didn't know I could get someone like that."

Robby had curly black hair and his eyes were hazel. She noticed
this because whenever he talked about his girlfriend, they lit up. He
had a round jaw and was thin, almost too thin, which made Gaby
worry he wasn't eating.

"What does she like?" Gaby asked. "Start there. Notice what she talks about. That's the best way to think about gifts."

He was a cute guy. She rubbed her palms against her warm belly that looked as though it was getting bigger by the minute. She pictured the little one inside. A growing, juicy apple ready to drop from the tree. She was terrified of the thought that it could be born a Robby but moulded into something else.

A light dusting of snow had fallen overnight, which was unusual for April, and the morning air sent a chill up her spine when she left the house on her way to her weekly visit to the café and Robby. But the bright sun shone down on her face like a beacon of hope. Her nose shrivelled as the cold wind blew off the water and wrapped around her hair. She was glad of the puffy jacket Adam had bought for her last November, for her birthday.

"I don't want you both out there catching your death," he had said.

It was expensive, Gaby guessed, but Adam didn't let on. Thick fabric lined the hood and feathers filled the puffs. In that jacket, Gaby felt loved. When she pulled open the doors to the café, Robby looked up from the counter and then down to his feet. She could feel her face thawing as she broke out into a smile, but Robby turned and fiddled with something at the back end of the counter. She waited for him to turn around, but when he didn't, another barista, a young girl with long braided red hair, asked, "What can I get you?"

Gaby's eyes hovered on the back of Robby's head. "Decaf Americano, please."

The girl nodded and pressed ground beans into the portafilter, sending the aroma of bitter espresso Gaby's way. Robby looked over his shoulder, but when he caught her eye, he turned and walked into the back room. Gaby sat in her usual spot, drank her watery decaf and grimaced at her sudden change in drink choice. She went to the milk station at the far side of the counter and dunked in a few tablespoons of sugar and a hefty glug of cream. Robby re-emerged from the staff room door, but when he saw her, he froze. Gaby smiled.

"You okay?"

He dropped his head, looking at his white Converse high-tops. "I'm not supposed to talk to you." It was a whisper.

"What do you mean?"

He shook his head, eyes still glued to the tops of his shoes. "I can't."

Gaby studied his posture. His head bowed and disgraced. "Did your girlfriend tell you this?"

Robby glanced up.

"That's not okay. Do you hear me? It's not okay."

He shook his head like a schoolboy being disciplined, the acne scars standing out on his pale face.

"Then what?" She said that too loudly, concern in her voice. She saw the red-haired barista shoot them a glance. Eyes from others in the coffee shop turned their way. But Gaby didn't care. The only thing that concerned her was the boy in front of her who refused to look her in the eye. What had she done wrong? How could she have been so stupid as to upset this perfectly nice guy?

Robby glanced over his shoulder at the dining area and then through the large glass windows. When he spoke, she heard the quiver in his voice. "Your husband came in," he finally said. "I can't talk to you anymore."

The doctor glanced down at Gaby's chart, sighed, and took off her gold wire-framed glasses. She placed them on her desk, metal tapping against pine. The office was all white and sterile with cotton swabs and cotton balls in glass jars along the side of the wall. Thin crinkly paper covered the long bed slammed up against a heater.

"There are a few things we can do," Dr. Gray said. She had curly blond hair, and her skin was wrinkly but moisturized, like sagging leather covered in Vaseline. She had a constant sweet smile on her face and her voice was sing-song, which made it seem as though all the words out of her mouth were pleasant and true. "We can put you on a benzodiazepine which will help with the anxiety. I find that many of my patients who are having issues find them to be incredibly helpful."

Gaby had given birth to her baby in June. A baby girl. Evangeline. Stomach pains ruptured through her belly while making a salad one evening while Adam was still at the garage, but she'd had them so many times before, she thought it was nothing. She hoped it was nothing. Her breathing became shallow, tiny sucks of air as she leaned against the sink. The backs of her eyelids and their shiny stars comforted her as she tried to push down the pain, rocking back and forth. When she opened her eyes, she saw her linen dress below swaying between her legs, her bare toes purple and swollen.

Gaby had begun having nightmares about the whole ordeal. Giving birth on the kitchen floor, shivering in her own sick while a purple screaming baby quivered in her arms. Even in her dreams she could feel the sharp convulsions up her spine and the ripping. In some dreams, Adam was there, kissing her sweat-soaked forehead. In other dreams, her baby was snatched away by phantom hands. In reality, she had enough time to call an ambulance. The baby was kicking down the door the minute she lay down in the back of the truck—no patience! A release of pressure, Gaby thought she'd peed herself. And with the next bolt of lightning in her belly, the only thing she could think to say to the paramedics hovering over her was, "I'm sorry for the mess!"

The paramedic, who had already ripped off her underwear and sat straddling the bed with his hands ready, as if to catch a football, laughed. "Nothing to worry about except getting this baby out."

The baby shot out, screaming her tiny head off, all purple and goblin-like. Another paramedic wrapped her in a towel, wiping the milky coating off her hands and face. She sat cradled in Gaby's arms, eyes crunched together and a full head of hair wet and swirly. When the baby stopped crying, Gaby started, feeling the water pool in her eyes. The paramedics both crouched beside her, folding mom and baby up in blankets and making sure they didn't fall when the ambulance turned sharp corners and bounced over potholes.

The baby was asleep next to her in a tiny plastic cradle on top of a pushcart when Adam rushed into the hospital room, sweaty and exuding panic.

"Hi, my love," Gaby said in a tired, light voice.

Adam's face brightened, his smile insecure. He fidgeted with his shirt before rubbing his hands on his jeans. He walked up to the baby like she was royalty, bending at the knee, head bowed.

"She's beautiful," he said. Gaby stretched into her tiredness and felt her body glowing. There was an emptiness inside of her—or more a tranquillity. Still water. Placid tree branches gentle in their breeze. Gaby fell asleep and stayed asleep for what felt like an eternity. In that moment, all was well.

"I can refer you to a psychiatrist, which could take a few months," Dr. Gray said. "Are you hearing voices?"

"No."

"Do you believe anybody is following you?"

"No."

"Okay, well. Do you believe you're at risk of harming yourself or others?"

"No."

"I'll fill out a prescription for you. Take them once a day or any time you start to feel anxious."

She watched as Dr. Gray scribbled a few words on a piece of

paper. "Um." Gaby cleared her throat. "I think I might be gaining weight."

Dr. Gray placed her glasses back over her eyes and glanced at Gaby from head to toe.

"You just had a baby."

"I know, but I feel like the weight should be coming off quicker."

The doctor stood and beckoned Gaby to follow her to the scale located in the hallway by the receptionist's office. While she stood on the scale, she could feel the eyes of the waiting patients on the back of her skull. Dr. Gray took a pen and flicked the weights so that they fell level. She made an approving noise and told Gaby to follow her back to the room.

"Your BMI is normal," Dr. Gray said.

Gaby squirmed in her chair. "Is there a way to lose more weight? I'm just feeling. I'm feeling very full. You know? Like, I'm feeling like . . . not eating makes me feel better and I think if I had some kind of meal plan? And my husband says that I could lose a few more pounds and I think I could. You know?"

Dr. Gray looked over the tops of her glasses and gave her a little smile. "The weight will come off in time." She ripped the script from her notepad and handed it to Gaby.

"Remember. Once a day," she said. "Or whenever you're feeling anxious."

"What about breastfeeding? Will it hurt the baby?"

"It's safe. But if you're worried, lots of babies grow up on formula."

All babies are difficult but Eva was a really difficult baby. She had colic and cried all the time and she wouldn't eat. She lost so much weight Gaby screamed in anger when Adam told her there was no need to take the baby to the doctor. She spent every waking moment with Eva, cleaning her and soothing her and trying to feed her to no avail. Gaby eventually learned the only way Eva would eat was if they were out of the house. She fed her on walks and at cafés. She would breastfeed in parks and in malls, receiving both kind and disgusted looks from strangers. She tried her best to not overuse her medication. She tried. But every now and then, she'd allow herself a taste. No, a breath. That's what it was. Like taking the biggest breath she'd taken all day. A rest. For the first year, Gaby's brain was Eva. Adam spent most of his time at the garage, coming home just in time to help put Eva to bed. But he never really held her, only when Gaby asked him if he wanted to. It stunned Gaby. He had wanted the child and was so happy when she was pregnant. But now, it was like he thought of her as some nuisance—an object in the house that he could ignore. She tried to think about what had changed. Had she done something wrong? Was it her fault? Did he secretly want a boy? Thoughts swirled through her mind that was already loopy from lack of sleep and food caused by the new diet she'd put herself on. She told herself that she would stick to 1,200 calories a day on Mondays and Tuesdays, 900 on Wednesdays and Thursdays, 800 on Fridays and Saturdays, and on Sundays she would only drink chicken broth. When her concern about Adam's indifference to Eva consumed her, it felt comforting to occupy herself with food. It made the anxious thoughts go away.

"You've put on weight," he said one afternoon while she sat in the kitchen spooning mushed carrots into Eva's gurgling mouth. Her little arms smacked the highchair's plastic table, sending loud claps through the kitchen.

"Can you get her to stop?" Adam opened the fridge and pulled out a carton of milk. He poured himself a glass.

"She's a baby," Gaby said.

"I'm going to take a nap. Lie down with me?"

"I'm feeding her."

"Come on."

"Adam. Please."

She felt him stiffen. The glass of milk flew across the kitchen and shattered on the tile wall. Eva belly-wailed, her eyes blubbering. Gaby, covering her head with her hands, smelled the mushed carrots in her hair. Adam stood, arms by his sides, glaring white. He swept out of the room, leaving the milk carton on the table. That's when she began cleaning up all her messes. Her mistake messes. Her fault messes. Her stupid messes. Her messes that weren't there one moment and then, like magic, appeared before her like forgotten phone calls or steak prepared wrong. You-owe-it-to-me-tonight messes. When she talked about moving back home to live with her mom, just for some help with the baby, just for a while, Adam would resist. *All we need is each other. Why would you want to be with anyone else but me? You can't trust anybody else.*

On Eva's second birthday, nobody showed up for the party. Gaby had purchased a giant pink balloon in the shape of the number two and taped blue and green streamers from wall to wall. Even Maddie, who said that she would show up, called just hours before and cancelled. "I'm not feeling well," she said. "She's two. She won't even notice."

Gaby sat on the couch feeling ridiculous with a paper crown pushed lopsided on her head. She'd purchased them from the discount store. She was going to make everyone wear them.

"People are busy," Adam said when Gaby began to cry. Eva slept quietly next to her on the couch with her yellow velvet blanket over her.

"I think I need to go back to work," Gaby said. "I can't do this. I feel so alone."

"Come on," Adam said. "Haven't I given you a good home? A married mother working as a waitress? It's not a good look."

She looked around at the sterile house she once believed would be filled with laughter.

"What about college courses? Something else."

"Why do you need anything else? Are you unhappy with me?"

"No, that's . . ."

"I give you everything. What else could you need?"

"Just something that . . ."

"Come on. Let's not be greedy. I have everything you need."

At the time, it made sense to Gaby. At the time it seemed reasonable because Eva needed her. But loneliness crept around her like a snake, squeezing tight. While Eva slept, Gaby would pop only one pill, but after that didn't work, she'd sneak two and then three. It was never enough to let herself fall away from Eva, but just enough to take the edge off. Enough to numb. Enough to pretend the snake wasn't coiling tighter around her neck.

It was an abnormally hot night in late July when Eva couldn't sleep. Gaby decided to drive her around the block a few times while Adam slept soundly. In the car, she let the hum force the baby's eyes closed. It was relaxing for both of them. She drove by the pub. Would Brandon or Jill be working? Gaby ached for the times when they would stay up late after closing down the bar and drink and talk; they would listen to every word that fell off of her tongue as though it were magic. Gaby kept the car running in the parking lot for the air-con, letting Eva sleep. She was only going to be a few minutes—a quick hello, then she would leave. Brandon was behind the bar and when he saw her, he broke out into a huge grin welcoming her into his big arms. She melted into the comfort of his cotton shirt smelling like tobacco and sweat. She wanted to keep her face pressed to him forever. The place was deserted except for a few regulars hunched over their beers.

"You should stay," Brandon said.

"I can't."

"Come on. Just one!"

"I have . . ."

"What? You have what? I haven't seen you in forever."

She was about to say no when he popped her a bottle of Schooner. She stayed for one beer, drinking it fast. Then three. Then five. Brandon kept popping them open and smiling and Gaby didn't know how to say no because how could she say no to love? The lights were warm and the familiar shitty country songs played on the speaker. Even the beer-stained hardwood floors made Gaby feel nostalgic—the same way she felt when she looked at old photos of her dad wearing his thick wool fisherman's sweater on the docks. Gaby drank more and she was loved.

"Who owns the vehicle out back?" A police officer stood in the shadow of the entrance, incandescent light shining down on his face.

"Shit." Gaby stood and caught her balance. She tried to run for the door, but the officer grabbed her upper arm.

"Is that your kid?"

"Is she okay?" Gaby knew she was slurring. She couldn't breathe.

"How many drinks have you had tonight?"

She looked over at Brandon, who was talking to another officer.

"Where is she?"

"You worried about her now? The fuck were you thinking?"

Outside the bar, she heard Eva crying. A cop held her, bouncing her up and down, a blankie wrapped around her tiny body. Gaby felt the other officer's hands on her back, guiding her to the police car. He stood in front of her while she swayed, arms crossed and face red. She couldn't believe how much of an idiot she'd been. The cop looked down at the ID she'd given him and paused.

"You're Adam's girl, aren't you?"

"What?"

"Adam Lawrence?"

"Yeah."

The officer handed her back the ID and told her to get into the back of the car. He slammed the door and Gaby sat quietly in the still dark of the cruiser, her heart pounding. She watched as the two cops spoke to each other, and then grabbed Eva's car seat.

"We're going to drive you home," the cop said when he opened the door again, placing Eva next to her in the back. "You do this again, and we'll take you in."

It was the first and only time Adam ever hit her. When she got through the door that night and put Eva to bed, she came back downstairs and felt his closed fist collide with her cheekbone. She lost her balance and dropped to the floor, smacking her knee on the tile in the kitchen. He didn't call her a name. He didn't tell her how disappointed he was in her. He just stood over top of her with his hands hanging down by his sides.

"I'm going back to bed," he said. And then he left.

A line of drool fell from her mouth and landed sticky on the pillow. Gaby wiped her lips with the back of her hand and sat up. She'd fallen asleep on the couch. The clock on the wall read quarter after six. She'd missed Eva's supper.

"I'm going out." Adam grabbed his jacket from the coat rack.

Gaby sat up, feeling the pill bottle in her pocket pinch up against her hip.

"You're leaving? You just got home." Her throat felt hoarse and dry.

Adam's eyes flickered. "Maybe try to be a mom tonight."

It had been a year since the bar incident, and he held her mistake over her head like a concrete block he was ready to drop.

You could have killed her.

You know, I do the right thing. I take care of you.

You're so irresponsible.

He was right. Gaby apologized over and over, and each time he would hug her tight and tell her that it was alright and he knew she could be a good mother. His arms were so strong and when he wrapped them around her, she felt as though he could hold her up forever. She'd never have to stand on her own as long as she had him. But right after, the concrete block found its way up over her head again. He would leave for days and come back in the middle of the night to sleep on the couch. She noticed messages started piling up on their answering machine from women she didn't know. When she asked him about it, he told her there was nothing to worry about. "Are you still taking your medication? Maybe up the dose."

The days blended. Gaby felt as though she were awake when dreaming and dreaming while awake—as if she'd fallen through the looking glass. Sparkles drifted across her face and her muscles liquified. She lost track of time and either fed Eva too much or not at all. She was almost four, and her cheeks were still fat, and her hair blew silky and dark in the cool spring air while she played outside. She giggled and smiled when Gaby walked over, reaching up to her with her tiny little fingers, wanting to be picked up. Her jeans were already too small for her, the hems landing just above her ankles. Her big, brown eyes looked up into Gaby's face as if she were calculating something.

"We're having the funeral Sunday," Maddie's voice sounded solemn on the other line. "You can at least try and make it down."

Their mother had died. Heart attack. Gaby's head swirled with the echoes of Jacques Brel's voice as she watched Eva play in the backyard, running in circles and giggling to herself.

Ne me quitte pas. Ne me quitte pas.

"You didn't even like her," Adam said. "She was a horrible woman. The things she did to you kids!"

It was his excuse for not allowing her to have the car—not that she needed one given her past mistake.

"I think I should at least show my face," Gaby wilted. "She was my mom."

Adam shook his head and tsked. He held an apple in one hand and a paring knife in the other, stripping the peel off in one long strand, round and round.

"It's like you're trying to be a child," he said. "She doesn't deserve your presence. Matter of fact, she doesn't deserve your sister's presence either. When will she come to her senses?"

Gaby opened the back door and shouted for Eva to come inside. She stopped running and shouted back.

"Why?"

"Because I said so."

"No!"

"Evangeline, get inside right now."

"Come on baby, here have some apple," Adam leaned forward and dangled the long, red peel in the air for Eva to see. The little girl smiled and ran toward her father, giggling before grabbing the peel and munching on it with her tiny baby teeth.

Sitting on a bench with Eva in the Halifax Commons one foggy afternoon, watching bleakly as a group threw a frisbee back and forth, Gaby spotted her old friend. "Jill, Jill!" she waved and shouted. "Come on over, girl!"

Jill responded with a hesitant wave but didn't move. Gaby grabbed Eva's hand and began to walk over, but Eva was holding back, so she picked her up and broke into an awkward run.

"I haven't seen you in forever," she said, catching her breath. She tucked her long hair behind one ear, embarrassed. She must have looked rough. Tousled, unwashed hair, sweatpants covered in green pea stains, a shirt that was two sizes too big, falling off her shoulders.

"Hi, Gaby," said Jill, who took a step back, then looked over her shoulder.

Who's she looking for, thought Gaby. Jill kept glancing back as if waiting for someone to jump up behind her.

"How've you been?" Gaby moved Eva onto her hip and bounced her up and down with a big grin. "This is Eva. Eva, tell her how old you are."

"Put me down, Mom?"

"Alright," Gaby set Eva down on the grass and let her hide behind her legs.

"I'm kind of surprised you're talking to me," Jill said.

"Why?"

"After what happened."

"What happened? The bar thing? You heard about it? That was nothing, I mean . . . I made a bad mistake. Never happened again."

"No, not that."

Gaby filled the uncomfortable silence growing between them with a forced laugh, finding it difficult to look Jill in the eye. "I'm not sure . . . I'm not sure I know what you mean."

Jill rubbed her hands on her pants. "Adam called me. After Eva was born."

Gaby felt a shiver run up along the back of her neck.

"He told me that you both knew I'd stolen jewellery from you and that you never wanted to speak to me again."

"That's crazy," she said.

"You never came back to work. At least not while I was there. I didn't take anything, Gaby. Why would you think that about me?"

"I don't! I didn't!"

Jill shook her head and looked down at her boots. She shrugged her shoulders. "I have to go."

A girl kicking a soccer ball ran in front of Gaby and told her to watch out as Jill shrank smaller and smaller in the distance, leaving her alone. She felt Eva kicking gently at her legs, asking if they could get ice cream. The fog seemed to thicken around them, warping their bodies and covering the tops of the apartment buildings off to the side. There was no sky. No horizon. Just grey.

XV
Eva

Smoke plumes filled the air as people passed around a joint. Speakers pumped out music and shook the floor, vibrations travelling up Eva's legs as she let the smoke leave her lungs. It burned at first, and then her mouth got all cottony and dry. She took a shot of whisky, her whole body tingling and light. A door hung loose on one of the cupboards and the floor felt sticky underneath her shoes. Alma was by the counter, talking to someone Eva didn't know. Then she turned, locked eyes with Eva, and smiled. She grabbed a red apple from a bowl, spun and walked backward down the hallway, a beer in one hand and waving the apple as if tantalizing Eva to follow.

She followed Alma down the hall to a bedroom where two girls lay side by side on a bed, holding their phones in front of their faces. Their phones looked different than Eva's, who had to slide her screen up in order to access the keypad. Their phones were glassy and smooth. Alma sat on the floor, her long legs in sheer black tights stretched out in front, combat boots tied tight. From her tote bag, she dug out a yellow pencil with a sewing needle stuck into the pink eraser tip and a pot of black ink.

"What do you want done?" She threw the red apple onto the bed. "What?"

"I'll do it for you." She pulled Eva's hand forward and made her

126

sit on the corner of the bed. Alma's legs swung out to her side, and she sat with her legs in hooked triangles on the floor. She clipped a lighter and slid the sewing needle through the orange flame.

"You choose," Eva said.

"Where you from?" one of the girls asked.

"Nova Scotia."

"Newfie!"

"No, the other one," Eva said.

"I'm gonna do a circle." Alma dipped the needle into the pot of sticky black ink. "'cause I don't know how to do anything else."

"Why'd you ask me what I wanted then?"

Her eyes went wide. "I didn't think you'd say yes." She held Eva's hand down on the bed, gripping it tight and spreading her thumb and forefinger wide. She felt the needle pierce the meaty bit of flesh on her hand. Eva watched the black ink spread and it felt like her hand was being tenderized. She grabbed the beer that Alma had set down on the floor and took a long swig. The red apple on the bed shone in the smoky light, juicy and crimson.

"Do you like it there?" one of the girls on the bed asked.

"Where?"

"Nova Scotia. I hear it's beautiful."

"Do you have one of those farmhouses?" The other girl sat up. "With a big farm kitchen?"

Eva's hand got hot and itchy from the pinpricks as Alma dug the needle in and out of her flesh, the tip of her tongue just past her lips in concentration. She was ignoring the conversation.

"Do you guys do a lot of fishing?"

"I don't know how," Eva said.

"I thought you all knew how to fish."

"I get seasick."

"The people there seem so nice and simple."

"Not in a bad way." The other girl backtracked. "Just happier."

"Do you go back a lot?"

"No."

"Why? I'd buy a house there in a heartbeat."

"I'm waiting for it to break off from the mainland and sink into the Atlantic." Eva smirked at Alma, who giggled.

"I think my uncle has a home there."

"From the pictures it looks so idyllic."

"So beautiful."

Eva knew the tattoo was finished when Alma sat back against the wall and let out a big yawn, cracking open a Colt 45 she pulled from her tote bag. The circle on Eva's hand was strangely perfect and thick. Little dots of blood collected on top.

"What should we do tonight?" Alma tossed the makeshift tattoo gun onto the floor. She pulled a screwdriver out from her bag and snagged the red apple she'd thrown on the bed. The tip of the screwdriver punctured the crisp flesh at the top and she shoved the metal in, juice bubbling up around the sides. She tugged it out and then stabbed the side of the apple, creating another hole. She popped open a tiny case she'd taken out from her bag and pinched what looked like tiny pieces of green lint. She sprinkled the pieces on top of the apple and smiled, satisfied at her creation. Eva was curious, and Alma must have spotted the confused look on her face.

"Ever smoke weed from an apple pipe before?" She beamed.

Their sharp teeth were invasive. Spit flew at her, marking their territory with terrible jokes. They ended up at Peel Pub. Eva hated watching people laugh over pitchers of beer and soggy fries. She thought they were all miserable and lying. Aggressive music strained through the speakers and she could smell cigarette smoke wafting in from the sidewalk, sending her head into a frenzy. The walls were brick and lined with TV screens projecting a soccer game. Small tables filled the floor and people sat squished together under framed hockey jerseys, sweating and jostling one another. A waitress came over to their long, crowded table and placed a massive tower of yellow beer in the middle of them. There was a spout at the tube's base, and when it landed, everyone cheered.

Eva left to find the bathroom but, on her way, felt a hand tap her shoulder. When she turned, she saw Dex standing by the bar with two pints.

"Want one?"

Eva shook her head, but he smiled and pushed one of the blond beers forward. Her fingertips left marks in the frost on the glass.

"When did you move here?"

"About five months ago."

"You and Alma became friends fast."

"I like her."

"She's fun."

Eva drank from the glass. She felt unsettled and wrong. She kept glancing over at Alma who was engaged in a conversation with a girl named Anna who was studying fine art and had just recently created a portrait of Quebec's minister of education with blood coming out of her eyes. Eva knew this because the girl had shown her pictures of it on her phone.

"Listen. I think you might have seen something that night at the party and I just want to make sure we're cool."

"What do you mean?"

"You didn't see anything that night? You know it . . . might have looked weird at the time but—"

"I saw you on top of someone and—"

"It probably looked like that, but that's not really what was happening."

"I mean I'm sure it was something that I shouldn't—"

"If you say anything about this to her, she'll be really confused and I think it will waste a lot of her time. Because it wasn't anything. Really."

Eva wiped the condensation off her glass with her thumb, feeling her skin grow numb and the cold disappear. "Yeah, I mean. I'm sure it wasn't anything."

Dex nodded and took a drink. He smiled at her and gave her a playful shove. "I appreciate it." He let out a laugh, cocked his head and said, "Now I don't have to hurt you." But then he stopped laughing and stared at her, wide-eyed. Eva saw levity disappear from his eyes while his smile remained small.

Eva left her beer on the counter and found the bathroom. She couldn't hear anything except for a fuzzy, high-pitched buzz, as if someone shoved a mosquito wrapped in a cotton ball into her ear canal. She leaned against the wall and caught a glimpse of herself in the mirror. A grey face, downturned mouth. Her tongue sticky from the beer. She felt the slam of a stall vibrate down her back and watched a girl with smudged makeup waltz out. She had on tiny black shorts that exposed her ass and a strappy bodysuit that tightened across her nipples. Her long dark hair was wrapped in multi-coloured headbands. She was about a foot shorter than Eva and bubbly.

"Do you want some?" The girl held up a small white bag and then began tapping the powder onto a compact mirror balanced on the sink. She cut a few lines and sniffed hard, leaning back to let Eva have a turn. Eva leaned over and breathed in. The inside of her nose turned red hot, and she felt the back of her throat close. The girl giggled.

"That was a fat one."

"I've never done coke before." Eva smiled and rubbed her nose.

"I have that too," the girl reached into her purse and took out another small bag of white powder.

Eva pointed to the lines. "Isn't that coke?"

130

"Oh, girl, no." She giggled manically and shook her head. Eva continued to rub her nose. She looked in the mirror and saw grey skin, grey eyes and grey lips.

Bar was elongated. Stretched tight like cooling caramel taffy. Pull the caramel rope and meet your partner in the middle. Remembered her little hands grabbing the sugary candy rope. Big grin as she leaned her whole body away, strong. Ear to ear. Pulled back until it was about to break. Was on a raft in the ocean, completely alone. Fear dissolved like sugar in hot water. Clouds in her ears grew. Could get punched over and over and never feel. Pulled toward the heavy traffic in the street. Cold. Ground covered in sparkling white. A shadow from another realm. Grabbing. Grabbing. Ringing and felt pulled out of her shoes left and right, a piece of kelp flowing in the waves. Saw the shadow of her mother across from her in the park. *No.* Waves crashing over. Bending lights. Cars honking. Saw her mother's body ripping apart like smoke in front of her. Light waxing and waning. Her mother in a white dress peering out from behind a tree, her crooked finger beckoning. *Come.* A shadow. A demon. *Come with me.* Her eyes onyx moons of dread. Walked to the park across the street. Don't get hit. Lean back on a bench. Head rolling back beyond the heart.

"Hey."

She parted her fingers and squinted up through them. Something ominous. Teeth. A mouth. Alma looked down at her, face all swirly.

"Do you think he's cheating on me?" Alma's voice was big neon violet bass strings vibrating through a starry night.

Silence.

"Do *you* think he's cheating on you?"

"I don't know."

"I don't think he is," Eva lied.

Alma sat on top of Eva's toes on the bench. Her hair was a mess, her profile devastation. Eva lay on her back and opened and closed her knees like a child playing peek-a-boo. She couldn't feel her feet planted on the hard wooden bench under Alma.

"Are you okay?"

"I think so."

"You're lying on a bench alone in the snow."

"Oh."

"Here's your jacket."

"Thanks."

"I can take you home."

"I love you."

"Yeah?"

"I'm sorry."

"Don't be sorry about loving people."

"Not that way though. You know?"

"I know. I love you not that way too."

She tried to study Alma's face, but she couldn't pin it down. It kept skating off into the darkness, profile shifting like lights captured on film in the dark, stretching in space.

"I feel like I'm in a horror movie."

"I can take you home, Eva."

"Who?"

"You."

She shook her head. "I don't think I am."

Her armpits felt as though they were burning as Alma grabbed underneath and hoisted her up.

"I don't want to go back," she said.

"To your apartment? Why?"

"I don't want to go back there."

"Come to my place."

"Dex."

"He'll find his way home. Don't worry about him."

They made it into a cab and it was there that she saw Alma's face turn to her, illuminated by the city lights—fluorescent fairies streaming through black velvet. A dark shadow fell over half of Alma's face and Eva squinted at the sudden change.

"You know my criminology elective?" Alma's voice was soft underneath the hum of the cab. "Last week, we looked at domestic violence cases that lead to murder. And there was this one from where you're from. I looked it up online afterwards because it was so strange. The woman had never reported being physically abused. At least, it was never talked about in court. I did some digging. Lawrence. They had a daughter. His eyes . . . I mean, they looked exactly like yours."

The cab slowed to a stop at a light. Eva clicked open the car door and walked into the oncoming traffic, drivers leaning on their horns and shouting. The cab driver growled something and she heard Alma shout for her to come back. Stomping to the alley, Eva pulled back her hair and splashed vomit on the side of a late-night pizza joint. Alma hovered behind, leaning over to hold her hair away from her face while rubbing her back.

XVI
Mathilde

The way you needed me. The way you loved me. The way you jumped in after me, crashing the calm into chaos. The way you spoke to me. The way you held me. The way your eyes changed into diamonds when they looked into mine. The way you spoke to your daughter in that caring tone. The way you held me. The way you cried with me. Your tears are tattoos on my shoulders. The way you spoke my name over the years. Mathilde. Mah-tild-ah. It dripped out of your mouth like molasses. The way you dipped your fingers into me like dipping your fingers into a cup of sugar and then tasting it. The way you laughed at my jokes. The way you made me feel like I was the only one who could ever make anyone laugh. The way you slept. So soundly. Next to me. Exposing your chest and belly to me. Your mouth open. Your face so soft. Your skin so warm and naked and perfect. The way your neck looked, thick, and your Adam's apple rubbing up and down underneath your skin when you swallowed. The way your lips parted. You looked so beautiful.

XVII
Eva

The ceiling spun rays of orange and pale yellow light. Her eyes ached from the brightness; Eva slammed them shut and buried her head into the pillow. Wiping sweat off her chest, her skin seemed both cold and hot; it felt like someone was stabbing her brain with an ice pick. She heard someone moving in the distance and checked under the duvet that covered her to make sure she was still wearing pants and a shirt.

"Do you want coffee?" Alma's voice hit her ear and travelled down into her stomach, making it queasy. She looked up from her pillow as if that would somehow help her hide from Dex if he were home. Alma held a mug in her hand, steam rising lazily in front of her face. Her hair was tangled. She placed the mug on the coffee table and sat down next to it, pulling her heels in toward her.

Eva pushed herself up to sit, her head spinning, ready to fall off and roll down her chest and onto the floor. She could smell something foul drifting up toward her nose and it took her a second to realize it was coming from her own armpits.

"I don't remember her voice." She didn't want to say it, but she couldn't stop.

"Who?"

"My mom."

Her lungs felt as though they were about to collapse, but she forced a breath. Alma leaned forward. She refused to cry. She couldn't cry. She stared ahead at a small crack snaking up the baseboard.

"Where is she?"

"I never knew I couldn't hear her voice in my head anymore."

"Where's your mom?" she asked again. Eva knew Alma knew the answer, but she wanted Eva to say it. Eva looked up at the ceiling and rubbed her forearms. She felt like a small, cornered rodent.

"It was winter," Eva began.

When she was six, Eva's mother threw her and a pile of luggage into the backseat of their car one night. It was mid-winter and light snow dusted the driveway; their quiet street was blanketed by the milky streetlights, sugar coating over a chocolate cake. Eva almost slipped on the brick steps leading down to their driveway, but her mother caught her under the arm and yanked. In the car, she told Eva to wait. She sat shivering in the cold damp dark listening to growls and shouts coming from the house before eventually drifting off to sleep.

When she woke up, she saw the ocean. The sun rose behind them in the moving car, and her eyes lingered on the calm horizon in its periwinkle hue, the water rippling in the morning breeze. They were on a winding, single-lane highway that folded into rows of shorefront houses spaced so far apart from one another it made Eva feel disjointed. Some houses crept toward the ocean, small in stature and broad, while others sat right on the highway's edge, threatening to fall over in front of them with their rotting wood. Some looked as though they'd grown larger over the course of time, with small rooms added to the sides and porches lifted from the ground and extensions smacked onto the back. Red, white and blue stripes with a golden star were painted on the sides of houses and roofs. Flags were sparse during the winter months, but Eva remembered in the summer they would line emerald-green properties as if every day were the Tintamarre. Dune buggies sat proudly in restaurant parking lots and Eva counted each dirt bike, swearing she saw more of them than people.

The drive into Clare was desolate. The ocean was lonely and bare, and the landscape gleamed with ice and white frigid air.

When Eva stepped out of the car after her mother parked in the grocery store lot, a full gust of sea wind smacked her hard in the face and nearly knocked her over. The wind blew so hard and cold it took her breath away and her bones shivered. Her mother grabbed her by the arm and pulled. The grocery store smelled like hard clay and marsh. Eva followed her mother down the aisles, watching as her legs took long, determined steps. Her mother wore black boots and her black jeans were thin at the ankle. Eva tried to keep up with her, but her legs were too short, and she had to walk in double-time. She watched as her mother selected a bunch of fresh parsley and celery from the produce aisle, along with packaged fresh herbs Eva didn't recognize. She trailed along behind her mother who walked as if Eva was not there, making a sudden left down an aisle filled with packaged soaps and bottles of shampoo. Her mother grabbed a soft package from off the shelf.

"Why do you need diapers?" Eva asked.

Her mother's eyes flicked up and narrowed.

"They're not diapers," she said. "They're menstrual pads."

Eva didn't know that word. She kept quiet while her mom juggled the parsley and celery and herbs in her left arm, clutching the pads in her right.

"Come on." Her mother turned and Eva followed her to the checkout. The cashier smiled bright and chatted with the man in front of them while she bagged his giant bottles of Pepsi and a bunch of bananas. Their conversation was casual, French and boisterous, and Eva could tell the cashier ended with something to the effect of "see you later." But when her mom stepped up to the counter, the woman's face fell into a grouchy stare. She scanned the items and left them at the end of the conveyor belt.

The trailer was a burst of red and sat at the edge of Mavillette Beach.

"Where are we going?"

"Aunt Maddie's."

There were other houses in the village. It had a winding road passing through that ended at the top of a hill that looked out onto the Atlantic. Her aunt had moved into the trailer after Eva's grandmother passed away. She remembered her mother telling her about the funeral. There'd been tears in her eyes. Eva wanted to go, but her dad told her that her mother didn't want to, so they all stayed home.

There were no trees along the road. Only frost sprinkled over brittle faded yellow grass. A bridge led to the beach's parking lot flanked by large stones and overgrown prickly thick bushes brown and hay coloured. The houses were mid-sized and wooden, painted white and yellow and grey and blue, with some having red or blue roofs. A rocky dam jutted out from the edge and shielded the bridge from the large waves. Eva heard the constant beating of the waves on the shoreline, thunderous and lulling with the wind. But after a while, the sound of the ocean and the wind took refuge in her ears, and she barely noticed. It wasn't until she and her mother left the seaside town that she recognized the absence of the ocean—the dull ache of city silence. But that didn't happen for another few days.

Mathilde stood at the front of the trailer with her arms crossed, leaning her shoulder on the door frame. Her mother parked the car in the lot next to Mathilde's truck and got out. They did not say a word to each other. Her mother held the groceries in her arms and squeezed herself through the door and into the trailer. When Eva climbed the white steps up onto the front porch, her aunt held out her arms in lazy welcome.

The front door opened up into a small kitchenette. The floor felt like bubbled plastic underneath Eva's stocking feet, and the place smelled like lavender and gasoline. Eva sat at the small round table in the corner while her mother filled a kettle with water from the tap. "Go to the den and watch TV," she said to Eva without looking at her.

Eva stood back up and took the three steps required for her to land in the small den off the side of the kitchen. There was an orange-flowered sofa in the corner, a reclining chair, and a small TV mounted high on the wall. The other wall had a large sliding glass door that led to the side porch, with steps running down to unkempt grass and a sideways-leaning barn with holes in the side. Eva sat down cross-legged on the dark green shag carpet and turned on the TV, found a channel that played cartoons, but kept the volume low. She leaned her head against the wall and listened while her aunt spoke in rapid French to her mother, who didn't say anything. Then, Mathilde spoke in English.

"I'll be back tonight."

Eva heard the door open and slam, then heard the sound of her aunt's truck rev and back out of the gravel driveway. In the kitchen, her mom chopped vegetables on a cutting board. The ripping of leaves. Plastic containers clawed open with hurried hands. The front door opened again and, through the sliding glass door, she saw her mother walk down the steps onto the grass and disappear into the barn. When she reappeared, she was carrying a fistful of something scraggly and dark green. Seaweed. Eva smelled something bitter in the air after her mom arrived back in the kitchen. The kettle whistled and then died, and water poured.

After a few moments of silence, Eva stood up and peered into the kitchenette. She saw her mother sitting at the small round table with a large mug in front of her that had steam rising from it. A half-empty bottle of whisky sat in front of her too. Her eyes were closed. The package of menstrual pads had been ripped open, and they sat at her feet. A tube of something deep green wrapped in cheesecloth and a white string dangling from it sat on a plate in the middle of the table. Eva's mother picked it up and gazed at it, turning it over in her fingers. She held it delicately, like some expensive jewel. With her elbows on the table, she rubbed her temples and then looked up at Eva, as if only then noticing that she was there. The tips of Eva's toes were touching the cool tile, but she did not dare step over the threshold until her mother held out her hand and moved it in such a way that told Eva to come forward. She leaned into her mother's side. She had strong arms, and her hugs were never lacklustre. She felt held and secure in her mother's arms, and when she felt her warm lips kiss the top of her head, Eva knew everything was okay. The smell from the mug was rotten and her mother sipped the hot liquid. Then, after placing the mug down on the table, she unlatched herself from Eva and reached for the bottle of whisky. Her mother stood.

"My tummy hurts. I need to lie down for a while." The green thing in mesh cloth dangled from her fingertips.

Her mother jostled her awake from her slumber on the couch and told her to get ready. Her smile seemed to go on forever. "Let's go for an adventure," she said. Before they left, her mother went into the small bathroom and picked up the trashcan, bringing it out with her. Eva could see what looked like bloody bandages crumpled up inside.

"What's that?" Eva asked.

"Freedom," her mother said.

At first, Eva's eyes wilted from the cold, tearing up and fizzing from the harsh sea wind. But after a while, she grew used to the smell of organic, frosty air and the feeling of cold biting her nose. Her mother ventured up into the high dunes covered in spiky, dry seagrass. The dunes were packed thick, a wall of khaki-coloured sand that was double the height of Eva, who chose to walk on the beach where she could find strangely shaped rocks, broken crab legs and the tops of beached jellyfish. The jellyfish tops were amethyst and milky-white, and she jiggled them with the tips of her booted toe, then felt bad for disturbing them even though she knew they were dead.

"Look!" Her mother shouted over the winter ocean wind. "Sea Pepsi!"

Eva looked up and saw her mom's head covered in her winter coat, cheeks red from the cold, holding up cans in her gloved hands. Eva giggled and ran, muscling her way through the sand in her thick winter boots up the dunes, slipping when cold sand gave way. Her mom caught her hand and pulled her up. On top of the dune, she could see the full view of the ocean, tide out. White lace lazily rolled over the top of the grey water and was erased by the small waves rolling into the shore, which smoothed like melting butter over the wet sand, flat and solid as a chalkboard.

Her mother bent down again. "A sea lighter!" She picked up the black plastic rectangle and clipped it alight, beaming. Eva's face hurt from the cold and from smiling. She roamed through the sea grass and the dried primrose and the beach rosehips, trying to match her mother.

"Sea barbeque sauce!" Eva yelled proudly, picking up a bottle of burgundy plastic. This made her mother keel over with laughter. They continued down the shore with their game.

"Sea rope!"

"Sea granola wrappers!"

"Sea beer!"

"A sea shoe!'

Eva ran and jumped and slid down the dunes to a corner of the beach covered in rocks that crunched under her weight like shattering glass. The wind floated by, an unsteady breath, high and causing her nose to drip. There were so many rocks. All that had not been beaten by the waves just yet, keeping whole and clustered. The waves rolled in like a deep sigh and bubbled at her feet before dragging themselves back out, leaving broken bits of crab, white foam, and thick seaweed. She made sure to keep a few paces behind her mom, not to lose sight of her. Down in the rocks, she searched for more treasure. That's when she noticed it. A green, almost perfect sphere glistening under the cloudy sun. When she picked it up, it was hard and smooth, though she expected it to be jelly.

"Mom!" she yelled. "A sea marble!"

Her mother whipped around and held her hand up to her eyes to block the sun. Eva shone the marble up overhead between her fingers with pride. She sniffed back the drops coming out of her nose and breathed through her mouth, holding her hands out so that Eva could let the green marble fall into her dry palms.

"Look at that." Her mother's deep brown eyes sparkled. She held the marble up to the sky between her thumb and pointer finger. "That's one in a million."

Eva felt herself glow.

She remembered the dead deer. The following morning, she was sitting on the couch wrapped in a quilt and shivering in pajamas that always seemed damp. Mathilde sat at the kitchen table with her sketchbook, drawing one of the dried weeds Eva had ripped out from the ground on her way back from the ocean. That's when she heard the car wheels on gravel and the squeaking of brakes. Her aunt's head lifted to look out the kitchen window. Eva could see the truck parked between the porch and the barn. Her mother jumped out of the cab and walked around to the bed of the truck, slamming down the tailgate. Mathilde grabbed her boots and her jacket and a large knife from the drawer. Eva's breath pulsated on the glass as she pulled the quilt tighter around herself. She watched as her aunt stomped through the snow in her untied boots to meet her mom. They looked as though they were arguing, Mathilde's arms bouncing up and down, her mom unimpressed and lighting a cigarette. She looked irritated and kept pointing to the bed of the truck. Eva liked the way her mother's long hair looked, silky chocolate.

The two women disappeared behind the truck and returned carrying a dead deer. Her mother held the front legs and her aunt held the back. They swung the dead animal onto the snow at the side of the house. Eva, in her pink Barbie pajamas, shoved on her boots and ran out into the snow, dragging the quilt. Her breath caught outside, a thick cloud hovering in front of her face.

She watched her mother take the knife from Mathilde and cut a circle around the animal's backside. The two flipped the deer onto its back and her mother used her thighs to hold the deer's legs open. She gripped the skin of the belly and made an incision down along the middle, opening the flaps and exposing the white, veiny stomach balloon, the smoke from her cigarette billowing up above her head. She reached her hand up into the cavity and tugged something back. Eva heard the knife blade scrape against bone and watched as Mathilde pulled out a blood-soaked glob of guts and threw it in the snow. Her aunt looked up and stared straight at Eva, whose teeth were chattering. A light snow had begun to fall silently around them.

"Your mom hit a deer," Mathilde said.

Eva watched her mother stand tall and broad. It was a mother she'd never seen before. Her hand did not shake as she held the knife. She stared deep into Eva's eyes. Her mother's eyes were bright and steady, and Eva felt her belly flip in a queasy motion that told her simultaneously that she was safe and to be careful.

They cut up the meat and stored it in the freezer. Her mom showed her how to cut the layer of fat and tissue off the raw heart with a sharp knife, slicing from the top and removing the sack. It was solid purple, the size of a large orange. The top tube was open and raw, a straw burrowing down into the organ. The muscle came to a point at the bottom, a thin vein running through to the tip with small lines jutting out at the sides along thin white fatty tissue.

Her mother had the heart on a cutting board on the counter and evening was seeping into the trailer. The kitchen had a coil-top stove, white and clean, with a timer that looked like a chicken placed in the middle. The floor was brown linoleum, starbursts of caramel and ochre. Eva noticed how different it was from their own kitchen, which was large and had stone countertops and an island in the middle and was very white. Mathilde's kitchen had wooden counters the colour of rust and wallpaper above the sink.

"You gotta cut out the veins here," her mother said, pointing to the top cluster of tubes that jiggled when she ran her finger over them. She drank from a can of beer, keeping a second one unopened and close. She took the small knife, made a cut through the valves and used her fingers to peel back the meat. The holes in the top of the heart were deep and looked like a bruise, thick and purple. She dug her fingers into the sockets of the heart, using her knife to make small incisions in the wall. Eva saw how her mom's fingers slowly coated with blood.

"See the heartstrings?" She opened up the muscle and picked at the small fibres that strained between the meat. She continued to cut, her fingers getting bloodier while the heart sliced into smaller and smaller pieces. Then she roughly chopped some white onions and put a pan on the stove. She threw in globs of butter and waited for them to melt before shoving in the onions, using the same knife to push them around. She threw salt and pepper on the heart pieces and called for Mathilde, who was in her room. Her mother told Eva to grab the paper plates from the cupboard, and she watched as her mother cracked another cold can of beer and brought the pan of meat to the table. Mathilde sat next to Eva and gave a small smile.

"If you don't like it, we'll get something sweet later," her aunt said.

"She'll like it." Her mother sat down and stabbed a forkful of onions and meat and shoved it into her mouth. She watched her mother's eyes close as she chewed, taking a big breath. Mathilde took out a knife and cut the meat on Eva's plate into small pieces. Eva stabbed the heart with her fork and took a bite. It was tough and tasted like blood. The way her aunt looked at her made her feel as though she were meant to spit it out, but she didn't want to. Her stomach growled with hunger and her mother looked so happy.

"You don't have to finish it," Mathilde said.

"Why wouldn't she?" Her mom shot back.

"I'm just saying. *C'est fine si qu'al'aime point ça.*"

Her mom dropped her fork on the table and glared.

"Why wouldn't she like it?"

"It's deer heart." Mathilde's words were stone. "She hasn't had it before."

"How do you know?"

Her aunt said nothing. Her mother shoved a piece of heart into her mouth and chewed, staring at Mathilde without blinking. She turned to Eva. "Show your aunt how good you are at French."

Eva chewed on a piece of soft onion before it melted away in the salty butter between her teeth. She looked from her mother to her aunt.

"*Essaie-la,*" her mother said encouragingly.

"I . . ." Eva stuttered.

"Say anything," her mother said smugly. "Say your name."

"*Zche . . . zchee ma pelle Eva,*" she stumbled.

Her mother smiled broadly while chewing. Mathilde gave a gentle nod. "*Très bien.*"

"Tell her something else," her mother said. "Tell her your favourite colour."

Eva cleared her throat. "Mom," she said. "I don't know—"

"Go on," she said.

Eva looked at her aunt whose eyes were fixed on her plate.

"*Zche*," Eva said. "*Zche ma chem the couleur bluh.*"

Mathilde cleared her throat and glanced up, first at Eva then at her mother. Eva wanted to shrink down small and hide under the table. Her mother leaned back in her chair and stared daggers at her sister. She chewed the meat slowly, her jaw muscles strong, then pushed away from the table, knocking the chair to the floor. She picked up her empty plate and threw it in the sink.

"It's paper," Mathilde said.

Eva's mom halted just as she was about to leave the trailer. She spun on her heel, grabbed the plate from out of the sink and shoved it into the loose garbage bag on the side of the counter. Mathilde turned to Eva with a gentle smile.

"*T'es okay, chère.*"

That night, Eva awoke to hear Mathilde whispering to someone on the phone.

"She did what?" Her aunt said. "Are you . . . Adam. I'm so sorry. I didn't know."

Eva pretended to be asleep, closing her eyes tight as she shivered under the quilt in the den. The deadly wind blew outside so hard it felt like it would knock the trailer on its side. In between gusts, Eva heard her mother's voice, low at first, then screaming in French. Eva tore off the quilt and padded out to the dark kitchen, then retraced her steps and peered out from behind the doorframe. Her mother and her aunt were standing at opposite ends of the kitchen shouting at each other in French. Eva didn't understand what was going on. But when her mother dove at Mathilde and pulled at her hair, pushing her into the kitchen counter, Eva couldn't help herself. "Stop!" she shouted.

Her mother whipped around and scowled at her. She looked as if she were possessed.

"You're going back tonight." Mathilde pushed herself away and pointed. "Get out."

"This was my house too."

"It's not anymore."

"Maddie, you don't understand."

"I can't believe how stupid you are," Mathilde said. "This is crazy. Even for you."

"I'm not going back."

"Then he'll come get you."

Alma's sock feet glided to the floor. Eva felt a warm squeeze on her arm and looked up. Her face was bare and fresh but her eyes were pools of concern. Eva pulled her hair up into a short ponytail. Her hair had grown since the summer, and it felt tangled and more unruly from the dry, winter air.

"I never visited her. In prison. I remember sitting with my aunt and crying. She told me it was okay to miss my dad. I was allowed to be sad. But I wasn't crying about him. I did miss him. Like, I guess I still miss him because he was my dad and I want my dad. But I missed her more. I felt so dirty for wanting her back, like my brain was wrong. I couldn't see her the way other people saw her."

"I'm sorry," Alma said.

Eva tugged up her shirt to let the air chill her skin. She excused herself, hurrying to the bathroom to splash cold water on her face. She used toilet paper to sop up the sweat collecting underneath her arms. She saw that Alma had left gold bracelets in a small, crystal dish on the sink. Beside the bracelets, a necklace dangled from a tiny hook. Eva touched the delicate bracelets and shimmied one over her wrist. The marks from the handcuff she'd pulled off her wrist a few months before were gone, except for small white lines where scars had formed. She tried on the necklace and let the gold pendant drop cold on her skin. She gazed at herself in the mirror, wrapped in Alma's expensive jewellery, and tried to slow her breathing. Eva realized that the necklace was a locket, which she opened to reveal Dex's face. A handsome smile. Eva returned the necklace to the hook and removed the gold bracelet that felt right around her wrist. She tried to make a face that Alma would make. She tried to stand the way Alma would stand. She stood still in the mirror, looking at her own reflection and wishing it was someone else staring back at her.

"Are you going away for Christmas break?" Eva asked, coming out of the bathroom and trying to wipe her face discreetly. She sat down on the couch and took a sip of coffee.

"What? Oh. I guess. It's still a few weeks away. I'll be in Toronto."

"Do you know if the university will be closed?"

"It will be. Why?"

"And the library?"

"I think so, yeah. I think it closes."

"Is Dex going with you?"

"Are you okay? We can talk more about your mom. It sounds like she had a really hard time."

"She didn't," Eva said. "She was, like, a monster."

"She was a monster?"

Eva pulled back. "I don't think what she did was good."

"I know," Alma said. "I know. You're right. I'm really sorry, Eva. That must have been hard."

"She was selfish."

Alma looked as though she wanted to say something but held back, tightening her lips around her teeth. The sadness Eva tried so hard to hide suddenly erupted from her belly. She hugged herself and crossed her legs and tried to believe the words that came out of her mouth so that she would truly feel them and know them to be true so that it was easier.

"He was a good person," Eva said.

Alma leaned forward and hugged Eva tight to her chest. Eva felt clammy and cramped, and her eyes grew wet. She hated herself for that. She wiped them on Alma's shoulders, apologized, and stood.

"I'm gonna go home now," she said. "Thanks for letting me stay over."

While she laced up her winter boots, she saw a shadow hovering in the corner of the loft, extending long up the wall.

Alma reached out her arms and enveloped her in a hug. She saw the side of Dex's face appear and then disappear.

She left the apartment more embarrassed than she'd ever felt in her entire life. Worse than the time she accidentally wet her pants at school. Worse than the time one of the other kids asked her if she was stupid in class because she got a math equation wrong. Worse than the time nobody threw her the ball in a game of catch. She hated how she had exposed herself to Alma in such a crude way. She knew her aunt would have been so ashamed.

XVIII
Gaby

The metal door opened. A guard shouted a name. Someone in the distance cried and the cry bounced from one wall to the other until it twirled through the air like a spinning top and died falling to the floor.

Sign here.

Sign there.

"Can count everything you have to your name on one hand."

"What's the first thing you're gonna do when you get outside?"

"Drink?"

"Smoke?"

"Go to church?"

"See the ocean?"

No. I'm going to lie on the ground and stare up at the sky and drift off into the deepest sleep of my life.

Gaby's breath expanded across the window of the Greyhound as it rocked back and forth down the busy highway. The glass was cold and dewy under her fingertips. She drew a smiley face and then wiped it away, staring out at the passing trees bending to winter. Hair fell in her face. She desperately needed a cut. A good cut from a real salon. Maybe get her nails done. If she could find the money. She feared little things. What if she tripped and fell and nobody helped her? What if a car hit her? And then, the little things she longed for. The grass tickling her ankles. Buying a two-litre bottle of Orange Crush and drinking it all herself. The first thing she noticed when she left prison? The smell. It smelled fresh outside. No toilet cleaner mixed with cigarettes and bleach.

When she arrived at the halfway house in Dartmouth, she hugged her garbage bag full of clothes tight to her chest. A woman named Monica greeted her.

"You can follow me," she said. "My office is on the ground floor." She had on a brown, pilled blouse, the ends shoved into black slacks.

"You'll have the first room on the left on the second floor," she said. Monica sat at a small desk that faced a bright window with a yellow curtain hanging from a silver rod. The curtain had three patches stitched into it, and they were all different patterns and colours.

Monica had black hair, and at the end of every sentence, she wiped away some invisible hair from her nose. "Every time you leave, you need to check in with us." *Wipe.* "Every time you change locations during the day, you need to call us and tell us where you're going." *Wipe.* "You cannot use a cellphone to do this." *Wipe.* "You must use a landline." *Wipe.*

More rules. No drinking. No drugs. No visitors. Absolutely no travelling outside the province.

The room on the second floor had enough space for two single beds and two bedside tables smashed together. Her roommate was an older woman named Tori who had spiked purple hair and wrinkles all across her face.

"From the crystal," she said.

Gaby herself had aged. When she was alone in the room, she stared into the mirror, gazing into her own eyes as if at any moment she'd drown. Her cheekbones were still high, and she had that long nose. That long, beautiful nose everyone had always complimented her on as a kid. But deep lines cut up around her eyes and when she smiled she thought she looked ugly. What an ugly smile. She should never be allowed to smile ever again.

The backyard had planters and bird feeders made by the women at the house. In the summer, it must have been lush and green, but with the onslaught of winter, it had decayed. There were fifteen women at the house, all released from prison at one time or another. There was a junior high school up the street on one side and, on the other, a cemetery. The house stood slanted on a hill. It had yellow wooden siding that needed a paint job. Large empty trees lined the street, curving over the road. In the back, snow-covered garden, Gaby roamed alone to get fresh air and saw a single small tree standing next to one of the flower beds. She stepped on something big and heard it crunch underneath her foot. She looked down and saw a decomposing apple. It was rotted black, dotted with oozing white spots.

The first night, Gaby couldn't sleep. She heard an AM radio somewhere down the hall. Tori slept with ease on her side, her boney hips sticking up under the sheets. Gaby turned on her back with her hands clasped over her belly, still wearing her day clothes. The ceiling was calm. She heard cars roll by outside her window. Whenever she thought she had drifted off to sleep, there was blood. Handcuffs scraping. Prisoners screaming. It was easy to go back, harder to move forward. When she thought she'd fallen asleep, she'd feel the lid of her left eye peel open, staring dead straight at the door. Old habits.

"I got drunk one night and we got in the car. I didn't even think about it," one woman said. "We got into a fight while I was driving. He hit me. Right in the face. I remember waking up in the hospital the next day. He got thrown. Hit by an oncoming truck."

In the circle of women, Gaby listened as they all told their side.

Some said a lot. Some said two words. Either way, they were not used to being listened to.

"It feels like I'm stuck in an endless loop, you know? I don't want to go back to prison. I don't want to go anywhere near—you couldn't pay me! You couldn't pay me to go back. But sometimes it feels like it's . . . this sounds awful, but sometimes it feels like it's the only place I can go. There's nowhere else to go."

"It's easy to feel good with that one thing you got. Drugs, gambling, whatever. But it's the one thing that sends you back."

The thought of drinking made Gaby long for some forgotten dream of brighter, more twisted times. She didn't miss it. It wasn't a case of missing. It wasn't a case of wanting. It was a case of easing pain in this strange new world.

"Gaby, would you like to say a few words?"

Expectant eyes zoned in. Partially opened mouths held their tongues. *They're waiting.*

"I always wanted to be a mom." Those were the first words that came to her because they were true. "I thought I was good at it when it was happening. Or. You know, when I had her. I'm still a mom. I'm still her mom. I have an older sister. I don't think she ever liked me very much." Gaby waved her hands back and forth and forced a smile. "I'm sorry, I can't."

"It's okay."

"No, because if I keep talking I'm gonna faint."

"It's okay."

"I hate when people say that." That's when the flood of rage came. She was shouting. She wanted to throw all the chairs away from her to prevent the room from collapsing. "I hate when people say that it's okay when it's not."

Gaby was allowed to excuse herself. She cried alone in the bathroom but wet herself before she could make it to the toilet. Her body felt broken into the compartments of her life—each limb a different time when she fucked up. Her right arm was being born bad. Her left arm was not being able to hold onto Eva. Her left leg was being a whore. Her right leg was meeting Adam. Falling in love with Adam. Believing what he showed her was love. Her toes were all the times she couldn't say no. Her fingers were all the times she should have shut up.

There was no way to escape.

There was a fish plant an hour away from the group home that needed warm bodies. Gaby showed up for her first shift and was given a hairnet and a lab coat-style coverall. The room was large and white, and the floors were covered in pools of water. Voices echoed along with the sounds of pallets being moved by large machines, motors spinning around and hydraulic pistons pushing in and out. She was told to stand in line next to a conveyor belt that pushed along hundreds of lobster tails.

"Don't break them. Don't crush them. Don't overfill the buckets. Just almost to the top."

Gaby picked up the chubby, scaly tails and lined the bins. She stood next to a young man who couldn't have been more than fifteen. Across from her, an older woman with glasses stuck to the tip of her nose worked with such speed that Gaby felt completely inadequate. Gaby stood for five hours packing lobster tails into the clear fish buckets, then pushing them down the line.

She didn't mind the work. In fact, she liked the repetition. It was soothing. She didn't have to talk to anyone. Her mind could be at peace by focusing on the task at hand. Pick up the tails and sort them in a row, don't pack them too tight. The tails were a deep greyish-brown and they glistened up at Gaby as she packed. With each tail she held, she imagined a bright green dollar sign springing up over her head. Sometimes, she'd take three in her hand at the same time and place them in a line, perfectly clean. But she also made sure she wasn't too rough with them. She didn't want to knock them around too much in case she damaged the tails.

It was while packing the lobsters Gaby concocted her plan. She was going to save up all the money she could and weasel her way into borrowing a car. She wasn't sure who would lend her one or how much it would cost her, but she assumed that, if she could save up a few hundred dollars, a car wouldn't be too difficult to find. She even convinced herself that, if she found a guy willing to let her use his car, but he needed a bit more bang for his buck, she'd be willing.

A trip to Montreal and back, Gaby imagined, could be done in under three days if she drove through the night. Her parole officer probably wouldn't even realize she was missing, and even if he did, Gaby could make up an excuse—she was in the hospital or something. Maybe she could convince her roommate to cover for her if Monica asked about her. No, that wouldn't work. She'd have to think of a way to get Monica off her back. Maybe she could pay her. The only other thing she needed was Maddie's address.

The last of the lobster tails were packed and sent down the line. A long, low whistle sounded and everyone stopped what they were doing. The conveyor belt slowed and came to a halt. The workers made their way to the loading docks where they could smoke and eat their lunch. Gaby decided to go into the break room instead. She took off her gloves and coat and sat on a plastic chair with her pre-packed peanut butter and jelly sandwich and stared at the bulletin board covered with notices on hygiene, safety, statutory holidays and time theft. She felt her feet and calves tingle and relax.

The older woman with the glasses who had stood across from Gaby sat next to her and began reading the newspaper. She didn't look up at Gaby or ask her for her name. She didn't even seem to register her. Her eyes just went back and forth over the page, flipping through the rustling paper. Then, her eyebrows raised. "Did you hear about this one?"

Gaby chewed her sandwich, the bread soft and the peanut butter and jelly sweet.

"A woman killed her poor husband, just down the road. Stabbed him in his sleep, no chance to defend himself." She shook her head and tsked. "Bring back hanging, I say. Or let her die in prison."

The bread almost dropped out of Gaby's mouth. She inhaled sharply, choking on her sweetened spit. Her throat burned.

"Are you okay, dear?" The woman stood up, holding out her arms. "Oh dear, come on. Breathe. Do you need me to knock on your back?"

"No," Gaby held up her hands. "No. Thank you." She found her way to the bathroom and locked the door, hacking up the rest of the brown and red spit into the porcelain sink. She saw blood that wasn't there. She felt cold ghost hands wrap around her neck.

Everyone in the house had a chore schedule. On Mondays, Gaby cleaned the bathrooms. On Thursdays, she cleaned the hallways. On Fridays, she worked in the kitchen. House meals brought people together. They ate canned beans with garlic and tuna mixed in with mashed potatoes. She found herself enjoying serving the most, spooning out globs of potatoes onto passing plates, a woman's arms stretched out and a soft smile on her face.

"Let's talk about our thorns and roses," Monica said after the food had disappeared from the plates, leaving nothing but traces of green bean stems and sauce streaks.

"I'll go," said Anne. She was a stately woman with ruddy cheeks. "Thorn: I found out my friend died, and I can't go to his funeral. Rose: I'm grateful to be surrounded by all of you."

"Thorn: I can't do drugs. Rose: I can't do drugs," said Angela.

"Thorn: my husband's getting full custody," this from Roberta, who had a ring piercing her left eyebrow. She didn't have a rose to add.

When it was Gaby's turn, she cleared her throat. It was her first time talking for the day and she sounded like a tiny woman at the bottom of a well.

"Thorn: I haven't seen my daughter in almost twelve years. Rose would be, um, I found something I enjoy doing. Making food for all of you."

A woman raised her glass of juice. "It was edible."

The table, including Gaby, burst into laughter. Someone else raised her empty plate. "Not trash."

"Adequate mush!" Gaby leaned to her right, giggling. Tori, next to her, put her arms around her shoulders. Gaby rested her head on her roommate's shoulder.

But it wasn't all roses.

While washing the floors in the hallway, Gaby saw Tori lunge out of their room with a crazy look on her face.

"Did you take it, you thief?" She shoved her face in front of Gaby's, backing her into a corner.

"What are you talking about—"

"The pills," Tori whispered. Out of the corner of her eyes, Gaby saw Monica lean out of her office.

"Hey," she yelled. "Back off!"

"I don't know what you're talking about," Gaby whispered back. Her eyes felt stretched and shaky.

"Do you think I'm stupid?"

"I don't—"

That's when her skull collided with the wall. Over and over and over. Gaby slid to the floor and tried to kick at Tori's knees but that only enraged her further. The bottom of her boot hit Gaby's cheek and the side of her nose, crunching cartilage. She wrapped her arms around her head and curled up like a cooked shrimp. People pulled Tori off her and someone touched Gaby's back, which made her flinch. There were smears of blood on the wall and a pool on the floor; Gaby could feel it coating her teeth and dripping down the back of her throat like a clotting slug. Someone gave her a wad of paper towel, and she covered her nose, the rough fibres rubbing against her skin and the paper soaking with red.

She was escorted to the hospital by an officer who kept looking back at her through his rear-view mirror, his eyes shifting back and forth from her to the road. Gaby sat small, feeling like a child who had been picked up from detention, still holding up the red tissues to her face.

"I recognize you. From court."

She looked out the window at the road. It was cold in the car, but Gaby hadn't had time to change out of her clothes or grab a sweater.

"He was your husband."

Nothing but the wheels turning over pavement. She thought about jumping out of the car. How ridiculous would that be? Jumping out onto a road from a moving vehicle? The officer was waiting for the clown to deliver its tired old punchline. Gaby kept her eyes on the window. She removed the tissue and saw her nose in the soft reflection. It was no longer straight and pointed, slim. Now, it had a massive bump on one side, swollen purple.

It was an hour before a doctor came out into the emergency waiting room and told Gaby to follow her down a hallway that was lined with beds with white curtains wrapped around them. Gaby sat on a bed with the curtains drawn, the officer's shadow fluttering outside. The doctor sat down on a stool and rolled forward.

"What happened?" She was young, with dark black hair and a neutral expression on her face.

"A misunderstanding."

After that, the doctor said nothing. No small talk. No questions about kids. She didn't want to know what Gaby was going to do afterward or where she was living. Doing her job. Gaby was thankful. The doctor pressed on her nose with cold, soft hands and Gaby flinched. She took a needle and injected something into her face. After a few minutes, the doctor told her to lean back, then she gripped Gaby's head. She inserted what looked like a screwdriver up her nose and then pinched the bridge. The doctor squeezed hard. Gaby let out a grunt and squeezed her eyes as she heard cartilage cracking once again. The doctor stepped back and looked at her work and then went in once more, the screwdriver pressing against Gaby's nasal cavity, fizzing her nose and making her eyes water. The doctor rolled back, wrote something on her chart and left.

"Good as new?" The officer opened the curtain.

"Good as new."

They drove back to the group home in silence—until the officer opened his mouth again.

"How could you do it?"

Gaby pretended she didn't hear.

"Your daughter still around?"

"Yes."

"She proud of you?"

"He threatened her." She regretted saying it the minute it came out of her mouth. She couldn't help it.

"What did he say?"

"He was going to drown her if I left him."

"And what did you do?"

Gaby cleared her throat, but she said nothing. She kept her eye on the road and watched as the trees rolled by.

The officer whistled. "Must be hard for you to talk about."

"It is."

"I'm only asking 'cause I'm curious. You know, I see the worst of the worst in people. Disgusting things. Abuse. Rapes. Murders. All of it. Anything you can imagine. Crazy-people murderers. You know? Like real bat-shit crazy people. But at least they have an excuse. They're crazy."

Gaby kept her eye out the window.

"But you. I don't understand you."

"I don't know what to tell you."

He looked at her through the rear-view. "It's creepy," he said. "No remorse." He kept his eyes on her. "There must be something evil in you."

Back at the group home, Gaby needed to sleep. She was given permission to take the afternoon off and she fell onto her bed, looking up at the ceiling, her head spinning. *There must be something evil in you.* She couldn't worry about what people thought of her, but she did care deeply. Almost all her decisions in life had been made because she cared so much about what people thought. Her leg kicked up in frustration and crashed back on the bed in defeat, bouncing the mattress. She did it again and again and again as if exorcising a demon. She must have knocked the side table because, after her last kick, she felt something knock and hit the ground with a small splat. When she turned over, she saw it on the floor by her roommate's bed. A small, clear bag of white pills.

XIX
Eva

Gabrielle LeBlanc. Eva looked over her shoulder after hitting search.

Some singer from Louisiana. A nurse. An amateur photographer. Obituary. Obituary. Obituary. Her mother's name didn't lead to any photos of her, only to people with the same name, as if showing Eva all the other lives she could have had. All the great things she could have become.

Adam Lawrence

Too many results.

Adam Lawrence Halifax murder

Pages and pages and pages.

Images.

A wedding photo outside a stone building. She wore a simple dress, hemline grazing her ankles. She looked happy, leaning into her new husband. A cigar hung out of his mouth and his hair was longer than she remembered it, tucked behind his ears. She didn't remember him doing that.

A close-up. His eyes, sharp and smiling. Impish. Straight, perfect teeth that Eva had not inherited.

Her mother. Haunted eyes, still face. Long hair tied back. She didn't look anything like Eva remembered.

Their house. It looked massive, but it didn't look safe.

Newspaper articles.

Murder. Stabbed. Sociopath. Planned. Domestic abuse. Daughter.
A charity website. Pledges.

The books in Concordia's library sat lonely on their shelves as the holiday closure loomed and students left campus. But Eva hadn't bothered with books that day. Normally, she snuck into the library scanning her stolen student ID card, opening the turnstiles and finding her way to the section that housed poetry. She'd found Mina Loy particularly interesting after learning about the writer in a stolen lecture. *Are you prepared for the Wrench—? . . . the only method is Absolute Demolition.* Such strange words and horribly violent. They struck Eva like a hammer. She went to a computer that had been left logged on.

The search was supposed to be quick, a crude hunger in her belly to know. To look into the eye of what she'd been told her entire life was terrible. As a child, her aunt warned her about searching for answers to things she could never unhear or unsee. She said that there were people out there who believed that what her mother did shouldn't have landed her in prison. Her aunt also told her that there were people out there who believed that what happened was evil and that justice was served.

"Make sure you only listen to the truth," she said. "Don't look for the people who lie."

Eva didn't want to upset her aunt and had always kept her distance from the past, even though it haunted her at night, whispering made-up memories into her ear about how her mother had loved her. She tried to tamp down the whispers and recall only the good about her father. The candy. The toys. The Barbie. Making sure her mother took her medication. Draping a blanket over her while she slept on the couch so she wouldn't get cold. But since moving to Montreal, the whispers in her dreams grew harder to ignore.

You should be dead.

Dex leaned in and whispered in her ear in a deep voice.

Now I don't have to hurt you.

Her mother shouted downstairs.

I'll kill her.

A piece of clementine in her mouth, citrus syrup.

She doesn't need to know.

Alma leaning over her.

It sounds like she had a really hard time.

Scrolling the search results, Eva came across an online petition, started in September, against her mother's parole. There were hundreds of signatures and comments.

This woman shouldn't be allowed in society. – Diane

What about community safety? – Jess

I'm signing because she's a psychotic bitch who murdered a man for no reason. – Bryan

She killed somebody's son, brother, and father. – April

And then, a familiar name.

A life for a life – Mathilde.

Mirac paced back and forth in the kitchen with his shoulder-length black hair wrapped up in a bandana. He took orders from the receipt machine that spat out chits for the lunch rush and held a full mixing bowl of chicken thighs marinating in spices on one hip like a baby.

"Can you grab me another spoon?" He turned to Eva who was silently chewing on unsalted soda crackers in the corner to stop her stomach from growling. Even while he was stressed, Mirac had a gift of speaking calmly. Mirac handled himself. He handled his kitchen. During the lunch rush, Eva would help with the dishes. She had told him from the jump she had kitchen experience and knew how to clean quickly. Then, she moved on to vegetable prep. Mirac's cooks were always missing or quitting, so Eva learned the rhythm of absence. When he pursed his lips and patted his hand on his hip and looked at the fridge, Eva knew something was wrong. She would lean over the bar and say, "What can I do?"

Eva learned how to properly chop an onion with her thumb back and knuckles forward. She learned how to flip vegetable prep containers. She learned how to optimize counter space and prevent a cutting board from slipping while she chopped, placing a wet cloth underneath. Eva worked the line, taking orders and following the five recipes Mirac had drilled into her brain. *Low and slow with the eggs. Cut in the feta with a rubber spatula. If your heat is too high, we throw them out. Cut the chives softly. Your knife should sound like wind through grass while you slice them. Do not leave the kitchen counter dirty. This is an open kitchen. The guests should see nothing but spotless countertop. Weigh your dough. If the dough for the tahini rolls weighs twenty-one grams or nineteen grams, you are failing. It should be twenty grams. Only. Stir the tahini and place it upside-down in the fridge when you're done with it. If you don't, and you open it in the morning and there is oil on top, you've wasted five minutes by having to stir the damn thing.*

Usually, Eva loved how the scent of fried chorizo and scrambled eggs and melting butter filled her nose. She learned how to make simits, Turkish bagels, under Mirac's supervision, by stretching out long strands of dough and braiding them into circles before dunking them into a mixture of molasses, warm water and sesame seeds. He said that people told him he was crazy for making his own bagels in Montreal, but he didn't care. His were special. His were different. His were Turkish.

Eva handed Mirac a clean spoon and, once the dishwasher's cycle ended, she opened the door and let the steam fill the air around her. It pulled at her thick hair, and she could feel the strands bend to its will, curling and frizzing. She grabbed the hot clean plates, still chewing on her cracker, and sorted them on the shelves at the side of the counter where Mirac prepped five different sandwiches all at the same time. Eva looked out at the seating area and the guests. Maya floated between tables, picking up empty plates and smiling at the people who asked if they could have more water or tea. Eva watched as a child, maybe seven or eight, looked down at her plate of scrambled eggs and scrunched her nose. Maya looked like she was asking the mother if everything was okay, then picked up the plate and brought it to Eva.

"She says they're too runny."

"It's a French scramble," Eva said. "It's supposed to be runny."

Maya sighed. "She doesn't like them."

Eva felt herself scowling at the child who hadn't even looked at the kitchen the entire time she and her parents had been there.

"I'm not throwing this out," she said.

Maya shrugged. "You can have it if you want."

"It's okay," Mirac jumped in. "She's just a kid."

But Eva was annoyed. "She wants dry eggs? We can make the princess dry eggs."

Mirac gave a warm smile and patted her on the back. "Take a break and feed yourself. You look like you haven't eaten all day."

Eva reluctantly took the full plate of eggs into the storage room off to the side of the kitchen and stood with her back against the wall. She pushed the soft, bright yellow scramble around on the plate with her fork. Her stomach let out a low, painful moan. She picked up a forkful and touched the soft eggs to her lips and immediately felt sick.

"This is so fucking stupid," she said to herself as she forced the eggs into her mouth. They tasted like old, rancid butter, but she forced herself to chew and swallow before scraping the eggs into a large garbage bin and walking back to the kitchen.

After the lunch rush was over and Eva had cleaned most of the dishes that Maya had cleared, Maya asked if she had any plans for the holidays.

"My aunt and I usually go to church," she said. "And open presents in the evening. But that's about it."

Maya's gaze lingered on Eva's face, her square mouth moving with no sound coming out. It was as if she were trying to place her. Eva hated that look and decided she would quit if she kept it up, but instead Mirac said, "We're having a family dinner next Saturday. If you're not doing anything, you should come."

"My mother is visiting." He smiled. "I think she will love you."

Maya turned to Mirac and began speaking in Turkish. Then, the receptionist walked in and began speaking to the couple in French. They spoke back and forth, and Eva watched as the trio became more and more expressive and joyous. She tried to match their smiles. Her eyes volleyed from face to face. Their lips formed shapes Eva didn't understand, and the sounds were so foreign and fast she couldn't place them in her mind. And the wider Eva smiled in fake comprehension, the more her eyes threatened to sting with tears.

She dunked the ladle into a mucousy brine of kalamata olives that lived in a repurposed small black garbage bin, stuffed the pods into a plastic takeout container and dropped them in her basket. Pushing aside the heavy, clear plastic strands that hung in front of the chilled shelves, she grabbed a tub of hummus and another of plain yogurt. Segal's was overcrowded that afternoon and she wanted nothing more than to collapse in her bed. She couldn't get the thought of the wet, scrambled eggs out of her head. The mushy sounds they had made when she scraped them along the plate, slimy and cold. Looking at food, the thought of eating, made her stomach convulse. The tub of yogurt was cold and wet in her hand, and she could feel fine grains of dirt and sand on the side of the container. Stains and thin, hard pieces of organic matter stuck to the plastic strands hanging from the deli fridge. She placed the tubs of yogurt and hummus back, grabbed the olives and dropped them on the cold shelf, then slammed her basket in the pile by the door.

Outside the afternoon air was cool and she wrapped her acrylic blue scarf once more around her neck. The snow had turned from pristine white to grey chunks on the street corners. She kept walking up Saint Laurent, bumping into people, knocking shoulders with shoulders. She watched as people spat out their gum on the street, flicked cigarette butts into muddy puddles and sneezed into their hands. Buses heaved to a stop on each corner and dispelled streams of people out onto the sidewalk as if belching. Automatic doors opened and closed, convulsing out clusters of screaming children and bickering parents. Streams of brown, muddy water floated down the street, a lazy river of excrement. The smell of fresh bread wafting from bakeries made her gag.

Sociopath. Murderer. No remorse.

"In the name of the Father, the Son and the Holy Spirit"

Amen

"May the grace and peace of our lord Jesus Christ, the love of the Father, and the friendship of the Holy Spirit be with you all."

And with your spirit.

"Welcome to the celebration of the Mass of the Nativity of the Lord. As we begin this Eucharist let us ask the Prince of Peace to forgive us our sins."

A chorus of angelic voices permeated Eva's mind, singing for the Lord to have mercy and for Christ to have mercy. From fluffy white clouds, men with soft white long beards and dressed in red and green satin looked down at her sitting in the pew with her aunt. The scent of frankincense made her eyes water and, mixed with the chorus of voices, threatened to drift her off to sleep. Eva watched as a procession of men in white robes walked down the aisle, one swinging a thurible with smoke pooling out of it into the air. They approached the white marble altar and refilled the vessel with powder and covered the altar in the smoke, making the sign of the cross in front of their bodies.

"A reading from the book of the prophet Isaiah. The Lord has made a proclamation to the ends of the earth: Say to Daughter Zion, 'See, your Savior comes! See, his reward is with him, and his recompense accompanies him.' They shall be called, 'the Holy People, The Redeemed of the Lord.' And you shall be called, 'Sought Out, A City Not Forsaken.' The word of the Lord."

Thanks be to God.

Eva felt her chest bulge, involuntarily gasping for oxygen as she opened her mouth wide and yawned. She let her eyes wander around the golden arched ceilings, gazing at the chandeliers and the large dome that hung above the altar that illuminated the enormity of the church's power.

She felt her phone buzz in her back pocket and was about to reach for it when she was shocked back to life by Mathilde smacking her on the thigh. An older woman sitting behind her with a massive purple hat smacked the pew and whispered. *Shush!* Eva squirmed in the uncomfortable wooden pew that was causing her ass to fall asleep and pulled at the waist of her jeans that was too high. It filled her with dread to know that not only were there no lectures to attend for the next three weeks, but Alma was at her parent's place in Toronto with Dex.

That morning, Mathilde had woken her up early. Eva felt a hand shaking her leg and heard clapping.

"Rise and shine, *chère.*"

Her aunt ripped open the curtains in her room and the sun shocked Eva's eyes. She forced her head under the pillow and groaned.

"Don't be a lazybones. Not on Christ's Day! Come on. We'll have breakfast then get ready for mass. Then after, I have a present for you. Something special."

Eva couldn't bring herself to eat the plate of eggs that her aunt scrambled and covered in salt. She could only smell something acrid wafting off the plate and wondered if the dishes had been cleaned properly. She pushed the food around, and when her aunt wasn't looking, wrapped it in a wad of paper towel and took her plate to the sink.

"That was great. Thanks," she said. "I'm going to shower. When's Mass?"

"Not until five."

Eva turned. "Why did you wake me up so early?"

Mathilde beamed. "It's Christmas!"

"A reading from the letter of Saint Paul to Titus. 'When the goodness and loving-kindness of God, our Saviour, appeared, He saved us, not because of any works of righteousness, that we had done, but according to His mercy, through the water of rebirth and renewal by the Holy Spirit. This Spirit He poured out on us richly through Jesus Christ, our Saviour, so that having been justified by His grace we might become heirs according to the hope of eternal life.' The word of the Lord."

Outside, Eva stumbled down the snow-cleared steps as the yellow lights from the lamps hovered over the slick streets, forcing her to squint and shiver. Mathilde trailed behind, talking to a couple on the steps. A hunched old woman, her scarf tied over her head, hobbled with a rolling walker toward Eva and stopped at a corner, looking both ways multiple times before turning and letting out a soft, low grumble. Eva could see her red, swollen gums when she suddenly looked up and smiled under one of the lamps.

"Is this the way to the pharmacy?" Her accent was unrecognizable.

169

"Yes," Eva said, nodding. "Yes. But there's snow." Eva pointed to the woman's walker. "There's too much snow. It's slippery that way."

The woman smiled, her eyes glassy. She didn't truly seem to comprehend where she was, let alone understand what Eva was saying. She watched as the woman and her walker moved down the street, head down and back hump bobbing, still heading toward the thick patch of snow. Eva looked back up the stairs of the church—her aunt was talking to a different couple now. Then she looked back at the woman and jogged over, careful not to fall and trying not to let the sick feeling overtake her.

"Excuse me," Eva said. She got in view of the woman without blocking her. "Do you need help?" She motioned to the snow mound mixed with ice and gravel that was currently masquerading as a sidewalk. Eva could see her breath in front of her face. The woman had a gleam in her eye and smiled her gummy smile. She folded up her walker with the push of a button and, without any prompting, shoved it into Eva's hands. The woman then held out her arm so Eva could clasp onto it. The two traversed the snowy bank slow and steady, arms linked together. When they got to the other side, Eva handed the walker back to the woman, who looked at her without blinking.

"I am sorry for you to bother with me," the woman said, seemingly looking through her.

Eva smiled and nodded. But while the woman tottered away, her smile turned into a furrow of concern and confusion.

"I prefer *la messe en français*. You still don't understand the French services?" Mathilde asked once they arrived back at the apartment.

Eva sat on the couch and watched as her aunt pulled out the primary-coloured Pyrex mixing bowls, a sack of carrots and an onion. Mathilde took out a knife and a pile of spoons, paused, and then took out a bottle of wine, pouring glasses for herself and Eva.

"I should know by now," Eva said. "It just doesn't stick."

"*C'est point la mer à boire.*"

"What?"

"It's not that hard."

"It's translating everything from English to French. I can't think in French."

"You need to keep practising."

Eva approached the wine as if it were a sad lifeless animal she had to put out of its misery. Her back pocket buzzed again, and she glanced at her phone. Alma had wished her a Merry Christmas. Mathilde placed the carrots on a cutting board and made rough chops. Eva watched as the knife slid off the board with each slice, her aunt's fingers getting closer and closer to the blade.

"I love cooking on Christmas," Mathilde said.

"That knife's dull," she said. But Mathilde kept chopping. "You're gonna cut yourself."

"It's fine."

"Here. Give it."

"No!"

Her aunt turned, stretching the knife away. A tense silence hung in the air while Eva stood, arms hanging by her sides. She opened her mouth, then closed it. Dread brewed in her stomach like fermenting grain, bubbling and thick.

Mathilde placed the knife down on the cutting board. "I didn't want you to grab it," she said, "and cut yourself."

Her aunt stepped out from behind the counter, took her glass of wine and made her way over to the living room. Eva took a honing steel out from the drawer, wiped down the knife with a dry rag, and worked the blade over the pole. Mathilde sat on the couch, her eyes glassy and vacant, lingering in the distance. Eva chopped the rest of the carrots before moving onto the garlic, smashing the cloves with the flat side of the knife and then peeling off the husks.

"I learned how to properly mince an onion," she said. "Mirac taught me."

"Wonderful."

"Let me show you how."

"To chop an onion? Do you know how many onions I've chopped in my life?"

Eva sliced a fat, yellow onion in half and removed the outer layer. She placed the flat side down on the cutting board and held the knife so that the flat edge hovered parallel, and the blade faced the wall. Her nose and eyes shrank from the onion vapour, causing them to water. But she kept going. "Minced." She smiled to herself. Her aunt held her glass of wine to her lips.

"You should spend this kind of time on your French," Mathilde said. "Just cut the damn thing."

Eva ignored her and chopped the rest of the aromatics, adding in celery and ginger.

"I saw she was up for parole," Eva said.

A chill rippled through the air as Mathilde placed her glass of wine down on the coffee table. She picked up a magazine and leafed through it as if Eva had left the room.

"Do you think she's out?"

Her aunt was a scarecrow, unmoving.

"Did you ever visit her?"

"Enough."

"I'm just—"

"Enough!"

Eva opened the fridge and grabbed a container of chicken stock. She peeled back the lid and poured the contents into the pot, letting the steam fill her nostrils. The mixture of butter, garlic, carrots, and onion gave her a headache. She stirred the mixture in silence; the knocking sound of the wooden spoon filled the apartment.

"How long are you roasting the chicken for?" Mathilde asked.

"An hour. I'm just getting everything prepped."

"Good. Why don't you sit and open your present with me?"

Eva set down the knife and joined her aunt on the sofa, curling herself into the opposite side. She pulled out a small present she had hidden next to the couch and handed it to her aunt, who blushed.

"You didn't have to get me anything."

Eva shrugged. "I know. I wanted to."

Mathilde sat the present on her lap and played with the silver bow. She gently lifted the tape from one side, then the other, and pulled the red wrapping paper away in one smooth motion.

"We can save that for next year," she said placing the paper neatly on the floor. Her aunt lifted the top off the brown box, and Eva watched as her aunt's face went from excitement to feigned delight.

"Oh!" she said, "a book."

"It's a collection of Shakespeare's sonnets," Eva said. "I thought you might like to read them."

Mathilde nodded and set the book down on the coffee table. "Very nice. Thank you."

"I really like them. I thought maybe you'd like them too."

"Hmmhmm. Yes. Very thoughtful. Okay. My turn!"

Mathilde jumped up from the couch and went into her bedroom, closing the door behind her. She was gone for a few minutes, and Eva heard the sound of wrapping paper being cut and tape stretching out from the roll.

Her aunt reappeared with a big TV presenter smile on her face, holding up a large rectangle wrapped in shimmery blue paper that had Santa hats and bells printed on it. She handed it to Eva, who gently unstuck the piece of scotch tape at the top and glided her finger along the seam, opening the rest of the present and revealing the face of her father.

"Do you like it?"

Her father stared at her with gentle eyes. His face was round and she saw that Mathilde had portrayed him with stubble on his chin and cheeks. Eva remembered how it tickled when he hugged her. He appeared before a velvety purple background, looking poised and waiting to be complimented.

"I was thinking we could hang it in your bedroom."

Eva bit at the dry skin around one of her fingernails and pulled it back, chewing on the hard piece of flesh.

"Yeah. Okay."

Mathilde smiled, beaming bright with rose-pink cheeks. She grabbed the painting and walked quickly to Eva's bedroom.

"I was thinking this wall," she called from the other room. "Come see."

Eva stood and moved to the edge of the doorframe where she watched her aunt hold up the face of her father, a portrait of a saint being placed in a house of worship.

"That's fine," Eva said.

"It looks good?"

"Yeah. That looks good."

Her aunt looked pleased, and Eva turned back to the kitchen where she pulled out a whole pink chicken and slapped it on the counter, ripping open the plastic packaging. The pimpled skin felt slimy in her hands. She felt the eyes from the painting follow her wherever she moved and suddenly felt self-conscious.

"Why didn't you ever take me to see her?" She spoke the words down to the counter, but she could tell Mathilde had heard. Her aunt came out of the bedroom with empty hands.

"I don't have to explain myself to some kid who never finished high school."

Eva felt a burning sensation slither down her back as she held her tongue.

"Can't we just have a nice Christmas?" her aunt asked. "Just a nice Christmas?"

The phone rang and shook Eva out of the moment, releasing her from the anger and resentment she was feeling. When she picked up, she heard the voice of her uncle Marc on the other end of the line and smiled. Mathilde hovered over her shoulder, listening to their conversation that had to be in English despite Marc's disdain for the language.

"Merry Christmas to you too," Eva said. "Yeah, we just opened gifts and I'm making supper."

Eva, cradling the phone between her ear and her shoulder, placed the chicken on a sheet pan and rubbed it with olive oil. When she heard her uncle say the name Gabrielle, she froze.

"You were talking to her? What did she say?"

Mathilde looked like she wanted to hit Eva. Her nostrils flared.

"I hope she's having a good Christmas too." Eva pumped liquid soap onto her hands and rubbed them together, letting the warm water run over them as she scrubbed. That's when Mathilde ripped the phone away and held it up to her own ear. Her aunt spoke to her uncle in rapid-fire French while she finished prepping the chicken with salt and spices. After she stuck the chicken into the oven, Eva went into her room where the portrait of her father leaned up against the wall.

She picked it up and gazed down at his face. His eyes. Eva remembered those eyes. Mathilde had captured his slightly lazy left eye—Eva had forgotten that. The mole almost hidden by the stubble on the right side of his chin. The lines on his lips. He looked pleasant and warm, and Eva's heart hurt and her lips quivered slightly as she set the painting down on the floor.

After the roasted chicken and vegetable soup had been eaten, and Mathilde had passed out in her bed from too much wine, Eva needed to get out of the apartment. Outside, the Christmas lights were bright and dazzling, but there wasn't anybody else on the icy sidewalk. The buzz from the wine made her feel nothing and the nothing felt good. She didn't want to think about her father, where her mother might be, or why she felt so much anger.

She walked by a bar and smelled cigarette smoke and Old Spice from a man leaning up against the wall. She turned and looked in through the window. It was open, and a bartender was pouring a glass of beer for a lonely patron.

"*Joyeux Noël,*" she said sarcastically, entering the bar and waving at the bartender.

"*Oui, Joyeux Noël. Ça va?*"

"Oh, sorry," Eva turned red with embarrassment. "I don't actually speak French."

"Ah, I heard your accent." He wiped a beer glass with a white towel and looked at her coolly. "What would you like?"

"A beer, please." When he passed the glass to her, she said. "It's not real."

"Non?"

"*J'suis terrible.*"

"*Que tu veux dire?*"

Eva held her beer in front of her. She gnawed at the loose skin on her lower lip.

"It's like I'm from a French island in an English ocean."

"*Quelle île?*"

"No." Eva swayed. "That's not what I mean." She took a long swallow of the amber ale that he set down in front of her. "My family spoke French, but it was a weird French."

"*Un exemple.*"

Eva tried to think about a strange phrase she heard as a kid.

"*Worry pas ta brain.*"

He laughed.

"*C'est différent,*" he said. "*Un autre.*" He bent forward.

"Oh, I don't know."

"*Ouais, donne-moi un autre.*" He was leaning on his elbows waiting in anticipation for the punchline.

She swayed in her seat. "*Chus wayment pissé off.*" She grinned, happy with herself.

"*Wayment?*"

"I have no idea," she said and watched as he chuckled and poured her a shot of tequila and then poured one for himself.

"It's so stupid," Eva said, taking the shot. She thought back to the summer when she'd lived with Uncle Marc. How his large hands would delicately thread fishing wire through the pole. How he'd smile big smiles and point to something, and Eva knew exactly what he was saying. The low heat, raw on the salty coast, sharp rocks biting at her calves.

"It's so stupid."

"It's not," the bartender said, pouring another shot for Eva.

"I wish I knew more."

"You can learn."

"It doesn't stick. I really try, you know. Or maybe I could try harder. I just feel like I should know it. Like it should come easily to me. The one thing that should come easy to me."

"It's sad, no?"

"Maybe a little."

"We're losing our language."

"Oh, I don't know about that," she said. "How much sympathy should we really get?"

"Who?"

"The French," Eva laughed. "We shouldn't have been here in the first place." She fiddled with the shot glass, expecting the bartender to agree. But his face turned dark. He pulled back, took the other shot that he'd poured for her and dumped it in the sink. He turned to the side and began pulling out glasses from the sanitizing machine, then turned to the other man seated at the bar a few feet away, shooting glances at her while he spoke in a hushed tone. Eva drank the rest of her beer and slapped a few bills on the table.

"I meant fuck *les anglais*," she said, lazily waving her hand good-bye. But the bartender had already turned his back.

XX
Gaby

Tori brought Gaby a Jos Louis one afternoon as an olive branch. Gaby was lying on the bed and Tori threw it at her. It landed next to her thigh. "You still mad at me?"

"No."

"I'm sorry I broke your face."

"It's okay."

"Your nose still looks pretty bad."

"It's healing."

Tori sat on her bed and crossed her arms. "Thanks for not telling them why."

"It's okay."

"I just freaked out. I think Sheila took them."

"You're still looking?"

"It's bullshit. It was just a small bag."

Gaby looked up at the ceiling at a yellow water stain that had been slowly expanding across the tile ever since she arrived. Her eyes were heavy, and she blinked slowly, feeling her chest lift as she breathed.

"You okay?" Tori asked.

"I'm good."

"You gonna eat the Jos Louis?"

Gaby looked down at the packaged chocolate cake. The plastic wrapper crinkled as she picked it up and held it out to Tori who leaned forward and accepted it.

"Seriously, what's going on?"

"Nothing. I'm tired," Gaby said. "And thinking."

"Uh oh."

"Nothing bad. Just remembering things. Like I found out that I was pregnant again before . . . it happened. I was a week late, which is strange for me because I'm always on time. It's the only thing about me that's on time. But I didn't think much of it then. I gave it another week in case my body was being weird, you know, stress or something. Adam had started throwing beer bottles at the wall in the garage so I was on edge that month. But after two weeks, still nothing. That's when I thought it could have been the pills. I had these pills, you know, that my doctor gave me and they made me so drowsy."

Tori nodded.

"You know, at the beginning they were great because I didn't feel . . . weird anymore. You know, like there are butterflies in your stomach all the time or you're just about to fall into a hole. I'd take one in the evening after supper and it would just knock me out. And maybe I was drinking too much back then too, I don't know. I ended up taking more pills than I was supposed to. But Adam kept . . . he kept changing and I didn't know how to understand him or make him happy anymore. And he'd get into these moods that were . . . he treated me like I was crazy. He acted like, when I was off the meds, I was hallucinating. I wasn't crazy. He somehow got me back on them again and I just broke down and took one and then another and another and he was right because I could breathe again. I just drifted. Into a sleep and it was like the world was sighing.

"But as Eva got older, I didn't like her little brown eyes watching me. How quiet she got. And Maddie always judging me. So, I told myself I'd stop. But I didn't. I couldn't. And Adam . . ."

"Why are you telling me this?"

"Look, all I'm saying is that I was a really fucked up mom. Okay? And I was weirded out because my body was doing something it never did and I thought I'd messed myself up with the drugs and I was . . . dying or something. I didn't want to be a bad mom and a dead mom."

"Okay, but two weeks isn't that long. Even if you were pregnant, it wouldn't have been that bad. I know worse moms."

Gaby sat up and wrapped her arms around her bent legs, bringing her shoulders up to her knees. "I found some guy who would sell other things to me and . . . Anyway, they made my memory shit. I would fall asleep at random hours and wake up in bed not remembering how I got there. But you know what? Things got better. Adam stopped having these crazy moods. He stopped yelling. Eva was smiling again. Do you know what it's like to not see your daughter smile for a month? Only to see her eyes light up talking to her dad? I knew it was wrong in its own way, but the drugs, the medication. It was helping make things better. But when I didn't get my period I thought, I really fucked it up. I really fucked myself up this time, not eating properly, getting sick—you know I was down to 115 pounds two years after Eva was born. So, I went to the doctor's office, and she tells me to get on the scale and she makes me pee in a cup and she checks my blood pressure and she asks me to cough and she looks into my ears and then she checks the pregnancy test and tells me I'm pregnant."

Tori looked at Gaby with her head angled sideways and her arms folded over her chest, waiting patiently. "Okay. So. You were pregnant."

"I hadn't had sex in over a year," Gaby said. "That I remembered at least. When I confronted him about it—you know when you see a weasel trying to run away backward? And they do that little wiggle with their bodies? He tried to get away so fast, and I let him. At first. I let him back off and then I told him if he ever touched me again while I was sleeping . . .while I was unconscious . . . I would kill him. And then I left with Eva. We went to my sister's place. I didn't know what I was going to do, I just needed to get away from him. I ended up making myself miscarry. I knew he'd find a way to stop me from getting an abortion. Anyway, he threatened to call the cops and tell them that I'd abducted our child and my sister told me that I should go back to him and that it wasn't that bad and every pregnancy is a blessing. So I drove back home with my daughter, made her a sandwich and gave her a cheese string and a few chocolates for a snack, put her to bed, and then while I was in the kitchen Adam told me that if I ever left again he would kill her—to save her from me, I was such a horrible mother. He kept shouting at me and shouting at me and so when he was asleep, I stabbed him. I kept stabbing him. Until I knew he would never get up again."

Gaby looked at the pictures of Eva tacked to the wall by her bed. Her favourite was the one of Eva in her highchair eating spaghetti. It was her first time trying it, and she'd placed the half-empty bowl on top of her head and the pasta hung down like strands of hair. Her fat cheeks were stained orange and her tiny teeth stuck out of her gums. When Gaby hugged herself tighter, she could hear the gentle crinkle of the pill bag in her breast pocket.

"What's gotten into you?" Tori asked.

> *You're going to make me lose my fucking mind!*
> She'd always felt so swollen in the morning.
> *Mom?*
> He had passed out on the couch. She knew it was her
> hand reaching for the knife.
> *You're a child.*
> Eva had said something about the juice.
> *Maybe up your medication?*

So much rage she felt as if her skin would rip open.

*al allait mourrir, al allait mourri al allait mourrir she was
going to die al allait mourrir al allait mourrir she was going
to die*

Gaby didn't look at her when she asked the question. She kept staring at the picture, hating each time she blinked. She had to look
away.

"My brother called me a week ago and told me that she'd wished
me a Merry Christmas. Well, he said that she said she hoped I had
one. And it made me feel so . . . It made me feel so good, you know?
And, it was like the disgusting snowbanks outside all of a sudden
looked like blocks of marble and the lights were sparkling and I just
felt so good in my skin. And then I went to the mall and there's a
toy store there—you know that big one at the top of the escalators?
I must have lasted two minutes in there. I wanted to buy something for her, something she would like and that would make her
dimples shine. And there was this stuffed toy of Oscar the Grouch.
This stupid little fuzzy green monster sticking out of a trashcan.
And then I . . . I dunno I just shut down. I didn't get her anything because I didn't know where to send it. She's not a little girl
anymore. She's eighteen. All these years she was growing up. I don't
even know what she looks like anymore. I don't know what she likes
anymore. I don't even know if she's eating. What if she's not eating?"

Gaby felt tears fall on her forearms. Tori kneeled beside her,
stretching her arms along the bed and grasping her legs, giving them
a tight squeeze. Gaby wiped away her snot with her shirt collar,
careful not to push too hard.

Tori leaned back on her heels and didn't shift her eyes or say anything. She only shook her head.

XXI
Eva

The cold snap that had fallen over the city during the second week of February finally lifted on the day that the first groups of Quebec students began voting in favour of a walkout. Over the weekend, it had fallen to -17°C, though it felt much colder.

Once Monday came, the sun peered out behind the clouds and shone down on the city so brightly that Eva felt like she would melt in her winter coat. She had been hungry to be back in the lecture hall during the holiday break, so much so that when classes opened back up in January, she arrived before anybody else and sat alone in the giant, echoey chamber.

But as the weeks went on, she noticed that the once-full lecture halls were diminishing in size. Alma walked down the lecture hall steps and gave Eva a hug before sitting down. But before they had a chance to talk, Eva heard shouting and the banging of pots and pans. Booing erupted from the hallway as some students opened the door and found their seats. The protestors made as much noise as they possibly could and, when that didn't get a reaction, they followed the students into the room, filling it with noise and clamour.

Professor Moore entered the lecture hall and put his briefcase on the desk without saying anything. The protestors were all shouting, and when they marched to the front, Eva noticed they all wore small red squares pinned to their chests. Then she saw that the professor had one pinned to his shirt as well.

"Seventy-five percent over five years is garbage, and we as students have a right to demand affordable education. But it's not just that. It's public services. This government thinks it can privatize public services."

"Challenge the government! Challenge the austerity measures!"

Once the protestors had said their piece and left, Professor Moore turned to the students who sat quietly in their seats. "I don't mean to rip you all away from the forest primeval," he said. "But today's class is cancelled."

Eva heard someone behind her curse under their breath and saw one student roll their eyes.

"You joining them?" Alma asked as the students all filtered out and the noise in the hall dulled to an aching silence.

"Why are they so upset?" Eva asked. "Can't they, like, do something different? Or like, just take the increase."

Alma shrugged. "Dex's classes have already been cancelled so I think we're going to just get away for a bit and wait for it to stop. I walked down Sainte-Catherine's yesterday and it looked like a war'd ripped through the streets. So much broken glass and trash. The rioting is crazy."

"You're leaving?"

"Only for a bit," Alma said. "We might go to Mexico or, I don't know, maybe Portugal. Dex's parents offered to pay for the flight. I don't think this is going to end soon."

"You're just going to leave?"

"Yeah, I mean, I don't want to be pelted with tomatoes every time I try to enter a classroom."

"So you don't care."

Alma looked jolted at the change in Eva's tone, but Eva couldn't help herself.

"Are you mad at me?"

"No, I'm not mad," Eva said. "It's fine. Go to Mexico or whatever. With *Dex*." She couldn't help but say his name that way. *Dex*.

"Okay," Alma said. "I'm gonna go. Let me know if you want to hang out before we leave."

"I saw him having sex with someone. At that party."

"What party?"

"That party. October. He was on top of her but it was weird. She seemed like, I don't know. She didn't seem awake. And he was like, on top of her on the floor. And he told me not to say anything so I didn't."

Alma's face displayed an expression that Eva had never seen before. It was rough and her nostrils flared. Eva registered her friend's pain—and then saw her anger. "Why would you say that?"

"Because it's true."

"And you're just telling me now."

"I wanted to tell you."

"You kept that from me for how many months?"

Eva didn't know what to do with her hands, so she clasped them in front of her and motioned them as if praying.

"I wanted to tell you, but he made it seem like if I did . . . like he would do something bad."

"Are you kidding me? Dex would hurt you? What the fuck are you saying?"

"You're mad at me?"

"I don't understand you, Eva! Okay, whatever. I'm gonna go."

Eva watched as she walked out of the swinging doors, leaving her alone in the lecture hall that, when empty, looked so cold and uncaring. She wanted nothing more than for the students to all rush in at once and take back their seats. She stood, imagining them running back through the doors and moving on as if nothing had happened. But Eva was alone and on the wrong side of the door.

She felt it in the walls of the auditorium and how the empty silence grew to become a loud ringing in her ears.

Eva decided to get a bottle of wine. Or two. Something cheap with a bicycle on the label at the *dép* near the apartment. When she opened the door, she called, "Mathilde?" The silence told her that her aunt was at work. She turned on the faucet and let the waterfall fill the tub. She sat on the edge and drank the wine straight from the bottle.

At first, she couldn't get the painting of her father in the tub. The canvas in its frame was too big, and the sides squeaked against the tile wall when she tried to force it to bend. Out of frustration and with a slight buzz, Eva rammed her foot through the centre of the painting, ripping a hole through the middle and splashing water all over herself as her foot landed in the tub. She snapped one side of the canvas in half, the wood splitting on the top of her thigh, then began pacing around the apartment to see what else she could add to the soup. She found sketches Mathilde had drawn for the portrait of her father. She threw them into the tub as well. When the floor began to pool with water, leaking out from the bathroom and onto the hardwood of the living room, she poured more wine into a glass and shut off the faucet. When Eva opened the tall cupboard door in the kitchen to grab a mop, the artist's portfolio that had been balanced on the top ever since they moved in fell to the floor. The contents spilled out—watercolours, canvas boards, sketchbooks. And an envelope.

Eva swept everything back into the portfolio except the unsealed envelope, which she opened, unfolded the pages and read. The more she read, the more she wanted to look away, to *not* read, but her eyes wouldn't leave the pages. The words made no sense. Passionate words dripping in desire and longing for the wrong person. A switch flipped, and Eva's confusion became rage. She crumbled the pages up in her fists, feeling how sharp paper could get when bent. Eva lit a match and watched as the orange burst pulsated and caught on the wrinkled paper before letting it fall into the history soup. Mathilde's laptop that sat on the kitchen table was next. She dropped it in the bath as if dropping a chicken carcass into a pot. Eva tried to remember her mother's voice, but nothing came. Everything swirled together, like looking at a face through a kaleidoscope.

Dors, dors, dors, dors
Dors, dors, p'tit bébé à maman

XXII
Mathilde

The colour wouldn't have been her first choice. The style of leaf was very strange and did not look like any leaf Mathilde had ever seen. She didn't even think any leaf in the world had that many irregular points on it. Who in their right mind would paint a leaf that shade of green, place it on a tree in Parc La Fontaine with that many points, and believe that nobody would notice? The children don't have to know what every tree in the world looks like, but they should at least know the types of trees that exist in the city. That tree would never grow in Parc La Fontaine, and not only that, but the tree also looks to be completely made up. Fabricated! Why couldn't they have painted a real tree?

"Hasn't Brian done a good job!" said Brenda. "What do you think of the painting, Mathilde?"

"Oh, it's very nice," she said. "Wonderful display of colour."

"Let's take a look at Wesley's next."

Parents, families and teachers milled around the gymnasium where proud art students stood behind their creations.

Wesley stood behind a table covered with a white cotton sheet, his painting propped on an easel: a wash of green with a giant red circle in the middle. It looked like the paint had been smeared on with fingers. The boy had a short fringe cut straight across his forehead and looked up at Mathilde with giant, brown eyes.

"Very nice," Brenda said. She peered down at the display tag that talked about the artist's work. Wesley scratched at his nose.

"Rembrandt," Brenda said.

"Sorry?"

"Rembrandt. The name of his piece is Rembrandt."

Mathilde felt her throat tighten and she let out a scoff. "Rembrandt? That's a . . . that's a silly name for a painting."

Wesley blinked. "Why?"

"I think it's a bit . . . much. Where did you hear that name?"

"What?"

"Rembrandt."

"My mother tells me that I could be as good as him."

"Your mother."

"Yeah."

"As good as Rembrandt."

"Yes."

"Do you know who Rembrandt is?"

"He painted the Mona Lisa."

Mathilde stepped back and stood against the wall, while Brenda engaged a parent whose child had just slipped on a puddle of melted ice cream on her way to see her brother's sculpture of the Leaning Tower of Pisa, which he created by taking a hammer to an empty can of pizza-flavoured Pringles. Mathilde had had enough. She grabbed her coat from the rack on the wall and waved to Brenda, who looked confused, but Mathilde didn't stick around to explain.

In the black night filled with cars honking and people shouting, and the smell of city snow, Mathilde walked away from the noise and the reality of her wasted effort.

She wanted to get home and escape into the portraits. The soft eyes of Adam. The brown hair of Adam. The plush lips of Adam. The easy outline of Adam. She craved the paints that sat next to the kitchen table. She longed for the brushes that brought her memories to life. She hungered for him. For the love he'd made her feel. The happiness. *Not Gabrielle, never Gabrielle.*

Then Mathilde remembered the community hall. The last week of school, at their high school dance. Her sister pulling her onto the dance floor, cajoling and laughing and teasing. How the two of them had danced to a song they'd never heard before, hypnotized by the hard beat, and Gabrielle moved her shoulders instinctively to the rhythm. Beneath the Christmas lights that were stapled on the walls and the ceiling of the hall all year round, even in June, Gabrielle looked like every boy's dream and bounced with a levity that Mathilde hoped other people were just born with and she, unnaturally, was lacking. Her sister held out her hands and grabbed Mathilde's and pushed her body away so that their arms were taut and the grip on their fingers tightened. Gabrielle leaned back and then began to spin, swinging Mathilde into her personal tornado. Her sister tilted her head back and let out a holler as the two of them spun out into the middle of the room while the music still blasted and Mathilde almost knocked over Henry from history class. She wanted to beg Gabrielle to stop until everyone around them began to clap. And cheer. They laughed. Not at them, but with them. And Mathilde leaned back, trusting her sister to not let go as she spun them even faster and laughed even louder and gripped even tighter.

For the first time in a very long time, Mathilde missed her sister. She missed her smile. She missed the way that she always spoke her mind. Mathilde knew if her sister was there at the children's art exposition, she would have lit two cigarettes in her mouth, handed one to Mathilde and taken a long drag of her own. She knew her sister would have snuck a mickey in her purse and would have offered her a sip while the other art teachers gossiped in a circle in a corner. She knew her sister would have made sure Mathilde didn't have lipstick on her teeth, pulling her discreetly to the side and telling her to "go like this" while she mimed rubbing her teeth with her finger. She knew her sister would have hated all the kids' paintings too.

Adam was the first to buy one of Mathilde's paintings—and he hung it on the white living room wall in their house in Halifax. The two had been married a year, and Adam had called, asking to buy something, as an extra anniversary present for his wife. Mathilde had driven to the city to deliver the gift—a painting of Mavillette Beach from the shore in the evening while birds glided over the water in the distance and the sun had almost disappeared below the horizon.

"Isn't my sister the greatest artist ever, Adam? Isn't she the best?" Gabrielle's praise made her blush, and she knew that her sister was being hyperbolic, but at that moment it felt as though it *could* be true. Adam told her that it was the most beautiful painting of a sunset he'd ever seen and couldn't believe that she'd created something like that with her own hands. He marvelled at how long it had taken her.

"Five days?" he exclaimed. "This took you five days?"

It had actually been one of her quicker pieces as acrylics were more forgiving than oil. It was the first time she'd used the expensive acrylic paints that she'd purchased with her first paycheque from the community centre in Clare.

"Will two hundred do?"

"Two hundred?" The number shocked her. "I was thinking more like fifty."

"You can't sell this for less than the materials are worth. Come on, Maddie, you need to up your prices."

She hated that nickname, except when it came from his mouth. He could call her Maddie all he wanted.

"I bet I can help you sell them," he said. "I bet I can get them in a gallery or something. Hey, give me a few of your best ones. I'll see what I can do."

She kept her expectations low, knowing that even if her paintings were good, it didn't mean they would be accepted. But Adam had called her a few months later, excitement beaming through the phone.

"They want you," he said. "They want you!"

She didn't notice the water leaking from underneath the bathroom door until she stepped closer to her bedroom and felt something cold and wet underneath her sock feet. Pushing open the door, Mathilde saw the tub overflowing with water, then the broken wood and torn canvas of Adam, crushed under her laptop while torn paper swirled on the surface. She pulled the broken painting out of the tub; water dripped from Adam's lips.

"Eva?" she shouted. But there was no answer. She held the canvas tight in her fist and pushed open her niece's bedroom door. Eva was sitting on the bed, leaning her back against the wall and staring at her toes. Her lips were purple and Mathilde saw two empty bottles of wine, one on the floor and the other tilted on its side next to her hip. She didn't look up when Mathilde said her name again, but closed her eyes and let her head lean to one side as if listening to soft music in her head.

"Did you do this?" Mathilde raised the broken portrait and shook it.

"I didn't want it in my room."

"Why?"

"It's a lie."

Mathilde shook her head. "What's a lie?"

Eva opened her eyes and glared at her.

Mathilde suddenly felt a deep shame in the pit of her stomach. "Eva, did you go through my things?"

"No."

"Don't lie."

"I can't believe you did that. That he did that."

Mathilde threw the broken canvas at her niece who put her hands up to push it away.

"Get out," Mathilde said. She felt her face growing hot. Her voice was loud and scratchy, a shrill tone she'd never heard come out of her mouth before. "Get out of my apartment."

She left Eva's room and began pulling everything out of the tub. Disintegrated pieces of paper. Her destroyed computer. Burnt matches that floated on top of the water like the stick bugs that sailed through marshes—water skeeters. A bit of canvas. Adam's eye suspended in the water. *All my love.* A fire of fury burned inside and melted her. Mathilde ripped out the plug at the bottom of the tub, and when she went back into the hallway, she saw that Eva hadn't moved from her bed. She ran into the room and grabbed a fistful of Eva's hair with a hand that didn't feel like her own. And she pulled and pulled until she heard the sound of bone slamming against the floor. Eva was screaming, on her knees on the floor. Mathilde dragged her up by the arm and to the front door, pushed her out and slammed it. Gasping, she turned and grabbed Eva's winter coat from the rack and opened the door and threw it into the hallway where it landed at Eva's feet. She slammed the door again before Eva could say anything. In the kitchen, she flicked on the radio and turned up the volume so that the music drowned out the sounds of Eva screaming and banging on the front door.

XXIII
Eva

An exile without a destination, Eva felt as scattered as the snow-flakes that were falling thick and wet, soaking through her skin as she walked from Mathilde's apartment to Hôtel Champ de Mars. Her feet froze in her thick socks as she made her way down Saint-Denis, passing the crowded restaurants where people sat warm and full. It was a long way down, and the trees were turning white from the thick lines of snow that collected on their branches. The grey stone buildings looked cold and desolate, and Eva didn't know how much longer she could walk but then the numbness set in and she was thankful.

When she turned down Rue Berri, she saw white sheets hung on fences with black and red spray-painted letters. Suddenly, the bare streets were filled with a horde of people, as if she'd been transported to another city. The people in the street had their faces covered with bandanas and were chanting something in French. She saw someone throw a bottle at a glass storefront and heard the crowd cheer. A line of armed police with clear shields and masks covering their faces approached the protestors. Imminent danger rippled through the air and hit Eva like a riptide and she was pulled by the current into the middle of the demonstration, banners and posters swaying in the air while people in cars sped by and pounded on their horns. She could feel their anger penetrate her skull as everyone around her chanted and taunted the police. A flare gun shot off and soared above the crowd's heads as they all booed. Window glass shattered and the crowd picked up their pace, rushing forward toward the unknown as camera crews followed on the sidelines. Smoke billowed in front of her. A trashcan was on fire, bursting with large orange flames that rippled up to the sky. Her hair cascaded over her shoulders as she choked and coughed her way through the middle of the fight. Finding a side street, she maneuvered her way through the crowd of people and away from the demonstration.

Eva found two twenties in her pocket and walked to a liquor store, purchasing a mickey of gin and sensing the judging eyes of the other customers drilling into her back. The sky crystallized into a slate grey, mixing with the smog from the city and the tall buildings that towered over her, blue and white fleur-de-lis billowing. Her hands slick and cold, clutching her jacket tight around her body, the bottle of gin bouncing in her pocket.

The hotel lobby was empty when she finally arrived at Champ de Mars, the sky outside blue-black. Mirac was carrying a bag of soiled kitchen rags when Eva stepped into the lobby.

"You're not working tonight," he said.

"I'd like to. If I can."

"Where are your shoes?"

"Can I help?"

"Did you walk here in your sock feet?"

"Please?"

Mirac paused and shifted the bag of towels from one hand to the other.

"I'm just finishing up."

"I can do it for you."

"There's no need. Go home." He waved his hand. But when he turned to go down into the basement, Eva followed.

"Eva, what's going on?" Mirac asked.

"Nothing."

"Do you need money?"

She forced a laugh. The dryer let out a monotone rusted beep and she watched as Mirac emptied the barrel, digging out strands of hot kitchen towels and rags, and clumping them into a pile. The hum of the other dryer and the furnace blended together and whispered for her to fall asleep. Eva had never noticed that the ceiling was only inches above her head and bright yellow insulation wool hung in pockets.

"Can I just stay here? Tonight?"

Mirac stopped folding and squinted. He nodded his head and moved on to the soiled towels, dumping them in the washing machine, sprinkling in off-brand OxiClean. Eva walked into the side room where they stored cleaning products and toilet paper and all the small toiletries people steal from hotel rooms. The smell of evergreen hit her nose as she began to open and close different boxes stacked around the room. She found a fresh pair of sweatpants and a T-shirt that had been left by one of the other girls. The stale, dry fabric warmed her skin. She also found two shoes, though mismatched, hidden on opposite sides of the room behind buckets of detergent. Her coat dangled from her arm as she walked back to Mirac.

"We have an extra bed at our place," he said. "You could stay."

"I just got locked out of my place," Eva lied. "My landlord is away but will be back tomorrow. I need a place to stay tonight. This will be fine."

"I'm not letting you sleep down here."

Eva set her coat down on the floor, but when she let it go, the bottle of gin hidden away in the pocket rolled out and into Mirac's toes. He picked up the bottle and looked up at her with a sad face.

"It was given to me as a gift." Eva couldn't think of anything else to say.

Mirac placed the bottle down on the counter next to the folded towels. "I can't help you if you don't tell me what's going on."

He stared at her with an expression Eva found hard to read until, in the silence of the basement, she felt something worse than death. Pity.

"Stay with us," he said. "Until you figure something out."

Eva placed the bottle of gin back in her coat pocket, stomped up the stairs and left.

She decided to spend the rest of the money on beer. She made her way to a park and sat alone and numb and drinking when a woman with a red vest came up to her and asked if she needed help finding a place to sleep.

"I thought I'd sleep here."

"In the park?" The woman's eyes were a deep brown, and the streetlight that only then turned on as the sun sank low, made her eyes twinkle with a soft concern. "It's snowing."

The falling snow seemed to muffle the noise around them, and Eva felt as if she were trapped in a snow globe.

"I think I'll be okay," she said, embarrassed by how her voice shook.

The woman moved in closer, kneeling. "You could freeze to death. I can help you find something."

"I can find a place," Eva said. "I'm okay. It's fine."

"Please," the woman's eyebrows turned up and her pale face grew rosy from the cold. "It's not safe here. There might be space at a shelter."

The intake coordinator said there was usually a long waitlist, but a few people had left that morning. Her name was Diane, and she had a short red pixie cut and wore an old brown pilled cardigan over a T-shirt that displayed a cartoon character called *Little Miss Bossy*. She told her they had to go through a list of questions before she could take a shower and go to her bed. Eva sat in a small white room that had a framed picture of a sunset hanging on the wall. Diane sat behind her desk and took out a clipboard and asked Eva for her full name and date of birth. She asked her about her family and Eva said that she had lived with her aunt but not anymore. Diane asked Eva if she was working and Eva said no. She asked if Eva was taking any drugs or was on any medication and Eva said no. She asked if Eva was pregnant, and Eva said no. She asked if she had an intimate partner and Eva said no. She asked if Eva had recently been the victim of physical violence and Eva fell silent. Diane looked up from her clipboard, waiting for her response.

"No."

"You sure?"

"I'm sure."

"You don't sound sure."

"I'm done," Eva said. "I don't . . . I'm not doing this anymore. Okay? I don't need to be here."

"Okay. It's okay. Stay here, it's safe. You're making the right decision. You're doing good. I have the information I need for now. We can get you to the showers."

She was assigned a locker to store her clothes and directed to the showers. The warm water made her muscles ache even more knowing she'd have to leave the steam and step out into the new reality. The shampoo was minty as she lathered it up into her hair, scrubbing her scalp until it felt raw, and the water rained down hard on her shoulders, almost like pinpricks. She was given a freshly cleaned sweatshirt, a pair of sweatpants and slippers. The shelter reminded Eva of a hotel, but not as welcoming. Instead of rooms, they were little open pens with bunk beds, the lights were too bright and the floors were dirty.

"Keep an eye on your shoes," Diane said. "Most of the women . . . they mind their own business. Just keep your things close."

Eva was issued a bottom bunk and sat on the floor, leaning against it and picking at her slippers, oblivious to the other women huddling on their beds as the evening trickled in.

Underneath one of the bunks, Eva saw golden letters and leather. She reached under to see what it was and pulled out a copy of the Bible. She held it in her hand. It was heavy and thick, and the pages were thin. Eva smacked her face hard with it and then punched her head. She hit her temples again and again and again. For the idiot she was. For the games she played. For fucking up in school. She hit her face for being a stupid little girl. She hit her head until her nose bled and her tears mixed with sweat on her face and it felt like her forehead split down the centre like a crack in the earth.

Hands grabbed onto her arms and lifted her up. Two shelter workers had come up behind her. She hadn't heard a woman screaming for her to stop and shouting for someone to come help. Eva kept trying to punch her own face, wriggling away from the workers' grasp and crying out for them to leave her alone. They finally managed to calm her down, setting her in one of the recreational rooms with a blanket and some water. Diane wrapped her arms around Eva and rocked with her, back and forth.

"Everything will be fine, dear," she said. "It's just a hiccup, come on. Everything will be okay." After that, Eva was told it would be best for her to get some rest, so they showed her to her bunk again. The woman on the top bunk snored. Her left leg hung down off the bed, giving Eva a full view of her spider veins. The woman stopped snoring, choked, gagged and then started snoring again.

Lying there, Eva had a map of all the little broken pieces of her life. They all expanded out before her. Her father was no longer a historical painting, an icon never to be tarnished. Mathilde was no longer a saint, the good woman who'd taken care of her and protected her. And her mother? Was she still a phantom? Or someone who now only existed in her head?

Through the window up above, she watched the skeleton branches swaying, begging to be hugged in warmer weather. She rolled over onto her side and pulled her knees up to her chest, hugging them tight, then caught the eye of an older woman in the bunk across from her. The two mirrored each other.

"*Quel âge as-tu?*" The woman asked in a low, husky voice. From the streetlamp outside, Eva could see that her hair was white.

"*Une. Huit.*" Eva mimed along with her hands.

The woman's body jiggled as she chuckled. "*Dix-huit?*"

Eva nodded.

The woman's laugh grew raspier. "*T'as l'temps de me er'trapper.*"

Eva turned onto her back and looked up at the ceiling. She repeated what the woman said in French, letting her mouth move slow and exaggerated, trying to break down the sentence and figure out its meaning.

"Hey." She heard the woman say in a softer tone. "You have time."

XXIV
Mathilde

A couple of hours after she had pushed Eva out of the apartment, Mathilde went looking for her. There had been a light snow, and a fresh layer had dusted the old mounds of snow and ice. She wrapped her thick coat around her body and called for Eva down alleyways and side streets, asking passersby if they happened to see a teenaged girl with no shoes on her feet. But people shook their heads. She considered calling the police but knew that she would have to explain that she was the one responsible for throwing her out in the first place, and it filled her with shame. She cringed at the thought and slapped her head once she made her way back to the warmth of the apartment, seeing, without a lens of anger, what Eva had done. The floor was still covered in water. Mathilde held the mop in her hands and moved the grey, braided strings across the floor, sopping up the worst of it. She wrapped her hands in paper towel and got down on her hands and knees, wiping up the rest of the water that floated between the tiles. She packed the broken canvas and the mushy papers into a garbage bag and sealed it, placing it in the corner by the front door.

At midnight, Mathilde poured herself a large glass of wine and drank it while clipping her toenails and her fingernails. She washed her face and plucked the tiny hairs that grew dark in between her eyebrows. She sat at the edge of the tub and lathered her legs with soap, since she believed shaving cream was a scam, and glided the sharp blade over her skin. She rubbed herself all over with thick lotion, allowing the moisture to absorb into her skin before picking up a piece of paper and writing down that she loved him. She had always loved him. And she was sorry.

XXV
Eva

She left the shelter during the day—everyone did. It had been a few weeks and Eva couldn't stand staying there longer than she needed to. It was now March, and she wandered the streets without any direction. Some people were kind enough to give her some money to buy a coffee or a sandwich. Most people ignored her. They probably thought she was on drugs, but even if she was, who could blame her? She'd bum cigarettes from people. Smoking helped distract her from the cold and the hunger pains.

Finding a metro station, she hopped the turnstiles and ran down the stairs before realizing that she didn't have anywhere to go. She looked at one of the maps, but when the train rushed into the station, picking up her hair and tossing it around, she decided she might as well get on since it was warm on the train. She let her head rest against the window, the motion and hum lulling her to sleep.

She rode until she hit Guy-Concordia, and when the doors opened, Alma walked in. She was wearing a thick camel jacket with her usual tiny leather backpack hoisted up high. Her hair was shorter, and her eyes were darker. She was staring down at her phone, but when the doors closed, she looked up and made eye contact with Eva, who felt herself redden.

Even though Eva knew she saw her, Alma pretended not to and

looked away. She kept her head down, glancing up every few beats. When the doors opened at Peel, Alma rushed out of the car.

"Alma, wait," she said running after her. She watched Alma's hair bounce in the air while she hurried away. Alma tried to run up a down escalator but was blocked by a sea of angry commuters who shouted at her to get out of their way. Eva waited at the bottom of the escalator as the electronic steps carried Alma back to her.

"I'm sorry," Eva said. She didn't know what else she could say. Every word seemed wrong and clunky.

But Alma wasn't looking at Eva's face. She was looking down at Eva's legs. "Why are your pants ripped?"

"I messed up."

"You're bleeding."

Eva looked down at her leg. She must have done it when she jumped the turnstile. Now she felt the pain of the graze, but she did not have the patience to listen to it.

"I should have told you sooner." Eva felt her nose fizz, forcing tears to accumulate in the corners of her eyes. She roughly wiped them away before Alma could see. But Alma was looking at her strangely. She didn't know what that expression was—it was like she was smelling rotting fish. Alma walked away slowly toward the platform, as if to let Eva catch up this time.

They stood in silence and waited for the next train. The concrete slab columns around them reminded Eva of the Cold War documentary she'd seen in a lecture. Across from them, a large tile circle, red and blue and grey, stared at them as if to encourage some kind of calm.

When the train slowed and the doors opened, Alma walked in first and stood, holding onto the railing. Eva stood in front of her, gently letting her fingers touch the cold metal. Others crammed in after, forcing them to huddle together like penguins. Alma stared in front of her, jaw clenched and eyes unmoving. The jolt of the train forced them to bump shoulders, and Alma readjusted, trying to make space between them.

Eva, hungry and tired, tried to keep her head up and her eyes from closing. She stared at the speckled floor. There was a Quaker Oats granola bar wrapper stuck under one of the seats and she told herself that as long as it never moved, she could keep herself from falling asleep. She had to stay upright. With another jolt of the train, Alma caught herself from falling. Eva could smell her deodorant. Fresh linen. When the train stopped again, everybody left the car except for Alma and Eva who stayed in their place, huddled close together, clutching the same handrail in a completely empty train.

Alma's new apartment smelled like fresh basil and artificial van-illa candles. The first thing she noticed when she walked into the one-bedroom unit in de Lorimier was that the floor was covered in clothes. Alma's clothes. Dishes were piled in the sink and the walls were decorated with posters and pictures Eva hadn't seen in the old place. Alma told Eva to lie down, throwing her a cushion and motioning to the couch. The minute Eva's head hit the soft, velvet cushion, she was asleep.

She was covered in a cloud of fog and sunk deeper and deeper and deeper into the warm, cozy black tunnel that embraced her. Moving her hand to brush a strand of hair away from her face was somehow the most difficult thing she could think to do in the moment; every limb in her body felt like it had been packed with wet sand. Maybe this was dying. The thought of dying was peaceful, and she thought that if this was dying, at least she was warm.

Eva pushed herself up on her elbows. It was dark outside, but lit candles burned on the coffee table. She could see more burning candles through the kitchen door. The apartment looked like a cave. Eva felt her stomach rumble and knew she had to eat something, even though the thought of food still made her sick.

"There's a towel in the bathroom," Alma said, coming out of the kitchen. "You can take a shower."

"Thank you," she said, sitting up on the couch and crossing her legs. "Are you still mad at me?"

"I was never mad. I was just . . ." Alma rubbed her face with her two hands and then picked at the corner of her eyes. "I was confused. And annoyed."

She walked back toward the kitchen. Eva followed her and watched as she pulled a large bowl from a cupboard, then a head of lettuce from the fridge. "Just go take a shower. You need to eat something. You look like shit."

Alma drank from a mug filled with wine as if it were water and chopped the lettuce into pieces on the cutting board. Eva could feel the absence of Dex in the socks splayed out on the chairs and the layer of dust she'd noticed on the coffee table. Shadows from the second-hand furniture hung on the walls looming over them. The kitchen smelled like compost.

"Thanks for letting me stay."

Alma poured wine into another mug and placed it on the counter, pointing to it and then to Eva.

"Is your aunt still around?"

"Yeah."

"You can't go back to her place?"

Eva picked up the mug and took a sip.

"She kicked me out."

"Why?"

"I ruined something of hers."

Alma let out a low belch and then took another drink of wine.

"You look homeless."

"I know."

Alma turned and snapped. "Stop being so understanding."

Eva pressed her lips together. She sat in Alma's silence.

"Take a shower," she finally said, shoving the chopped lettuce into the bowl.

The hot water from the shower made the hairs on her legs stand up, almost painfully, as she ran her hands over her skin to warm it. She massaged the coconut shampoo into her scalp, closing her eyes at the soothing smell. Her stomach growled once more and it felt as if it were biting itself, ripping her insides apart like a pack of dogs fighting over trash. Eva stared at the soap and shampoo lather as it swirled into a sudsy white cream down the drain, hypnotizing her while the water beat down on the back of her head and fell into her eyes.

Alma offered her sweatpants and a sweater. Eva wrapped the towel around her head and sat on the couch next to Alma who had placed two bowls of salad topped with canned tuna on the coffee table. She topped up their mugs with more wine.

"Did you end up going away?" Eva asked, picking up the bowl of greens. Alma shook her head and shoved a forkful of lettuce and tuna into her mouth.

"No," she said. "We were supposed to leave for a week. To Cancun. But I didn't go."

"Why?"

Alma shrugged her shoulders. She stared into her bowl of greens. "We had a fight and I told him what you told me and . . . we just . . . ended. He got all mad and told me I was an idiot for believing you and that you were delusional."

Eva punched her fork into the salad but didn't raise the food to her mouth.

"I didn't want to believe you," Alma said. "But something just didn't feel right. And now I'm here." She waved her arms around the apartment as if presenting a luxury prize to a gameshow audience. Her fake smile disappeared. It felt right to be sitting next to her again. Even though she knew Alma was defeated, and that she too was in pain, it felt right.

"Do you remember? What happened that night?"

"I remember seeing him on the floor. There was a girl underneath him."

"No," Alma said. "I mean the night with your mom. And your dad."

She felt her heart flutter in her chest. It was a question she'd lived in fear of since it happened, first refusing to speak to the police and then refusing to speak to Mathilde. She held the secret of that night high in her throat, trying as hard as she could to force it down further into her stomach and make it disappear forever. But it never left her. It threatened to spill out every time she caught a scent of her father's old cologne, or someone shot the same kind of look her mother used to give. Alma's eyes were unwavering.

"I remember leaving this place by the ocean where my aunt used to live—we'd stayed there a few days, just me, my mom and her. There was a phone call and my aunt picked up and . . . it made her really angry and my mom started fighting with her. She told us that we had to leave. We had to go back or else she'd call the cops or something. My mom had pretty much kidnapped me because she hadn't told my dad where she was going, and it seemed like she had no plans to return. She packed and we just left. But when my aunt found out she kicked us out. Or didn't kick us out, but sided with him."

"Right. What happened when you got back?"

"I remember getting back to the house and the veins in his neck were so swollen. His face was almost purple and I was so scared of him. I'd never seen him like that—his voice sounded the same, just growling, but louder—he just kept shouting 'You're going to make me lose my fucking mind.' Shit like that. And my mom told me to go up to my room, but I didn't. I sat at the top of the steps and listened to them fighting. He was so angry. I moved down the stairs a bit so I could lean forward and see them. His face . . . it didn't look like my dad. It wasn't my dad, my dad never looked like that.

I've never seen anybody look like that. Like he was possessed. Just fucking wild, you know? He shoved his finger into her face and said something like 'You belong to me. She belongs to me. Leave again and you're dead, both of you.' I didn't understand what he meant by that. And that always stuck with me. Like, he had all these rules she had to follow and I never questioned them because that's just how it was. But this was different. He said something like 'If you live in my house, spend my money, wear the clothes I buy for you, then you fucking better behave.' She had to obey him, no matter what, and then he threatened to drown me if she didn't. Sorry. I'm not crying, I just can't. I can't really breathe."

"It's okay. I'm sorry. I can't . . . I can't imagine."

"After that, I ran up to my room and someone locked the door from the outside. I tried the handle and it didn't open. I wasn't sure if it was my mom or him, but I stayed in my room until the sun went down. My mom used to make me these boxes. They had treats in them, little snacks. And she put them under my bed, so I'd have something to eat if I wasn't allowed downstairs. That happened a lot—I'd hear them fighting and my mom crying. Or I'd hear nothing. And I remember looking underneath my bed because I was getting hungry and she hadn't come up to get me yet. But there wasn't anything there.

"I remember the house being so quiet and cold, I don't think anybody had turned on the heat. I couldn't sleep. I was just listening for any small thing. For them to start fighting again. But nothing. And then my mom opened my door and knelt down next to me. Her eyes were so big it scared me. I remember her grabbing my arms and hands and gripping them so tight. She said, 'You know I love you? You know I love you?' She kept saying it over and over and then told me not to go downstairs and she kissed me. When she walked away I felt something sticky on the sheets and on my forehead. When I turned the light on, I saw that it was blood."

Eva paused. Her heart was beating so hard she was almost positive Alma could hear it. She shifted in her seat, sitting cross-legged and facing her with her mug of wine clutched between her hands. Eva drank from her cup and choked on the booze.

"Are you okay?"

"Yeah. Sorry. It's fine."

"Do you want more?" Alma held up the wine bottle.

"Yes. Please. Thank you. I dunno. After that, I remember going to the bathroom and getting a towel. I soaked it in water and started cleaning. Everything. I scrubbed my face until the blood was gone, but my skin was still red. I tried to get the stain out of my sheet, but I couldn't. I saw there were drops on the floor too. I started scrubbing and I think I scrubbed all night because after that, I saw them everywhere in my room. Small drops of blood. I cleaned and I cleaned. My mother never came back after that. I must have fallen asleep in the end, because a police officer woke me up."

Alma let out a long breath and refilled her mug. She rubbed her face with the palm of her hands, her eyebrows long and unruly, pointing in every direction when she leaned back on the arm of the couch. She looked like she hadn't been eating. Her arms were thin, and her cheeks were hollow. It was strange to see Alma without a smile on her face.

"I never finished high school." It shocked Eva when she said it. She hadn't planned to say it out loud ever, but it just fell out of her mouth like an old, dead seed falling out of rotting fruit. "I was only going to classes with you because I wanted to learn."

"Are you serious?"

"Do you think they'll still let me in?"

Eva woke up early the next morning and stood in the messy, dirty kitchen. The countertops were stained and dotted with clumps of candle wax. In the sink, a brown, half-eaten apple stared up at her.

Full garbage bags were piled on top of one another by the door of the apartment. Eva rummaged underneath the sink until she found turquoise dish gloves, sponges and cleaner. She started by clearing the dishes to one side of the sink, wiping down the counter to create space for the drying rack. Alma had a dishwasher, but Eva didn't know how to use one, so she did all the dishes by hand. She didn't mind it though, enjoying the feeling of the warm, soapy water over the gloves. To her, it was a meditation. After she carved through half of them, she dried the mugs and plates with a clean dishtowel and did her best to guess where they all belonged.

Scrubbing hard on the countertop to remove the stains, she made a mental note that she'd have to run to the store to find a stronger tile cleaner, maybe one with bleach. All the fruit peels and leftover food left out on the counter to rot went straight into the garbage, which she carried out into the hallway and threw down the garbage chute. When she stepped back into the apartment, Alma was leaning against the kitchen counter. Her face was softer than it had been last night, and she let her head tilt to the side. The bags underneath her eyes looked darker and puffier since the last time she saw her. A line of small purple pimples ran along her jaw.

"We should go to your aunt's place," Alma said. "To get your things."

That was the last thing Eva wanted to do. She still remembered the look on her aunt's face, that horrible seething anger, painful and wretched. Part of her resented, perhaps even hated her aunt but, deep down, Eva felt that she deserved to be kicked out. They got dressed and walked out into the crisp air. Snow was melting around them on the sidewalk so quickly, it was almost as if the winter hadn't happened at all. The tiniest green buds on the tips of trees offered a whisper of spring, and Eva was shocked by how warm and gentle the wind was when just days before it had been snowing. Puddles collected in front of the thin iron staircases that led up to brick townhouses along Alma's street. The trees on either side of the road leaned toward each other to create a skeletal tunnel of brown and black, casting shadows on the brick houses and small restaurants. A child wearing a green helmet rode by them on a tiny bike, crunching loose, wet snow underneath his wheels while his mother trailed behind. Eva breathed in when a cool breeze blew through her hair, closing her eyes and letting the sun shine through her eyelids.

Alma walked fast, reaching Parc La Fontaine where groups of people smoking cigarettes walked in packs and couples held hands and strolled along in the sun. Eva watched as two boys threw a frisbee back and forth, one stretching up in the air, jumping high to catch it before dropping and rolling to the mushy, wet ground. She felt her shoulders relax, and even Alma slowed as they both stared out at the still pond, a mirror to the sky and the tall trees lining the perimeter. Two massive grey squirrels chased each other up a tree, swirling around with their fuzzy tails twitching. They startled Alma, who laughed, which made Eva smile. Gravel crunched underneath their shoes as they walked through the park's path that warped over a steep hill and led down to the water. On the side of the hill, a couple walking with their scarves tied tight around their necks kissed each other slowly, broke apart and smiled. Alma lit a cigarette and offered one to Eva, who took it and breathed in the syrupy tobacco, skinning the back of her throat.

Mathilde didn't answer the buzzer when Eva rang. When their neighbour came out, Eva forced a smile and pretended that she'd lost her keys and slid in through the door before it could close. Alma followed on her heels as they walked to the door that led directly into the apartment. Eva raised her hand and knocked. They waited, and then knocked again. Eva tried the doorknob and was surprised when it turned.

Eva pushed the door open. "Mathilde?" There was something

about the stillness of the apartment that made Eva shiver. Stale air and the smell of unwashed clothes greeted her, along with an undernote of vomit. The apartment was unrecognizable, not just because of the unwashed dishes and mess. Torn canvasses littered the floor, the kitchen table was on its side, and a chair on its back, furniture blown over upside-down. This no longer looked like a place her aunt could ever have lived in. When she opened the bathroom door, she was hit with a queasy feeling and the walls began to slant sideways. Blood. The bathtub was streaked with deep red, accentuated by the bright white porcelain. She heard Alma gasp behind her. The white floor tiles were streaked and blotted with the same crimson.

"Mathilde!" Eva screamed, running to her aunt's room.

"Eva," Alma said quietly. "I don't think she's here." Her hands were covering her mouth and her eyes were filled with a message Eva didn't want to believe. Out in the hall, Eva banged on the building manager's door until Reggie, a tall man with thinning hair, opened his door. When he recognized Eva, his face fell.

"I didn't know how to reach you," he said. "We received a complaint about a smell. So much garbage had built up. I knocked on your door and it was open—I hadn't seen her in a few days, which was strange. I usually see her leaving for work. I knew I shouldn't have pried, but she wasn't answering when I called for her. I'm glad I went in. She was in her room . . . in her closet . . . lying there. I think she tried to . . . at first in the tub, and then crawled . . . she was so pale. I called an ambulance."

Reggie wiped his face. "It was like a nightmare. She was still breathing."

"Where is she?"

"I think they took her to Montreal General. I'm so sorry. I didn't know where you were."

Eva turned to Alma. Her mouth was open, trying to capture the right words.

"I'll get a cab," Alma said. "Come on."

The black coffee tasted sulphurous but it warmed her insides and kept her eyes open. Eva had curled up on a chair in the waiting room after the hospital staff had told her that her aunt was stable but wasn't ready for visitors.

"You can go home," Eva said to Alma.

"You sure?" Alma looked around at the pale walls with their undertone of yellow. A man and a kid, who couldn't have been older than ten, sat at the opposite end of the room. Eva had never seen a child look so defeated. She sat with her legs crossed up on the chair, her gaze locked on the wall.

"Yeah," Eva said. "Go home. We've been here a while. I'll find you later."

Alma leaned down and gave her a hug before waving goodbye. Eva fell backward into the hard chair and pulled her knees up to her chin. The TV monitor that hung from the ceiling played images of the news—a boy had been badly hurt during one of the protests a few weeks ago after clashing with police. The news anchor confirmed that the boy lost his eye. An aerial shot of downtown showed a sea of red as the street overflowed with protestors. Eva couldn't tell where the procession began and ended.

Her cellphone was dead, so she wandered up to the nurse's station and asked if she could use their phone to call her uncle.

"I think she's okay." She told Marc everything. "She's been here for a few days."

"Do you need me to come up?"

"I don't think so. I'm staying with my friend for now."

"She's awake." Eva jolted at the doctor's voice. He stood in front of her in his long white coat, his thin glasses slipping down his nose. "But she needs more time."

"I have to go," Eva said into the receiver. "I'll call you back."

She handed the phone back to one of the nurses and turned to the doctor. "Did she ask for me?"

"I told her you were here." He pulled his glasses off and rubbed the lenses with a cloth that he'd ripped out of his breast pocket, furrowing his brow. He was about to say something else before he was interrupted by someone screaming.

"*Sors-la! Sors-la de d'là!*" Her aunt's voice screeched down the hall. The doctor turned and ran toward the noise, and a nurse came up to Eva.

"Maybe come back tomorrow."

Eva felt her heart pound in her chest. *Get her out! Get her out of here!* Her aunt's scream shot panic in her belly and Eva didn't know what else to do but run. Her sneakers lost their grip on the tile as she turned, but she didn't stop until she was through the hospital's sliding doors and felt the bitter night air cool her salty tears. The large sienna-coloured hospital loomed over her as she walked down Côte des Neiges, a fortress of brick surrounding her and casting tall, black shadows from the streetlamps. She walked, spellbound by the bobbing of her shadow that stretched out in front of her like long vampire fingers. Bright neon ambulances sped by, their sirens screaming into her ears as red lights blinded her, soaking her in memories of blood. Every wail a *how could you how could you how could you.*

She thought about getting drunk. She walked by a castle-like house and thought how wonderful it would be to live at the base of the mountain. Along Penfield and toward McGill, an empty playground, its emptiness like a haunted dream. A memory of something so distant she couldn't name it. She couldn't see the cross at the top of Mont Royal, but she knew it was there, its presence demanding she turn around, that she stand in front of it and dare to ask the question: *Was it worth giving up everything for you?*

The further she walked, the more she became aware of sound

growing ahead of her. People shouting and rattling shakers. Tin mixed with stones and someone booing. A helicopter hovered overhead and when she turned down a side street, she saw a dark sea of people marching, their bodies taking up every free inch of space. They carried large red sheets flanked by wooden sticks above their heads, blew horns and smacked pots in the air with metal spoons. Flags from all different countries billowed up in the night air, a blue and white banner with the fleur-de-lis the largest of them all. Riot police lined up with frozen looks behind their masks. She heard someone yell and then saw undulating smoke shoot up. People in the crowd ran toward her, cursing and coughing, covering their faces. One guy threw a brick at the cops and shouted something she didn't understand.

The resentment inside her ruptured. It had been doused in gasoline and a match had been lit. The fury came alive in her arms and her chest and she felt it burn like a hot, sharp knife from the tip of her chin, slicing all the way down to her belly. She was filleted with vehemence. The once blue-black sky was now smoldering red and white. Firecrackers shot into the air as Eva elbowed her way through the throngs of people, picked a bottle off the ground and heaved it at a car window. The bottle shattered and people around her yelled a kind of frenzied cheer filled with anger. She shouted as loud as she could—a sound, not words, feeling the muscles in her throat snap, painful and alive. She was coming alive. She wanted blood. The group began to chant. A chorus of words Eva didn't understand but it didn't matter. She caught the words on her tongue and echoed them into the ether, letting them escape from a mouth full of blood. She let them blanket her teeth in defiance and she shouted until the words finally meant something.

XXVI
Gaby

The call came in the morning, while Gaby was drinking coffee. Marc's voice was low as he told his sister that Mathilde was in the hospital and that Eva was fine.

"Why would she do something so stupid?" Gaby shot back. Marc tsked into the phone, and she knew she should be more delicate. But she couldn't help herself. Shock had turned to anger and Gaby couldn't stop her head from shaking as she listened to Marc relate everything Eva had told him.

"Can you give me her number?"

Marc was silent.

"Marc. She's my daughter."

He told her that he didn't think it was a good idea for her to have it.

"Bullshit, Marc. Did you ask her if she wanted to speak with me?"

Marc was silent at first. Gaby heard a deep inhale and a short cough. He told her, in his soft, hesitant voice, that Eva did not want to talk to her.

"Not yet," he said.

"Did she say that or are you making that decision for her?"

Silence.

Gaby slammed the phone down.

She didn't understand the words at first. They sounded clunky and backward. She thought she misheard him. But then they sank deep into her skin. *Ta fille ne veux pas t'parler.* She felt as if her memories were being ripped out of her and lit on fire.

The pill sat on top of the pink pad of her palm. The lines underneath the white circle distinct, curving up to the web between her fingers and back down to the edge of her hand, folding skin. She couldn't remember what any of the lines meant. Which one was supposed to be her love line? Her life line? Did one of them tell her anything about her family, or did that come only in the form of a tree? The pill had an M etched into the top of it, framed by a square. There were ten in the bag. She wasn't sure how much she could take. She didn't know how much more she could take of everything else. She pinched the white button with the tips of her fingers and placed it on the table, crushing it with the base of an empty glass. She pushed the tiny, white sand around with her fingers to create a line, bent down with a single nostril and took a sharp, long inhale.

Gaby placed the tiny bag of pills back in her shirt pocket, folded herself up into a ball and found her home back on her side, staring at the baby picture of Eva tacked on her wall. A heavy, soothing wave washed over her body, coating her in sparkles from heaven. Gaby took in the deepest breath she'd ever taken in her whole life and melted into her pillow. She felt a tiny voice whisper in her ear—God of reassurance blessing his child with a loving hand. *Be still. Be soft. Be love.* The orange spaghetti sauce smelled as it did the day she made it. She watched the strands of pasta wriggle the way they did when Eva's baby belly shook with laughter, whole body vibrations. She heard her in the room. Gaby let out a small giggle, eyes drooping. She tried to keep them open for longer, but the voice consoled her and told her everything would be okay if she let the weight of her eyes drop. So warm in her body, this was more than bliss dreaming. Swaying in a power of alleviation, how could she have ever felt pain? Her skin was water, her tendons were honey, her nerves were elastic bands that could stretch forever, unfeeling. Her body gave up counting the number of times she failed and she caressed her own neck with her loose hands, feeling how soft and how light her skin was. Gaby cradled her pillow in her arms, hugged it underneath her chin and crossed over to the living dead.

XXVII
Eva

Spring came to Montreal like a warm blanket thrown over a shivering child. The warm air breathed life back into the city, sprouting bright green buds on the trees and shaking the cold out of the grass. People opened their windows and let the fresh smell of new blossoms and spilled gasoline enter their homes. Eva wiped the dust away from the empty spaces on Alma's bookcase with a piece of cloth before placing her textbooks on the shelf.

"Do you want help studying tonight?" Alma asked.

"Sure. I just need to pick something up from my aunt."

"How's she doing?"

"Better," Eva said. "I told her about trying to finish high school."

"When's your first test?"

"Not for another few weeks," Eva smiled. "*J'ai du temps.*"

"*Très bien.* Do you want me to come with you?"

"It's okay. She said she just has something she wants to give me."

"Do you know what it is?"

"I don't," Eva said. "I'm sure it's fine."

She had a new job, working as a cleaner at a big, impersonal hotel downtown on Sherbrooke. Alma told her she didn't need to pay rent while she slept on the couch, but Eva insisted—eventually they would find a larger, two-bedroom. She pulled her hoodie over her T-shirt and laced up her sneakers. She grabbed her yellow

Walkman and stuck the earbuds into her ears before leaving Alma's apartment.

The first week Mathilde was in the hospital, it had taken her a few days to understand what had happened. She wasn't completely coherent and would throw things at the wall, confused as to why she couldn't leave. Eva talked to her uncle Marc once a week since her aunt had landed in the hospital and each time he asked her if she would like him to fly to Montreal to be with her.

"No, don't worry," she said. "Unless you want to see her. I think they're going to hold her for a while."

He'd joked that her French must be getting better, because he could understand her when she talked. It made her laugh, and she told him that she would visit him when she could save up enough money to buy a ticket.

"I don't know what you think about this," she said. "But . . . I don't know . . . maybe I could go see her as well. See mom."

Eva could almost hear her uncle shrugging over the phone. "Why not? *Essaie-la.*"

"I think I might," she said. "I think I could. Eventually."

"Not a bad idea." He always said goodbye with a new phrase that made Eva chuckle. "*Betôt bergot.*"

Mathilde was still being kept under supervision in an inpatient unit at the hospital. Eva had to check in at the front desk, writing her name amongst the others who sat in the waiting room, tired and nervous. The person at the desk called her name and she followed a nurse down the clean, white halls to Mathilde's room. There was nothing on the walls, but a small green plant sat by the window, and her aunt was resting on a chair with her eyes closed. Her hair was short, and it looked as if she'd aged a few years even though it had only been about a month since she'd first been admitted to the hospital.

"Hey, Mathilde." Her voice was soft and raspy. "Tired?"

Mathilde blinked open her eyes and wiped a bit of drool that had dripped out of the corner of her mouth. Her eyes were glassy, but when she recognized Eva, she smiled.

"Hi, *chère*," she said. Her arms opened wide, and Eva stepped forward into the hug, gently wrapping her arms around Mathilde's body so they just barely touched her. It was the third time she'd come to visit her aunt in the hospital, and whenever she did, her knees never felt right. They wobbled when she walked over to the chair where her aunt sat, and her mind couldn't move away from images of split flesh, pale white.

"Marc says hi."

"You were speaking with him?"

"He asked if he should come up."

"I'll call him," Mathilde said. "I have something for you."

When Eva first got to see her aunt after she'd been admitted, Mathilde was still confused and seemed to have forgotten she'd kicked Eva out. She asked her to go home and get something for her. "My closet. There is a small box in there, make sure you bring it. It is important."

Eva hated going back. The apartment still smelled sour, even though the building manager had arranged for it to be cleaned. Rummaging through her aunt's things made Eva feel both dirty and ashamed. She wanted to get out as soon as possible and shoved random articles of clothing and books into a suitcase. She placed the small cardboard box in last. As she walked past the bathroom door, she expected to see blood still on the floor. There wasn't any.

Mathilde reached into the drawer of the cabinet by her bed, pulled something out and held it out to Eva. It was a plastic tape cassette box. When Eva took it, she saw her name written in white block letters on the black plastic.

"I'm sorry I kept you from her," she said. "I was only trying . . . I thought it was the right thing to do."

"What is it?"

"Don't listen to it here," Mathilde said. The spring sun was beaming through the window and collecting light on the side of her aunt's face. When she smiled, it looked forced but kind, and Eva thought she should hug her aunt again but knew in her body that she didn't truly want to. Not because she didn't forgive her. It was something else. She didn't want the waves to crash up over the rocks in her mind. She didn't trust herself to release.

"Do you want me to pick you up anything?"

"No, *chère*. I'm okay."

"I can bring you a tea."

Mathilde smiled. "I bet the landlord is chasing after me for rent. You can give him a call if you don't mind and tell him I need another week."

"Do you need money? I've got a new job. Full-time. I can spot you."

"No *chère*," she said. "I'll be okay."

Eva leaned forward, and this time, wrapped her arms around her aunt so tight that she heard her let out a grunt. Her hair smelled clean, like fresh linen sheets.

"I'm sorry," her aunt whispered. She heard Mathilde swallow, and Eva knew she was forcing herself not to cry. It made Eva only squeeze her tighter.

Outside the hospital, next to a giant green bush Eva sat on a bench and held the cassette case. Inside was a black cassette tape, and again, her name, in thick white Tipp-Ex. She popped open her Walkman and removed the Donna Summer tape from the holder, placing it in the pocket of her hoodie. Eva put the new tape inside the player and snapped it shut, sticking the earbuds in her ears before pressing play. Static filled her brain and then a nervous laugh.

"Go ahead," a voice said. "Take one." Eva heard a clap and then the sound of someone clearing their throat. A shuffling noise.

"Okay." A woman's voice. "Hi, sweetheart. Mom's gonna sing you a song so Auntie Maddie can play it for you while you sleep. I know I've been gone for a while, but I want you to know that I'm still thinking about you in here. I know you're probably too old for lullabies, but you always loved this one."

Her mother cleared her throat and began to sing:

Dors, dors, p'tit bébé
C'est le beau p'tit bébé à maman
Dors, dors, dors, dors
Dors, dors, p'tit bébé à maman.

Demain s'il fait beau,
J'irons au grand-père
Dors, dors, p'tit bébé
Dors, dors, dors, dors
Dors, dors, p'tit bébé à maman.

Acknowledgments

I would like to thank Lesley Trites for being the first person to edit my initial idea and for encouraging me to complete my manuscript. Thank you to Mikkel Frederiksen for honest and insightful feedback. Thank you to Clara Doucette for encouragement and tough conversations. I would also like to thank Leila Marshy, Nisha Coleman and Leslie Ting.

For consultation on this project, thank you to Catherine Leger and La Société Acadienne de Clare. A special thank you to Lise LeJeune and Philip Comeau for language support. For historical consultation, thank you to Victoria Thompson and Billy McMaster from the Northumberland Fisheries Museum and to Simon Thibault for writing the cookbook *Pantry and Palate* with the recipe for *fromage à la tête de cochon*.

Melani Wood, thank you for guidance with grant applications. I would also like to thank Tara Chown, Archie Kaiser, Teresa MacInnes, James Bray and Sara Tessier.

Thank you to Debbie Berlin, Ash Mogg, Juliana Bryn and the staff at the Jean Tweed Centre.

Thank you to Luke Adamski for saying "you should" every time I said, "I think I want to write tonight." Big thank you to my mom, my dad, and my sister. Thank you to my *mamère*, my incredible aunts, uncles, cousins and friends for your encouragement.

I would like to thank the Ontario Arts Council for help with funding and all those who offered their support. Last but not least, thank you Kilmeny and Lynn from Tidewater Press for all your hard work and support.